The Ghost Finders

Adam McOmber

JOURNALSTONE
YOUR LINK TO ARTIST TALENT

Copyright 2021 © Adam McOmber

ISBN: 978-1-950305-81-0 (sc)
ISBN: 978-1-950305-82-7 (ebook)
Library of Congress Control Number: 2021934958

First printing edition: June 4, 2021
Published by JournalStone Publishing in the United States of America.
Cover Design and Layout: Matthew Revert
Edited by Sean Leonard
Proofreading and Interior Layout by Scarlett R. Algee

JournalStone Publishing
3205 Sassafras Trail
Carbondale, Illinois 62901

JournalStone books may be ordered through booksellers or by contacting:
JournalStone | www.journalstone.com

For my parents, Denise and Michael

The Ghost Finders

ħEⁿRɥ ɡOXTOⁿ

STORM CLOUDS OVER the rookeries at Spitalfields.

Rainwater on broken cobbles flushing tattered roses and rotted mortar. The dead body of a starling, wings still spread.

I stepped down from the hansom cab to the street where my mentor, Phillip Langford, waited, thin fingers troubling the ivory handle of his cane. He looked as if he might be on his way to the opera in his brushed long-coat and oyster-colored vest. But we were far from Convent Garden, and far from our cozy offices on Bachelor Street too.

"Come, Henry," Phillip said. "Step quickly now."

I glanced toward a crowd of grim-faced men who'd gathered across the street in front of the theater known as The Dragon. In their threadbare frockcoats and black dreadnoughts, they looked like devils hovering in the storm. "Are you sure this is quite safe?"

"Not at all," Phillip replied, rather too lightly. Somehow, he was already halfway across the thoroughfare.

I frowned and pulled my hat low against the rain.

A playbill tacked near the paint-peeled door of the theater showed a languid female form draped across an etched tombstone. Her face, half in shadow, appeared to be that of a leering, hollow-eyed skull. "*Marvel at the GHASTLY DAME!*" the playbill shouted. "*Behold the Grand Mysteries of OUR LADY DEATH!*"

Phillip used the tip of his cane to part the motley crowd that blocked the theater's entrance, and by some miracle, these dock-laborers and costermongers permitted us passage. Inside, we ascended a ruined staircase that smelled of cigar smoke and vinegar. A man in moth-eaten military garb lay curled in one corner of the otherwise empty balcony. His left cheek bore an old wound, a ragged hole, perhaps inflicted by an enemy sword. Through the gash, a mouthful of crooked yellow teeth was visible. I attempted to ignore this grisly detail and instead stepped to the balustrade, gazing down at the mildewed curtain that hung at the back of The Dragon's modest stage. The crowd below rippled in drunken heat.

"This so-called Lady Death," Phillip said. "I believe she's precisely what we've been looking for, Henry."

"A medium?" I replied.

"Not exactly that."

"What, then?"

"I'm not going to tell you that, dear fellow. I want you to see for yourself."

Before I could ask a further question, the gaslights dimmed, yet no hush fell over the crowd. If anything, the patrons of The Dragon grew rowdier still. The curtain shifted, and a bearded man in a charcoal-colored undertaker's suit emerged. The undertaker raised his pallid hands. I heard nothing of what he said due to the general clamor. After he'd finished his speech, the undertaker went to the ruined curtain and parted it, tying off the edges with a rope and revealing a lone woman. She sat bolt-upright upon a chair made from human remains, femur and radius, phalange and skull, pelvis and spine, all bolted together in the shape of a hideous throne. A transparent veil was draped over her. And beneath the veil, she wore nothing more than a corset. White paint made her flesh appear to glow. Loose bones lay scattered at her feet.

The undertaker walked to the edge of the stage, speaking to the crowd and gesturing toward the woman. He then helped one of the lewd members of the audience, a burly figure dressed in bloodstained butcher's clothes, to crawl over the footlights onto the stage itself. The crowd cheered as if watching some sport. And perhaps sport it was, for the butcher drunkenly lurched at Lady Death like a man moving toward a goal line. Lady Death, in turn, raised one slim hand, and a skull from the pile of bones at her feet trembled and remarkably floated up from the ground unaided, flying at the head of the butcher. The man dodged the skull with more grace than I would have expected. Then, ten or twenty more bones flew at him, some of them striking the butcher in the face and chest, some striking his shins. He stumbled backward. The crowd howled with pleasure. Finally, after enduring a second and more significant battering, the butcher toppled backward off the stage and several men caught him, preventing him from cracking his own skull on the floor. The undertaker then helped two more stout-looking men onto the stage, and the same treatment was administered. Bones flew, quickly, furiously, until these men too could no longer keep their balance and fell backward.

"What the devil?" I said.

Phillip leaned over his cane. "Not a devil, Henry."

"You've seen this act before?"

"Several times."

"There must be hidden wires."

"I don't think so."

On the stage, a tall lean man wearing a black dreadnaught dodged flying bones and made his way to Lady Death herself. He clutched at the veil that covered her white-painted form and, as he tore it from her body, appeared to grope her too. The audience went mad. The undertaker attempted to rescue Lady Death, but the tall man had taken hold of her hair and was pulling her face toward him, making as if he was going to kiss her mouth. Suddenly, objects from all around the theater—ale cups, coins, firewood, drapery hooks—began to fly, raining down on both men. Lady Death tore herself from the grip of the tall man and, grimacing, lurched toward the dark curtain. The audience booed as she stumbled. The tall man, battered, bleeding, and now red-faced with anger, lunged at her. At this, the wooden floorboards of the stage itself appeared to ripple and leap, as if there'd been some trembling in the earth. The tall man was thrown backwards, landing with a great thud near the footlights.

"We can't let this go on," I said, standing.

Phillip took my arm. "And we won't, Henry. That's why we're here. We're going to bring Lady Death back to the world of the living."

"How?"

He removed a cigarette from his silver case, lighting it as he spoke. "Her name is Violet Asquith. I've learned that she comes from a family of some good standing. You will speak to her. Use your charm and bring her for an interview."

"Phillip, I wouldn't know the first thing about how to—"

"We need this woman. These skills of hers. I believe she'll finally make our little firm a success."

* * *

Backstage, I found Lady Death near a makeshift vanity, eyes swollen either from smoke or tears. She'd partially covered herself with a Chinese robe and was in the process of removing white greasepaint from her face with a rag. A cracked and tarnished mirror rested on the vanity, and I wondered why the young woman didn't look into the glass as she wiped at her makeup. She was beautiful, after all, marble-skinned and sable-haired, the small dart of a nose. There was an odd nobility about her too. She looked like the sort of woman who should have been surrounded by hyacinths in the garden of some manor house. "Miss," I said tentatively, "I saw what happened—"

Lady Death did not look at me. Instead, she finished removing the greasepaint and tossed the cloth onto the vanity.

"My name is Henry Coxton. If I might have a word."

"Are you a physician?" she asked brusquely.

"No. Why would you think—"

"A physician came to see me here last week."

"And what did he want, if I might ask?"

"To perform an examination, I suppose. As physicians do. Are you with Scotland Yard?"

"I'm not. I'm merely here to talk. Perhaps even to help."

She peered at me in her mirror, eyes dark and cold. "Do I look like the sort of person who needs help?"

"Well, truthfully—"

"The man on the stage tripped. They're all drunks here. They fall with great frequency. I haven't done anything wrong."

"I'm not saying you did. But I saw quite clearly what happened, Miss—may I know your name?"

"Death."

"All right, yes, Miss Death. You see, I'm in the business of—"

"Why don't you just go watch the rest of the show? The next act features a baboon. It's very popular."

"I want to talk about your apparent ability," I said. "Your *talent*. Are there wires or mirrors involved?"

She raised an eyebrow.

"It's authentic, then?" I asked. "You're a telekinetic."

"I wouldn't use that word."

"But you have a gift. You can affect matter. Isn't that right?" I paused. "There's money in this. I'm what you might call a dark detective."

She turned to glance at me.

"Ghost finding," I said. "But not merely ghosts. *Abnaturals* of every sort—that's the word I use. It comes from an excellent book of stories by Mr. Winslow Crouch Harrington called *Thomas Shadow: The Ghost Finder*. Do you know of it?"

"I don't..."

"Just last week, I received a letter from a woman who believes there are fairies haunting her garden. And the week before that, a man reported a pair of malevolent eyes staring out at him from his newly applied silk wallpaper. All quite fascinating variations on the theme."

"So you're mad?" she said.

"Mad?"

"Yes," she said. "An adult man, coming to talk to me about children's stories and haunted wallpaper."

"I merely have a proposition."

"Of course you do. You're all in the business of making *propositions*, aren't you?" But having said this, she appeared to consider me further. "Mister—Coxton, is it?"

"That's right."

"How long have we been speaking?"

"A minute. Perhaps two. What of it?"

"I am standing here nearly naked," she said.

I glanced down at the half-open robe, the white flesh and corset beneath. "I suppose you are, yes."

"And you haven't once even glanced at me."

"I've been preoccupied. My mentor—he's aging and has become dependent on my stewardship. Our firm is struggling, I'm afraid."

She took a step closer. I smelled the lilacs of her perfume. "That's not it, though." She tilted her head, using one hand to push her black hair behind her ear. "We both have our secrets, don't we, Mr. Coxton?"

"I'm afraid I don't take your meaning." My mouth grew dry. Phillip had warned me never to reveal my true nature to anyone. A confession of that sort, he said, would ruin things for us. Not that I needed to be warned of such outcomes after what had happened during my time on the merchant ship in my youth.

"Don't be afraid," she said, reaching out to brush my cheek with a delicate finger.

"Afraid?"

"There's a softness in your eyes, Mr. Coxton."

"I'm a reasonable man."

"You're an invert, aren't you?"

"An invert?" I took a step back from her.

She smiled. "I'm rarely wrong about such things."

"Be that as it may—"

"There are no ghosts in London," she continued. "But there *are* men such as yourself, aren't there? Men trying to distract themselves from their shameful little secrets."

"I shouldn't have bothered you. Good evening, Lady Death." I extended my hand toward her then as one man might extend his hand to another. I realized such an act was ridiculous, yet in that startled moment, I could think of no better recourse.

She stared down at my hand. Then, she looked at my face, and with only the briefest of pauses, she uttered a hard little laugh.

The sound of that laughter rang in my ears, for I believed this woman was laughing at *me*, the invert, incapable of taking proper leave of a lady. I'd failed at my task. Failed at this simple thing Phillip had asked me to do. And now I'd embarrassed myself as well.

But then, before I realized precisely what was happening, she'd taken my hand in her own.

"Violet," she said. "My name is Violet Asquith."

* * *

Nearly a year later and Violet Asquith stood smoking a cigarette in her black dressing gown before the tall arched window in our offices at Coxton & Co. She looked every bit as though she belonged there, every bit the dark detective. Over the course of the year, we'd gained a third member of our party too, a most unusual figure called Christopher X. And together, the three of us had garnered a certain notoriety in London. Phillip Langford had been so pleased with our progress he said he felt comfortable receding into semi-retirement, leaving the firm almost entirely under my control. And I was so emboldened by this, proud of myself in a way that my own father had never made me feel. Phillip had only recently returned from traveling abroad, searching for relics in the Italian countryside. And to be sure, I'd missed his reassuring presence. I wanted to go and knock on the door of his house in Mayfair and hear the stories of his travels. Yet, more than that, I wanted to continue proving to him that I could flourish in his absence. So I'd set my mind to making a go of things until Phillip decided it was time to pay us a visit once more.

On that particular sunlit morning in September—the very day when the curious solicitation from one Mrs. Eldora Tremmond arrived quietly at our offices—I sat at my desk, leaning back in my chair, fingers laced behind my head. The cheerful room, with its tattered velvet sofa and gleaming ornate fireplace, lent itself to a gentle sort of dreaming.

Violet turned from the window as she lit a second cigarette and said, "Are you *whistling*, Henry?"

"What's that?" I asked, sitting up to look at her.

"Whistling," she repeated. "Some horrid number from one of the dance halls."

I raised my brow, attempting to remember if I had indeed been whistling. "I suppose I might have been. 'Lazy Moon,' I think."

"Well, it's very irritating. Do you think you might stop?"

"Apologies, Violet." I considered her more carefully. The skin beneath her eyes appeared bruised, as if she hadn't slept. "Is there something on your mind?"

"Nothing that concerns you," she said.

The fact of the matter was that Violet had seemed rather on edge for the past few days. I knew from previous experience, though, not to pry. She still preferred to keep her secrets close. Yet, as always, I wondered if there was something more I could do.

I turned my attention briefly to an unopened blue envelope on my desk. I might have overlooked the missive entirely had it not been for the fastidious nature of our housekeeper, Mrs. Hastur, who'd cleared a space in the clutter. The envelope lay between my well-read copy of Mr. Crouch Harrington's *Thomas Shadow: The Ghost Finder* and a spectral compass (meant to suss out even the most difficult of abnaturals) gifted to me by Phillip Langford. I lifted the envelope and noted it was from a Mrs. Eldora Tremmond of No. 15 Castle Crescent. Mrs. Tremmond was not on our current list of clients, and I was pleased by the thought of new business. Though, for the briefest of moments, some part of me thought I already knew the name Tremmond. However, after some consideration, I dismissed the idea.

I heard then a sharp intake of breath from Violet at the window. She'd placed her hand on the glass and leaned forward as if to look below.

"Is there something on the street, Violet?" I asked.

She didn't respond. And I found myself concerned, not only because she was my valued associate, but also because Violet had (whether she knew it or not) become my closest friend in all of London. Even closer than Phillip. She understood me in ways that others could not, and I always hoped, in return, to understand her better too. I laid the unopened blue envelope on my desk and moved toward the window where she stood.

Lacquered carriages trundled below in the muddied thoroughfare of Bachelor Street alongside a few electric motorcars, emitting their unusual hum. The day was crisp after a week of rain. Water glistened between cobblestones. A handsome telegraph boy in a stiff blue uniform darted from the open door of Bridgeman's Office of Law. Women with osprey feathers spilling like smoke from wide brimmed hats admired the window display of a silversmith. A mange-eaten dog rummaged in a pile of lathe and rope heaped before the grim Hotel Walford. And finally, a woman in a stiff black bonnet glanced briefly up at the window where Violet and I stood. Perhaps she'd heard about our firm from the newspapers. We'd taken several remarked-upon cases as of late. The woman's clothing was curious, almost like a costume from another century—a gray, serviceable over-dress, a dark half-cape, all topped off with the coal-black bonnet. Yet none of this should raise alarms. In London, even the bonneted woman's eccentricity seemed somewhat *status quo*.

I considered the fact that Violet might be merely be suffering from exhaustion. We'd been out until three the night before, contending with a revenant known as the "Up-Train Terror." The spirit was said to inhabit the dark tunnel near Battersea Station, reportedly manifesting, at times, as a thin man and, at other times, as a white calf with bloodshot "nearly human" eyes. Animal specters had been surprisingly popular as of late. There was the pig that climbed trees in Grimstead, and the talking mongoose that inhabited a lonely farmhouse near Digbeth.

"I know these investigations can be difficult," I said to Violet at the window. "And you must understand, I'm only trying to keep things out in the open between all of us. We don't want any trouble like the sort we had in Penge."

"Penge—" Violet said vaguely, still gazing down at the street.

"When you nearly killed all of us. Because you were distracted."

This, for some reason, brought the curl of a smile to her lips. "What did you call the abnatural in Penge, Henry?"

"The Drowsy Maiden."

"Where do you come up with such names?"

"Stop trying to change the subject, please."

She sighed. "You think of us as children, don't you? Both Christopher and me. You believe we need your constant hand."

"That's not true," I said. Though Christopher X was, in fact, a kind of child, at least mentally. But I didn't think this was the best moment to mention that fact.

"Christopher smells, by the way," Violet said. "He's been hunting rats in the alley again. He should have a bath."

"This isn't about Christopher."

At that moment, an awkward shuffling sound came from the hall.

"Oh, here we are again." Violet shook her head. "You've *summoned* him."

"Chris?" I called.

There was no response.

"We know you're out there, Chris," I said, kindly. "It doesn't do you any good to hide in the shadows, old fellow."

Christopher X, the third member of Coxton & Co., appeared in the doorway. He was so tall that the top of his head nearly brushed the wooden doorframe as he entered the room. His was an eerie presence, to be sure. I often expected to hear organ music when he entered, Franz Liszt or one of Bach's more disquieting fugues. Christopher was some seven feet in height, and broad of shoulder. He always managed to look otherworldly, even in the brown clerk's suit he wore habitually. A white linen sack covered his head, concealing his features. It was customary for him to wear the sack, even in the house, due to the peculiarities of his face (though I suppose the word "peculiarity" was putting things too mildly). Two holes had been cut from the linen so he could see out, and his gold-rimmed eyes peered at Violet and me. The eyes were like two ancient yellow coins, shimmering there in the dark.

"Good morning, Henry," Christopher said, his voice an odd throaty growl. "I was just passing by the office."

"No need to explain. You're always welcome in this room or any other. I hope you slept well."

I was aware, admittedly, that Christopher often did not sleep well. Some nights, I awoke to find him sitting on the edge of my bed, face buried in his overlarge hands. At these moments, I had to remind myself I wasn't dreaming. Christopher, despite his impossible appearance, was quite real. He would ask questions I could not answer: "Who am I meant to be, Henry?" and "Did God fashion me as He fashioned you?"

I'd put my own hand on his shoulder. "I'm here to take care of you, Chris," I'd say. "You're like family to me. You and Violet both."

He'd gaze at me with sad golden eyes. "But I could not be your family, Henry. I am so very different."

"Different on the outside, yes. But on the inside, we're very much the same. You and me and Violet. Even Mrs. Hastur."

16

Standing in the office door, Christopher said, "I dreamed again of rabbits last night. Hundreds of rabbits there on Bachelor Street. Soft gray animals with white tails. I couldn't even see the cobblestones. They made me hungry. I found I wanted to eat every one of them."

I paused, unsure how to respond.

"Are there rabbits in the city?" Christopher asked.

"Very few, I should think, Chris."

"That's what I thought." He turned to Violet then. "I do not believe I have an odor, by the way. I bathed on Monday in the early afternoon. You can verify that with Mrs. Hastur."

"Oh, don't mind Violet," I said. "Something else is bothering her today."

"Is that right?" Christopher said, tilting his head inside the white sack. "Is it food, Violet? Are you in need of food?"

"Dear God," she said. "None of you are going to shut up this morning, are you?"

"Chris is only trying to be helpful," I said.

"Why don't you ring for tea, Henry?" Violet said. "If your mouths are full of biscuits, at least you won't be able to speak so profusely."

"That's a good idea. We haven't had our tea yet, have we?" I went to my desk and reached for the handbell that would summon Mrs. Hastur. The bell was a large old-fashioned thing with a brass bowl and a heavy clapper. I didn't remember where I'd acquired it, though my guess would have been that it came from Phillip. He continued to furnish Coxton & Co. with its many interesting artifacts (talismans, pentacles, and the like), which—though not particularly useful, I'd found—at least made clients feel as if they were engaging professionals in the field.

Just as my fingers were about to touch the wooden handle, the bell rang three times in quick succession of its own accord.

I pulled my hand back.

"It *tolls*," Christopher said with interest.

Violet too had turned her attention toward the bell.

"Did you cause it to ring?" I asked her. Our resident telekinetic was more than capable of using her talent to make the bell ring on its own.

"I didn't."

If I wasn't mistaken, I recognized something like fear in Violet's voice.

"Christopher, are there any spirits with us in the room now?" I asked.

He sniffed the air through his linen sack. Locating abnaturals was one of Christopher's gifts, invaluable to me on our hunts. "There is *something* here, Henry," he said. "But I cannot tell what."

I cleared my throat, feeling a certain excitement at the possibility of an entity in our midst. "If you rang the bell, could you please do it again for us?"

We all waited in silence.

The bell didn't make a sound.

Then suddenly, Mrs. Hastur's high clear voice pierced the air. "Did you ring for me, Mr. Coxton?" Our housekeeper entered the office, gray hair pulled into its customary bun and her dark uniform looking purposefully rumpled.

"Mrs. Hastur," I said, "have you experienced anything out of the ordinary in the house recently?"

"Nothing is ever *entirely* ordinary here, is it now?" she said.

"A presence," Violet said. "He means have you felt any kind of presence?"

Mrs. Hastur wiped her hands on the dishtowel she kept tucked in the belt at her waist. "A spirit wouldn't dare come to this house, would it? Not with the three of you about. Is something the matter? I've baked some fresh bread and—"

At this, the bell rang again, a single eerie chime.

Mrs. Hastur fell silent.

"The bell wants to answer questions," Christopher said. "Like the pipe organ at Holybrooke Hall. Do you remember, Henry?"

"Of course," I said, though in truth, we'd never been able to determine whether a spirit communicated through the ancient organ at Holybrooke or if there was simply an overly aggressive draft. At least we'd set the kindly abbot's nerves at ease. "Once for yes, then," I said to the bell. "And twice for no. Do you understand?"

The bell rang once. Yes.

"Do we know you?" I asked. "Have we encountered you before?"

The bell rang once. Then, after a pause, it rang twice.

"Yes and no," I muttered.

"Who is it, Henry?" Christopher asked. "Who do you think it might be? The Nun of Barking?"

I held up my hand to silence him. "I think we're quite through with the Nun of Barking, Chris." I turned to the bell again. "Are you the presence from the tunnel last night—the Up-Train Terror? Did you somehow follow us home?"

The bell rang twice. No.

"Mr. Coxton," Mrs. Hastur said, "do you really think you should be talking to spirits in the house? It will only make them feel at home. They won't ever leave."

"I'm sure it will be fine," I eyed the bell, trying to decide what to ask next. But it wasn't me who asked the question; it was Violet.

"Have you come for me?" she asked, voice quiet, almost child-like. "Is it *you* who's come?"

"What do you mean, Violet?" I said.

The bell rang once: yes.

"*Who* is coming for you?" Christopher boomed, looking around the room as if he expected some smoke-colored phantom to unfold.

Violet didn't respond. Instead she asked: "Are you going to hurt me?"

The bell rang once: yes.

"Oh no," Mrs. Hastur trilled. "Why would anyone want to hurt you, Miss Asquith? You're so lovely and—"

"Do you believe she's done something wrong?" I said to the bell.

The object fell silent then. And somehow this silence was more troubling than the ringing.

"The bell will not say yes or no," Christopher said.

"Ask again," Mrs. Hastur urged.

"No." Violet shook her head. "No more. All of you, stop." Her eyes were wet with tears. "This isn't one of your boy's games, Henry."

"Violet is upset," Christopher said. "The bell has upset Violet." He started toward the bell as if he intended to mangle it.

I stepped in front of the desk.

"It isn't the bell that's done anything wrong," I said. "Violet, what's going on here? Who has come for you?"

She shook her head. "Don't."

The bell began chiming furiously behind me then.

"Violet—"

"Leave me alone, Henry," she said over the clanging of the bell. "Please."

At this, the bell flew off the desk, flinging itself across the room toward Violet's head. She ducked, and it struck the large leaded window behind her with enough force to put a spidery crack in one of the panes. The bell fell to the floor, and Violet stood staring at it. Then, without another word, she rushed from the room.

"We should smash it," Christopher said.

"No," I said. "Perhaps you should go lie down for now, Chris."

"But it is morning. I am not tired."

"Yes," I said, "but *I* am."

"That does not make sense, Henry."

I went to the bell and lifted it carefully from the floor, half-expecting it to shift in my hand as if alive. "Very little about this does, I should say."

CHRISTOPHER X

HENRY ASKED US to lie down. But we knew we could not. We were restless. The ringing of the bell had made us so. And at such times, it was necessary to go against Henry's wishes. He was a good man, yes. But we also had to obey our own nature. Instead of lying down, we made our way through the narrow hall to the back of the house. We would go to the alley where the rats were known to hide. They were black rats that scuttled and screeched. Fat-bodied, fleshy-tailed, they smelled of London's shadows. We made a habit of prowling the alley behind the house and catching the squealing creatures. We held them in our teeth and licked their oily fur. We shook them. We liked to feel their spines break.

A white door in the kitchen led to the damp and dark of the alley. Near the door, a stock simmered on Mrs. Hastur's black stove, and we knew we must not let the smell distract us. Mrs. Hastur did not appreciate it when we tasted her stock without asking. She said our mouth was not dirty. ("And don't let anyone tell you it is, Christopher. You're not dirty at all. You're different, yes. But you're a *good* boy, aren't you?") And we were good. We knew we were. Yet the stock had a scent that compelled us. There was death in it. And there were the screams of the chickens before their heads were chopped. Screams had a delicious scent. We remembered how much we liked the screams of the dying. We liked blood too. But these were bygone pleasures. For more than screams and blood, we liked to live in the house with Henry and Violet and Mrs. Hastur. And, in order to live in the house, we had to wear a suit and talk English and be good.

The alley was dim, even in the morning light. Buildings cast long shadows. The Englishmen had made a mistake when they built their city. We remembered when we first awoke in the shipyard docks. We were frightened and cold. We were naked. We had no memory. No sense of our own history. It was as if we had been born from the black waters of that great and stinking river, the one we would later learn was called the Thames. We crawled on our hands and knees through the muck at the river's edge. And we cried to ourselves, feeling lost and wanting food. Then the sound of voices rose. Englishmen. Rough merchants and sailors, coming from the taverns. The great city opened to us at the sound of those voices. Shadows became a welcoming thing.

The first man we killed after we awoke (long before we met Henry and Violet and Mrs. Hastur) was a dockworker. We waited for him in the shadows of a warehouse. We chose the biggest man we could find because we wanted all of his meat. We were hungry. The big man whistled as he walked, a sweet, high song that hurt our ears. We tracked him, and then, when he was all alone in the shadow of a great ship, we leapt on him and felled him. We dragged him behind a stack of wooden crates. He was still alive. We tore out his throat, so he couldn't scream. Screams were good at times. But they were not good if other men were close. We liked the way the blood pumped from the hole in the man's throat. We put our mouth over the hole and lapped at the blood. The blood tasted good, like the big Englishman's life. We had to hold him in place so we could lick the blood. He rocked back and forth and tried to kick us. But we were strong. Much stronger than any Englishman. We remembered how his brown eyes grew large with fear. He looked at us as we lapped at him with our long tongue. We ate the fat from his stomach. It was sweet and full of juice. The Englishman made a hissing sound. Soon, we began to eat faster. We tore at his guts. We ate his delicious soft organs.

Such memories. They troubled us. For we would never want to hurt Henry or Violet or Mrs. Hastur. And we would never want them to know we were capable of causing such hurt. That's why we wore our suit and talked English. That's why we kept our secrets. Instead of hurting men, we hurt rats. No one liked the rats anyway.

In the alley, we took off our suit of English clothes—our jacket and our vest and our fine cotton shirt. A seamstress near London Bridge had made these things especially for us because our body was so large. Henry told us the story. The seamstress said: "You must be buying a suit for a monster, sir!" And Henry laughed. "My associate," he said. "He's large-boned. From the North." But we were not from the North. At least, we did not think we were. We did not, in fact, know where we had come from.

We knew we could not get our clothes dirty in the alley or Mrs. Hastur would have to clean them. Cleaning tired her. And we did not like it when she grew tired. It reminded us that she was old. That, one day, she would die. And if Mrs. Hastur died, there would be no one to treat us so kindly and give us bones from the chicken and let us taste the stock. We liked to break the bones and suck the marrow. Sometimes, Mrs. Hastur let us break the bones before we went to sleep. She would tuck us into bed and tell us stories. She was a good storyteller. Often, she recounted the old tales. Fairy stories, she called them. Our favorite was about a girl in a cape who went to deliver a package to her grandmother in the darkened woods. Foolishly, the girl spoke to a wolf. Later in the story, the wolf ate the girl.

We had many questions after Mrs. Hastur finished that particular story. "Why did the wolf not eat the girl immediately when he met her in the woods?" we asked.

Mrs. Hastur wrinkled her brow. She sat on the edge of our bed, hands folded in her lap. "I'm not sure how to answer that, Christopher dear."

"Perhaps he was not hungry."

"Well—"

"Or perhaps he took pleasure in the idea of tracking the girl."

Mrs. Hastur shook her head. "I don't know that you're supposed to think about it in quite that way."

At other times, usually late at night, Mrs. Hastur's stories grew odd. They were no longer about such common things as wolves and girls. In fact, they began to sound not so much like stories at all. There were no forests or dim-lit paths. No places for people to walk about at all. Instead, there was dark air and invisible currents and creatures that floated like great ships in a fog. The creatures howled to one another with voices that were too big for any man to hear. Voices bigger than London. Bigger than even the world. The rest was hard to remember. But Mrs. Hastur often spoke these stories late into the night. And then she would sit with us, staring with her dark eyes. And it seemed the stories carried on, even in her silence. Eventually, she would stand and pat our head. She would say, "Oh, my dear boy. My dear, sweet Christopher. What a night it has been."

And we did not tell her we were afraid of her odd stories. For we did not want to hurt her feelings. Henry and Violet were kind to us, yes. But they were not as kind as Mrs. Hastur. She said we were like a child to her. She had married once. That was why she was called "Mrs." She thought she loved the man. But he hurt her. He hit her with his hand. We wanted to find the man who struck Mrs. Hastur. We would allow ourselves to kill one last Englishman.

In the alley, we hung our English suit on a nail outside the white door of the kitchen. We still wore our undergarments because Henry said we must always wear our undergarments. And such things as undergarments did not bother us so much. Then, we did a thing we were not permitted to do. We took off the linen sack that covered our face. It was a dreadful sack. It rubbed our nose. It stifled our air. But the sack was necessary. Showing our features in the Englishmen's city was dangerous. We were different. Henry had warned us of removing the sack. He sat us down in his leather chair and said, "Chris, I need you to listen to me."

"I am listening," we said.

"Are you truly listening, or are you thinking of something else?"

"To be honest," we said, "I was thinking of something else. But now I am listening, Henry."

"Very good. Hear me well, old friend. Every time you go outdoors, every time you even so much as pass before a window, you must always be wearing your mask," Henry said. "For if anyone were to see your face, anyone at all, you'd be taken to a hospital or a prison or worse."

"Tell me again what a hospital is, Henry," we said.

"A place for the sick," he replied.

"And tell me again what a prison is."

"You already know that, Chris."

"Tell me again. Please."

"A prison is a place for villains."

"Well, I am neither sick nor a villain, am I?"

"You are not. But no one will realize that if you take off your mask. They won't be able to think about anything but—but your face."

"I have a sick face, don't I, Henry? A villainous face."

"No," Henry said in his kindest tone. "It's a lovely face, really. It's just very, very different. And people in London—they don't like things that are different."

We knew Henry told the truth.

For Henry always told the truth.

There'd been a recent incident with a flower girl in Mayfair. We'd taken off our mask, only for a moment, because we'd found it difficult to breathe. The flower girl saw our face and could not stop screaming. It was as if she had gone mad. We wanted to kill her, yes, but we did not kill her. Instead, we ran. She reported seeing us to the authorities. Henry showed us an article in the newspaper. The article was called "The Monster of Mayfair." He said this was a bad thing for us. There was an ink drawing along with the article. We could not read the article, but we could surely see the drawing. A great dark shadow loomed over a defenseless girl. But we had not loomed over her at all.

"The picture isn't true, Henry," we said. "I did not mean to frighten her."

"The essence of it is true, though," Henry replied. "That's how the girl felt when she looked at you."

It was difficult to make words come from our throat because we felt so unhappy. "Yes, Henry, I understand."

But in the darkness of the alley behind the house, we still dared to take off the mask. No man or woman ever ventured into the alley. And we could breathe freely there and smell *everything*, just as it was in the great English city. Scent was our way of understanding. Scent was never confusing. We smelled the nearby fat-boilers and glue renderers, the stable ash and dung. We smelled every sort of London animal, from dusty moth to fatted pig. There too was the smell of baked red bricks, and the aroma of carrion and maggots. We smelled the hard lines of human bones beneath the churchyards and the delicious breads in the nearby market square. We smelled the river from which we had been born and the fetid muck that clung to its edges. We smelled the updrafts of chimneys, the sparrows and falcons that flew. Scent connected us to every part of the city. It told us a story that made us feel as though we were not so different after all.

* * *

We inhaled deeply in the alley. We thought of Violet as we prowled for rats. We thought of how the bell had frightened her. She could be a difficult woman, yes. She could even be unkind. And she often smelled of the abnatural, as Henry called it. The abnatural had a strong scent. Something like the sky if the sky caught on fire. And Violet reeked of this burning at times. We thought this scent had something to do with her special talent. Her way of moving objects. Still, we cared for her. We didn't worry about her smell. We would always protect her just as Henry said he would always protect us. We were a family together.

We dropped to our hands and knees, sniffing at the slime-covered bricks. They smelled like things falling apart. Their smell told us that, one day, even London would no longer exist.

And it was as we thought of London's end that we heard a faint laughter. Someone stood at the far end of the alley, a woman in a gray skirt and plain black bonnet. She watched us. At first, we thought she might be another flower girl. She would begin to scream, to go mad from the sight of our unmasked face, sick and villainous as it was. We would have to run for the white door, to hide in the house once again.

But she was not a flower girl. She had a mouth that looked angry but somehow also smiled. The odd black bonnet without ruffle or lace cast a shadow over her face. It cast a shadow like the buildings of London. The bonnet made a place for her to hide. What was perhaps even more interesting than her bonnet was the fact that she smelled of the country. We had been to the country with Henry. The country was different than the city. It smelled like clover and hollyhocks, like clean water and healthy animals. The woman who smelled of the country watched us from the shadows of her bonnet. And she did not seem afraid. When she saw our face, she did not scream. Instead the woman widened her smile. We thought she had too many teeth.

We stared at her, knowing Henry would not be pleased that we'd revealed yourself.

"You're the one they call Christopher, aren't you?" the woman said.

"You know of me?"

"That *voice*. It's barely a voice at all, is it? How did you learn to speak?"

We had learned English from listening to Englishmen, as all people learn English. And then Henry had kindly taught us more words. But we weren't going to tell this woman our history. Our history was a private thing. "How do you know who I am?" we asked again.

"You'd be surprised what I know. I've been watching."

"Who are you?" we asked.

"You can call me Rose, if you'd like. Sister Rose. I'm not supposed to be here yet."

We did not like this woman. We did not think she should be near the house. We moved toward her, showing our own teeth.

She backed away. "Say hello to Violet for me, won't you? Tell her that I've missed her."

A shaft of sunlight fell upon the black bonnet in the street. The shadow over her face grew darker still. She raised one hand to wave at us. We knew we could not follow. Not without our suit or mask. And we could not tell Henry what we'd seen, because he would be angry. We could not even tell Violet because she would tell Henry. She always told Henry.

We stood watching the woman called Sister Rose until she disappeared from view.

We squatted in the shadows, thinking about what she'd said. That she had been watching us. That she was not supposed to be here yet.

Soon, we realized we'd forgotten all about the rats.

VIOLET ASQUITH

MY FATHER, LORD Asquith, was dead. I knew that well enough. And yet, I'd asked: *Have you come for me? Is it* you *who's come?*

And the bell rang once.

Then: *Are you going to hurt me?*

And, of course, he would. Father would relish the chance.

Leaving Henry's offices, I passed down the lamp lit hall, brushing my shoulder against the velvet wallpaper that no longer seemed comforting or familiar. I'd been detained in the offices for too long. My friends meant well, of course. But the woman in the black bonnet who'd been following me for weeks, the woman who I recognized as a sign of my father's impossible presence, would be gone before I reached Bachelor Street, quick-footed horror that she was, more ghost than any ghost. And what would I do if she escaped again? Wait another hour? Another day? Feel haunted forever by the prospect of her return?

I'd come too far for that. I'd slipped the grasp of Father's cold hand, escaped the trap of my ancestral home, Nethersea Hall. I lived in London now. I had my own means. There were people here who cared for me. And I, in turn, cared for them. Though, for their own good, I could not often show my devotion. I had to hold myself apart.

I'd catch the creeping woman this time. I'd move her tongue, force her to explain why she'd been pursuing me these many days. And more than that, I'd make her tell me why she wore the wide black bonnet, *memento mori*, the very sign of Death in Life.

I wiped tears from my eyes. Whether they were false tears or true, I couldn't be sure. But they would at least keep Henry at bay. He avoided extremes of emotion, likely because the poor man himself was so frightened of his own feelings. Henry, with his well-groomed mustache, his square jaw and his peasant's build. He looked like so many other Englishman. But in his heart, he was another thing. I knew his story. Love lost at sea. A drink and then another drink. Henry had returned to London a broken man, and Phillip Langford had put him back together again. The Henry we saw before us was half of flesh and half of fiction. A ghost finder indeed.

I adjusted my silk morning robe in the rear parlor, searching for some weapon, an instrument of force. I chose an iron fireplace poker with a fierce pointed tip and stood holding the thing at my side, compelling myself to wait. For if Henry heard the front door too soon, he might come after me (tears or no tears), thinking I'd be run down in the street by a carriage because I was blinded by the force of my own hysteria. I couldn't allow him to become involved. He wasn't the detective he believed himself to be. Christopher and Mrs. Hastur needed my protection too. They were innocents, all of them.

While I waited, I reconsidered the incident with the bell. Certainly, my dead father hadn't caused the bell to ring. That was too far-fetched. And I hadn't used my talent, what Henry called my "telekinesis," to move the clapper. At least, that's what I told myself. But some part of me wondered if I could even still make such a statement. Lately, the power I'd mastered as a child seemed less and less under my control. Objects shifted when I did not ask them to. Or, more troublingly, they refused to move when I *did* ask. This effect reminded me of a late-in-life episode of Mrs. Hastur's friend, a nursemaid called Mrs. Beale. She'd lost her rational faculties over the course of a year. First, her ability to use logic slipped. Then she began mixing memories. Finally, the poor woman lost her means of locomotion. In the end, Mrs. Beal did nothing but sit in her chair, staring at the wall. Doctors said her state was incurable. She would remain inert for the rest of her days. And I wondered if my talent could be lost in a similar way. The mind, or whatever apparatus within me that caused objects to move, might falter and decay. Abilities I'd once taken for granted would be lost.

You speak a grave truth, child, said a voice inside my head. I pictured Father, the formidable Lord Asquith, giant of a man, striding down the moonlit halls of Nethersea draped in his great fur mantle. His dark mane fell about his shoulders. His black eyes perpetually leaked tears due to some defect of the glands. *Your gift is nothing more than a remnant,* his voice continued. *A scar in your memory shaped like a great gray house in the country.*

I squeezed the handle of the fireplace poker: a great gray house, a crumbling ship upon the bleak and rolling downs. Nethersea Hall, a confusion of histories, Dutch gables and Gothic towers, the enormous circular window of a Norman cathedral. (As a child, I thought the window looked like a red eye that never blinked). In truth, I knew this was no house for men. It was a palace in Hell. A dwelling place for devils. And I'd once wandered its corridors alone. There were days I saw no one, not Father or Mother or even Anna, our maidservant (she herself had worn a black bonnet when she visited her family in the village beyond the great house). My singular duty at Nethersea, the only act that truly mattered, according to Father, was to climb the wide and blasted Cedar Stair and enter the round room at the top of the Western Tower each day. There, I would stand before my inheritance, the object that would one day become the mysterious source of all my abilities: Father's treasured mirror, his dark magician's glass.

I'd been six or seven years of age when Father and I first knelt together in the tower room. We both stared up at the polished black stone that hung on the wall above.

"Do you know what it is, Violet?" he asked.

"A rock."

"Obsidian," Father replied, taking my hand. I was glad for his touch. I still loved him then. "From the depths of a black volcano."

"It's round," I said. "Shaped like Mother's mirror. But it's a poor mirror. Too dark."

"A poor mirror, yes. But what if this object you're looking at is, in fact, no mirror at all?"

"What, then?"

"Nothing on its own, perhaps. But with the help of a priestess—"

"A priestess?"

"You, Violet."

"I don't understand."

"But you will, child," he replied. "You'll help us all to understand, in fact."

Father's dark mirror had been the size of a serving plate. In certain lights, it looked, to me, like the bulbous eye of some sea creature, a great whale or giant squid. From that blackish eye, Father said I would take my *education*. I would learn of my truest self. "The mirror is your birthright," he said. "Gazing into it is what you were born to do."

And gaze I did. For years.

If only the mirror had arms, I once thought. *It could reach for me. If only the mirror had hands, it could hold me as Mother and Father refused to do.*

* * *

A chill passed down the hall at Coxton & Co., and I squeezed the fireplace poker again. I was done with the past. Done with my dead father and his torments. And most of all, I was done with his mirror. I wouldn't allow the ringing bell or the woman in the black bonnet to unearth such ugly phantoms.

I listened as Christopher lumbered toward the kitchen. He'd be venturing into the alley to catch rats. Henry and Mrs. Hastur remained in the office, speaking in hushed tones. They shared some special bond, stronger than was common for master and maid. When they sounded as though they'd fallen deeply into conversation, I moved down the short flight of stairs to the foyer. I turned the brass door handle and left Coxton & Co., slipping silently out onto the walk.

The stink of the city burned my nostrils. I squinted my eyes against a haze of morning fumes, searching for the woman in the black bonnet. Bachelor Street was even more chaotic than usual. A carriage had broken down mid-thoroughfare, a wheel having slipped its axle. Now, there was a backup of every sort of conveyance, motorcar and horse-drawn pram, omnibus and farmer's cart. Cyclists attempted to edge their way around the scene. An itinerant minister had stopped to preach. But the stranger in the black bonnet was gone. Of course she was.

I'd first seen her in Berkeley Square some weeks ago on a day that had seemed like any other. I'd stopped at a flower cart to buy crocuses for Mrs. Hastur, and when I glanced up, the woman in the black bonnet was there. She looked as though she was roughly my age. She had a small square face and dirty hair pulled back in a farm wife's knot. Her gray overdress was stained, forlorn, as though she'd stitched it out of scraps. What troubled me most was the bonnet, the wide black shell. I was taken by a memory of riding in Father's carriage through the village at Nethersea so long ago. Groups of women on the roadside all had worn precisely the same black bonnet. They stood alongside their men, who wore wide-brimmed black hats. And all of them, the men and the women, gazed at our carriage with such an eerie expression of admiration.

"Why do they behave in such a way, Father?" I asked. As a girl who saw no one for most of her days, such attention felt uncomfortable.

"Because, for them, we represent hope," Father said. "*You* represent hope, Violet."

"Hope for what?"

"An absence of pain. An end of sorrow."

I wondered silently how I could ever end anyone's sorrow when I had so much of my own.

* * *

The black-bonneted woman had stood quite still there in London's busy market square, watching me as I purchased Mrs. Hastur's crocuses. I thought: *Surely she isn't from Nethersea Village, even though she wears their sign. Such a creature would not have been able to find me here in the swell of London. The people of the village, they were incapable idiots, led through the darkness by Father. And even if she could find me, what would be her point? All of it is lost to history now. Father is dead. His mirror, broken.*

Still, the woman in the black bonnet had watched.

And it wasn't hope I saw in her eyes that day in Berkeley Square. Instead, I saw an emotion that looked very much like loathing.

After that, the mysterious woman began appearing at odd moments, gazing always from beneath the shadow of her cap. She crept toward me in the market twice more and then at a bookstall where I shopped on

Milner Street. She followed me from some distance as I walked home alone from the theater one night, a vague shape in the yellow fog. The odd woman even went as far as following us to Battersea Station where we'd investigated the Up-Train Terror. She'd shown herself on the train platform and then again at a tavern. Henry and Christopher didn't notice her, of course. Only I understood this woman's significance.

* * *

A man in a checkered suit brushed past me on Bachelor Street, nearly knocking me forward and not excusing himself as he gawked at the broken pram. I considered causing a brick from one of the taller buildings to fall on his head. *Please should a stone crack his skull?* For that was how my ability worked. I spoke in a soft voice, asking for the world to move. It was the same voice I'd used to speak to Father's dark mirror ages ago: *Please should the mirror help me? Please should the mirror use its hand?*

Following the man with my gaze, I realized the woman in the black bonnet hadn't disappeared at all. She'd merely taken a temporary respite from her vigil.

She emerged from an alley near Coxton & Co. and waited for a motorcar to pass. Then, she moved carefully across the street, looking as if she wasn't quite sure how to navigate the crowded passage. The woman paused before the decaying Hotel Walford. She didn't appear to know I'd ventured out onto the street myself. She lifted her gaze and stared at the window of our second-floor offices where I'd been standing only minutes before. I moved toward her, slowly at first, then quickening my pace. Perhaps this movement drew her attention, for she looked at me and then at the fireplace poker in my hand. A cunning expression spread across her face. Not an intelligence, precisely, but rather a kind of shrewd understanding.

As I was still some forty paces away, I realized the woman could easily duck down another alley to escape. I had to find some way to slow her. I glanced toward the pile of wreckage before the Hotel Walford, pieces of lathe and rope left over from some refurbishment. "Please may the rope come forth?" I whispered.

Nothing happened. My talent, once again, wasn't behaving as I wanted it to.

I heard Father's voice: *You no longer control it, Violet. You've lost yourself, my girl.*

But he was wrong.

I only had to work a little harder now.

"Please should the rope entangle?" I asked, using my finger to gesture sharply toward the woman in the black bonnet.

A mustached financier emerged from a red carriage to my left. He glanced in my direction, likely believing I was mad. After all, I wore only a black silk robe and was talking to myself in the thoroughfare. But mad I was not. I watched as a piece of rope slithered, serpent-like, from the pile of lathe, moving of its own accord as I had once moved bones at The Dragon. The rope became entangled between the tall woman's boots, and I found this satisfying. I'd moved the world once again.

Rather than looking surprised, the woman calmly pointed at the rope and said something under her breath. The rope untangled, falling limp around her boots. She stepped free from its knots and smiled at me, lifting the edges of her skirt to make a weird curtsy.

It could not be.

The woman in the black bonnet had undone what I had done with my talent.

Was it possible that she was like me somehow?

"Wait," I called.

But the woman didn't pause. She lifted her gray skirts and ran.

I held my black dressing robe shut with one hand and launched myself across the street, chasing her down a winding cobbled path. She dodged carriages, pedestrians, a crowd of children. At one point, I drew close enough to almost touch her, but again the woman slipped away into the throng.

I wandered aimlessly, searching for the bonnet, the black sign. Then, turning a corner, I found myself in an odd pocket of silence—one of London's ancient, disused courtyards. A forgotten place from another age, dusty and desolate, walls rising high on every side. A few lanterns burned in iron casings. And what I saw in the lamplight there, some ten paces off, caused my breath to catch in my chest.

At the center of the courtyard stood the hulking vestige of a dream, a nightmare from which I'd awoken, time and again, drenched in my own sweat, clutching my bed sheets.

Here then was a true *phantom*. Not the ghost of a dead man, but the ghost of a physical object—a rotting black coach, drawn by two large horses. Etched onto the carriage wall in rough lines, like a blaze of virgin silver on a rock face, was a crest: a black unicorn passing through an ash forest. It was the crest of my own family, the ancient line of the Asquiths. This was the crest of Nethersea Hall.

The door of the coach swung open. Blue silk from the cab ceiling hung down in rotting, tattered strips. Several men dressed in country clothes—pale cotton shirts, wide braces, and, terribly enough, wide-brimmed black hats—helped the black-bonneted woman inside. She seemed weak in that moment. Perhaps even ill. One of the men glanced at me. He had rust-colored hair and bluish eyes, a faint cleft in his chin.

I felt frozen in place. For I knew this coach well enough. I'd ridden in it time and again as a child when I'd lived at the great gray house in the country. Father had taken me down to the village in that then-fine coach. All the men and women there had peered at us through its windows. And now this dream had come creaking out of the past. It had come, bringing the woman and these country men.

Father's voice spoke once more inside my head: *Now you see, I am not gone, Violet. What we began together so long ago, we shall soon together bring to an end.*

ħＥＮＲＵ ＣＯＸＴＯＮ

I TURNED THE dented brass bell in my hand, examining the clapper that had so recently moved of its own accord. There seemed nothing remarkable about the oblong piece of metal. It hung against the inner-bowl, pointing like some gray finger toward an inscription on the tarnished rim. Tilting the bell in the light, I read the script: *Fiat, fiat, fiat.* Then I glanced at Mrs. Hastur, who stood before my desk, hands clasped, eyes dark with concern. I'd invited her to sit, but as usual, she declined. "Any idea what this means?" I asked, turning the bell so she could read the inscription.

Mrs. Hastur peered down at the thing. "An incantation, if memory serves, Mr. Coxton. *So be it.*"

I wondered how many other houses in London could boast a housekeeper fluent in Latin.

"And what do you think is the bell's history?"

"Oh, that's difficult to say."

"Tell me what you can."

"It's a medieval relic, perhaps. The inscription—"

"Yes?"

"The bell might have been used by a priest to ward off devils."

I tilted my head. "And how much do you know about devils, Mrs. Hastur?"

"This and that, sir. This and that." The lilt in her voice comforted me, reminding me of my own mother's Warwickshire accent. I thought of the green hills and my life as a boy.

"Shall I enquire about the history of the bell with Mr. Langford?" she asked.

I rested the bell on the desk. "Phillip hasn't been particularly sociable as of late."

"That isn't like him, is it, sir?"

"No. I suppose it's not."

"Are you worried he might be ill?"

"Phillip's an eccentric, Mrs. Hastur. His behavior isn't always scrutable."

"Perhaps I should at least look in on him?" she said.

"I think not. We'll give Philip his privacy. When we truly need him, I'm sure he'll make himself available." I paused. "How likely is it that Violet herself caused the bell to ring?"

"Not *impossible*," Mrs. Hastur replied. "But I don't think so, Mr. Coxton."

"What, then?"

"I think someone—or something—was trying to send us a message."

"And what was the message?"

"Unclear, sir. Though it certainly disturbed Miss Asquith."

I leaned back in my chair. "Can you see Violet now?"

"You afforded Mister Langford his privacy—"

"Mrs. Hastur, please."

She closed her eyes and took a deep breath. I'd grown accustomed to this gesture that initiated her "seeing." Mrs. Hastur grew so still that she looked not like a woman made of flesh, but like some idol hewn from stone. The air around her trembled. Pressure built inside my own ears. And soon, the very plaster of the walls even appeared to ripple.

"Violet—" she said, eyes moving beneath pale lids, "she's some distance away. Greatly troubled."

I leaned forward. "Troubled by what?"

Mrs. Hastur frowned. "I can see the black clock that hangs in the window of Mr. Winterbottom's shop on Bradford Street."

"That's where she is, then?"

"Violet sits on the stoop, face buried in her hands."

"Why?" I asked.

"I can't see. Mr. Winterbottom himself has come out to comfort her."

"Violet's wearing the Japanese robe?" I asked. "She's gone out into the street in only that?"

"Yes, sir."

"She must have been driven half-mad."

Mrs. Hastur slowly opened her eyes. An eerie blue light shifted in their depths, reminding me of the storm that had hung over London on the day she arrived at Coxton & Co. There'd been such an odd flickering in the clouds, not exactly like lightning. And then a rapping on the door. I'd answered to find a woman in a woolen coat, near sixty, with apple-red cheeks and a pleasant look upon her face. "I'm answering the ad you placed for a domestic, sir," she said.

"I placed no such ad," I'd replied, feeling I had no time for foolishness. I'd lost two of my clients the week prior because they thought my investigations were a sham.

"Oh, but you did, sir," the woman said, producing a copy of the day's *Athenaeum* with a call for a domestic clearly outlined in red wax pencil.

"Curious." I took the paper from her to have a better look. "Perhaps it was my mentor who placed the ad."

"Whatever the case, sir, I'm here to be of service." She glanced over my shoulder into the foyer of Coxton & Co. My coat hung draped over the newel post and my hat rested upside-down on the hall table next to a vase of long-dead chrysanthemums.

"I warn you that my business may be not to your taste," I said.

"What business might that be, sir? If you don't mind my asking."

"Ghost finding. Like Thomas Shadow himself."

"Ghosts, is it? Well, I do like a good shiver from time to time."

* * *

In the office of Coxton & Co., the eerie light in Mrs. Hastur's eyes faded, and she looked, once more, like nothing but our kindly housemaid. I was left thinking about Violet on the stoop of Mr. Winterbottom's shop, her face buried in her hands.

"You won't be able to protect her forever, Mr. Coxton," Mrs. Hastur said. "She and Christopher—they each have their own struggle."

"I'll do for them for as long as I can."

"You have to take care of yourself too, sir."

"I'm just fine, Mrs. Hastur."

"You're weary. Your past intrudes."

"My past is simply that," I said. "The past."

"Sir, I beg to disagree."

I took a breath and held it, gathering my thoughts. Finally, I said, "Have there been any inquiries today?" New business was always a useful distraction.

"Only one, sir," Mrs. Hastur said, gesturing to the small, unopened blue envelope on my desk. I'd forgotten it because of all the strange goings-on of the morning. "A letter from a Mrs. Eldora Tremmond of Number 15, Castle Crescent."

I rubbed my forehead. "Do you know any of the details of the case?"

"A servant, the young woman who delivered the letter, did mention a few things."

"Do explain."

"Well, it's an odd business, sir."

"What business isn't?"

"Mrs. Tremmond's husband, a Mr. Morton Tremmond, passed away some weeks ago. An ailment of the liver."

"That's not very odd."

"No, sir. It's what comes next."

"The Widow Tremmond has experienced some visitation?"

"Quite the opposite," Mrs. Hastur said.

I raised my brow. "There's been no sighting?"

"No, sir."

"Then why would the Widow Tremmond have reason to contact us?"

"As I understand it, and mind you, I don't think I understand it very well, it wasn't the widow who made the choice to solicit your services. It was her husband, Morton. He knew of Coxton & Co.'s capacities. Apparently you helped his sister some time ago in Yorkshire."

"Yorkshire?" I said. "What was the case?"

"The servant wasn't very well informed. She said only that Morton Tremmond stated in his testament that you were to be contacted upon the advent of his death. He said, well, he said he would speak to you then."

"Speak to me?"

"That's right, sir."

"In what manner?"

"From beyond. He wished to speak to Mr. Henry Coxton from beyond."

"Unusual indeed. What method of communication is he to use?"

"The servant didn't say. Should I send word that you decline Mrs. Tremmond's offer?"

"We aren't in the practice of declining business, no matter how odd."

"No, sir," she said. "I suppose not."

"Coxton & Co. will schedule an interview."

"I'm afraid Mrs. Tremmond doesn't want to meet you in person, sir."

"How's that?"

"Provisions are listed in the letter," Mrs. Hastur said. "You'll find them quite interesting, I should think."

As soon as Mrs. Hastur took her leave, I slid my thumb beneath the sealed lip of the blue envelope, wondering why Eldora Tremmond didn't want to meet with me. Perhaps she herself was an eccentric. Sensation surrounding one's exploits did have its drawbacks. Celebrity—even of a mild case such as ours—drew the attention of an uncommon sort.

In recent months, Coxton & Co. had become even more of a name-about-town. There'd been reports of our adventures in various less-than-reputable newspapers, and, more significantly, our firm was written up in *The Strand*. The article entitled "An Ever Open Door" had set about to document the current boom in Psychical Research, and Coxton & Co. was named as a small, rather unique firm with members who were able to perform effective, impromptu séances. The word *séance* was a misnomer, of course, as the rituals that Violet, Christopher, and I performed were far less orthodox than that. The piece in *The Strand* appeared in direct proximity to a new story penned by the famed author, Mr. Arthur Conan

Doyle, happily guaranteeing a certain readership. The article concluded that our city had awakened to a new revolution in spiritism even as haunted houses, one by one, were being lit with electric lamps. It didn't matter that the sound of motorcars drowned out the rustle that had once risen from restless graves. There were still people who saw fit to gaze into the darkness.

Hoping this Eldora Tremmond proved a rational sort, I slid the blue stationery from its envelope and began to read.

* * *

That afternoon, I sent a careful response to the admittedly curious Tremmond letter, and during the week that followed—prior to our scheduled investigation of Number 15—we at Coxton & Co. interviewed several more prospective clients. A certain Lady Constance, the seventeen-year-old daughter of Lord and Lady Westfall of Orpington, came to us claiming she'd encountered in a Chiswick alehouse what could only be described as a "rakishly handsome vampire." "He was lithe of build and had the most luxuriant hair," Lady Constance said tearfully. "Bright *blue* eyes, Mr. Coxton. So very much alive in their appearance. Who would ever have thought—" Violet sat with me at the preliminary interview, during which Lady Constance borrowed my monogrammed handkerchief and, at one point, asked to rest her head on one of the tasseled pillows from the office sofa. Thankfully, Violet had returned to something of her normal demeanor after the incident with the bell. She continued, however, to refuse to speak about the questions she'd asked of the instrument or to divulge what precisely had been troubling her for so many weeks. After Lady Constance took her leave, Violet noted that the bruise-marks on the young woman's neck were less in line with an encounter styled by Bram Stoker and more indicative of a simple, if poorly thought out, night of passion. "The question we should likely put to Lady Constance," she said, "is not 'How long was the vampire's tooth?' but rather 'What precisely were you doing in a Chiswick alehouse to begin with, dear?'" Unfortunately, in this matter, I had to agree.

Apart from the Chiswick Vampire, there were a number of odd claims surrounding what some believed to be an animate scarecrow in

Islington. A young barrister by the name of Clyde Overholt wrote to us, saying he'd encountered the shambling creature on Dunhill Road late one moonlit evening. "Its head, Mr. Coxton, was akin to a misshapen gourd, rotting and caved on one side. And its hands—its reaching claw-like hands—were nothing more than twigs and sticks, all gathered. Still, I felt it might clutch me. I have a wife and child, sir. I cannot be seeing such things as scarecrows dragging themselves about." Mr. Overholt's plight and the image of the Islington Scarecrow appealed to me, and despite Violet's protestations of not wanting to chase "vegetation through the farmlands," I marked the case for follow-up.

Coxton & Co. also conducted a single on-scene investigation during the week before the Tremmond case began. We'd been summoned to Wycombe Hall, a venerable finishing school where girls of an elevated class were taught such things as needlework and housewifery. I must admit our group seemed less than cohesive on the evening we visited Wycombe. Violet's mood had slipped, and Christopher too appeared unusually lost in thought.

We arrived during a pounding rain. Christopher carried a heavy leather valise and held a large umbrella under which Violet and I huddled. Headmistress Aberdeen, a stern figure with a large bustle, greeted us at the door, and we followed her down a long bare hall where electric lights flickered in plain glass sconces.

"Wycombe does not invite any manner of foolishness," Headmistress Aberdeen said. "The majority of our girls here are as proud and sure as any from Cheltenham or Manchester."

"I have no doubt," I said.

"But the child I mentioned in my letter, Miss Elisabeth Dawson, has proved herself difficult from the start. Her parents are both deceased, you understand, an accident some years ago. Her uncle sits in Parliament and has paid a good sum to keep young Elisabeth in our care. She cannot, therefore, be dismissed no matter how ridiculous or distressing her stories."

I cleared my throat. "Might we interview the child?"

"Certainly not," Headmistress Aberdeen said. "Your presence here is not for her benefit, Mr. Coxton."

"Then why precisely are we here?" Violet asked, a bit too sharply.

Headmistress Aberdeen looked at Violet with prim suspicion, observing both the rather flattering cut of my associate's lavender dress as well as the ostentatious nature of her French curls that had somehow remained intact despite the pounding rain. "Miss *Asquith*, is it? Are you of some relation to the First Earl of Oxford, Mr. Herbert Asquith?"

Violet raised a dark eyebrow. "Do I look as though I'm related to an Earl of Oxford?"

"Violet," I said

"Henry," Christopher growled from behind us. The graveled baritone of his voice made me cringe, as it always did when he spoke in front of clients. It sounded particularly unnatural in the echoing halls of Wycombe. "I am hungry," he said. "Do you think we will have time for a second supper tonight?"

"Perhaps, Chris," I said. "But let's discuss that matter later on, if you don't mind."

"All right, Henry. I will bring it up again in an hour or so."

I returned my attention to Headmistress Aberdeen who now gazed up at Christopher X.

"That's your man who was disfigured in a fire, is it?" she asked. Even the most particular of clients tended to experience an awe of this kind in Christopher's presence.

"That's right." The lie about him being a burn victim was one I'd invented some time ago to explain the necessity of his mask. Recently, Violet had added a detail, saying the fire occurred at a country orphanage and Christopher had singlehandedly rescued every orphan. I thought that was a bit much, but people seemed to take to the embellishment.

"And is it true that he can locate so-called spirits using his sense of smell?" Headmistress Aberdeen asked.

"It's a gift," I said.

"It is not a *gift*," Christopher countered. "At times, it causes me to sneeze violently."

Violet patted Christopher's arm, gently. "There, there, old boy. We all have our afflictions, don't we?"

The headmistress looked rather vague about all of this. "The board is certain you'll lay to rest all of Elisabeth Dawson's foolish intimations," she said.

"I'm certain we'll try," I replied. "Perhaps it would make sense to get things started now."

"You'll provide some kind of documentation, won't you, Mr. Coxton?" Headmistress Aberdeen asked. "Something the board can put in its final report?"

I cleared my throat. "Of course," I said, thinking Headmistress Aberdeen might have confused our practices with those of the Society for Psychical Research. Coxton & Co. tended toward a less conventional and overall more *eclectic* method. I was thankful that I'd at least thought to bring my camera, which Christopher now carried in the leather valise.

We rounded a corner, and, just ahead in the hall, a door closed promptly. Girlish laughter ensued.

"We've cleared the hallways of the North and South Dormitories where the sightings have taken place so that you may have your run of them," Headmistress Aberdeen said. She turned to look at me, and I saw in her expression that, despite her upright manner, Headmistress Aberdeen was in fact bearing a significant weight on her shoulders. Even a woman as stalwart as she could be unraveled by an abnatural. And that was precisely the reason for Coxton & Co.'s existence. As Thomas Shadow himself would say in Mr. Winslow Crouch Harrington's book of stories: "The living must be rescued from the dead."

The details of the case at Wycombe were as follows. Two weeks prior to our visit, the aforementioned Elisabeth Dawson, niece of an esteemed member of Parliament, claimed to have been confronted by an apparition sometime after midnight in the hall of the South Dormitory. She'd described this encounter in earnest to her classmates the next morning. She'd seen a man seated upon a tall black horse, wearing what she described as a "military uniform." Though Elisabeth Dawson had been shown pictures of uniforms from various epochs throughout English history, she'd claimed that none of them quite depicted what she'd encountered. The Rider, as the entire school had come to call the figure, sat stiffly in his riding saddle, and when Miss Dawson cried out in fear, he jerked at his reins and turned. His face, Dawson claimed, was not like a face at all. In some versions, the features of Dawson's Rider looked blurred, as if submerged under a swiftly moving stream. In others, his eyes and mouth were too large. Finally, and most terribly perhaps, she claimed the Rider had a fold at the center of his head, a kind of crease, and his features had been "consumed" within. In all versions, he made the same gesture, extending a gloved hand toward Miss Dawson, as a man might do if he intended to help a girl climb into the saddle with him. Elisabeth Dawson said she had gripped the handle of her bedroom door and spoken boldly: "Is that why you've come riding?" she asked. "You want to take one of us away with you?"

We entered the South Dormitory hall, and I unpacked my tripod and an Eastman camera. Phillip had given me the camera some time ago with the instruction that I use it sparingly, as the film was quite costly. This had been only a few months after he'd taken me on as his protégé. We had been at the Savile Club in Mayfair, seated in the smoke-filled library and drinking caramel-colored brandy. A pianist played some light sonata. The camera sat between us on a table. Phillip peered at me over it, resting one hand on the head of his cane. "Cameras and electroscopes and devices of psychic imprint can all be quite useful, Henry. But the best tool in your kit will always be the surety of your manner. People want to feel as though they've been listened to. As though someone cares for them and understands their fears. In the end, that's what will make them feel no longer haunted, my boy."

"But I'm not like you, Phillip," I said, taking a sip of brandy and feeling the burn of it in my throat. "Not so personable or charming."

He smiled warmly and patted my knee. "Would you like to know a secret?" He leaned forward. "*I'm* not much like me either."

* * *

In the South Dormitory at Wycombe, I assembled the Box Brownie, as Violet passed her hands through the air as if playing a harp. She muttered something under her breath; I heard the word "please" repeated. We'd discovered that her special ability, which she still refused to call telekinesis, quite often disturbed abnaturals, causing them, in some manner, to betray themselves. An entire evening of such focus was often exhausting for Violet. But clients who insisted upon being present for the investigation were usually quite pleased. In performing her role, Violet often inadvertently caused doors to close and even a few tables to rap.

Christopher, in turn, inhaled deeply through the linen mask. In this way, he could usually lead us in the proper direction.

"Picking up anything, old friend?" I asked.

"This way, Henry," Christopher said, moving down the hall.

He walked quickly when he was on the trail of something. We sometimes had to maintain a light jog to keep up with him.

It was near the end of the narrow hall that he finally paused.

I raised my camera. "Is there something here?"

"It smells like—cinders," Christopher said.

I depressed the button on the Brownie, taking a picture, hoping some abnatural image might be imprinted on the film. As I pressed the button again, I heard a little cry from Violet. I turned, half-expecting to see the Rider himself glowering at us, but instead I saw a girl of some eight or nine years of age, a serious-looking child in a quilted housecoat and slippers. She stared at us with great curiosity.

"Mr. Coxton?" she said.

"That's right." I lowered my camera.

"My name is Elisabeth Dawson. I'm the girl who saw the—"

"Yes, of course," I said. "It's very good to meet you, Miss Dawson."

"I'm—I'm sorry to bother you at your work, but I felt I must ask—"

"Go ahead," Violet coaxed. "Mr. Coxton likes to answer questions."

"Some of the girls," Elisabeth Dawson said, "they don't believe me about what I saw. They say I'm mad, or that I'm searching for some kind of attention because—because of what happened to my parents."

"Miss Dawson," I said, "there will always be those who lack the imagination to believe."

"But these same girls, they also said that even if there is a Rider, people like you won't be able to get rid of him. They said you merely take foolish people's money."

"I can assure you that I've seen things with my own eyes. Inexplicable things."

"The Nun of Barking!" Christopher said loudly enough to wake everyone in the house.

"Henry wouldn't steer you wrong, dear," Violet added in an uncharacteristically kind tone.

Elisabeth Dawson appeared relieved.

"Now go back to bed," I said. "And when you wake up in the morning, things will be better here."

No Rider appeared that night to us. Christopher did not smell cinders again. We left just as the sun was rising with the camera in tow. And when Headmistress Aberdeen asked us if the ghost was gone, I told it her was, though, in truth, I had no idea.

* * *

On Monday, the following week, our carriage arrived at the Widow Tremmond's row house, Number 15 Castle Crescent. Dusk had fallen, and the air was cool. The arc lamps along the street were yet to be lit, and smoke from a nearby refinery had painted the sky a sullen shade. Law clerks and bankers' aides, a relatively new class of wealth, had gathered with their families in sturdy brick homes for dinner. Warm light spilled from the windows of those houses onto the stone walk. This was not a fashionable neighborhood, not yet at least; nevertheless, a sense of good and homely cheer pervaded. Death did not belong in a place like this. And neither, of course, did my associates and I.

Violet, in a dark suit-dress with a long coat and pearl-buttoned black gloves, drew back the carriage curtain to peer up at Number 15. Unlike the rest of the street, the Tremmond house remained shuttered. No warm lamps flickered there, and the oaken door was firmly shut. The house had an *injured* look, seeming to linger in some incurable and melancholy state.

"The widow isn't home?" Violet said.

"She isn't," I replied.

I hadn't allowed Violet to read Eldora Tremmond's curious letter of solicitation. Instead, I'd provided vague details. It was sometimes better not to give Christopher or her too much information. Such divulgences could conflict with their special talents. And more than that, I was concerned about the way Violet would react to the idea that the house was not yet haunted.

"No housekeeper to light the lamps?" she asked.

"Doesn't appear so."

"What exactly are you getting us into, Henry?"

I thought back to the letter, admitting to myself that even I wasn't entirely sure. As Mrs. Hastur said, Morton Tremmond had requested his wife absent herself from our initial investigation. The widow's letter explained that her husband wanted something he called a "clear channel." He'd also specified that all of Coxton & Co. must be present on the expedition. *My husband thought you were at your strongest as a group*, the widow wrote in her careful script. *As I've mentioned, Morton took an enormous interest in your exploits. He kept up with the doings of the Golden Dawn and the SPR, but you and your little band were his favorites.*

There'd also been mention of a housekeeper in the Widow Tremmond's note, perhaps the very woman who'd delivered the blue envelope: *Our Lucy* should *see you in. But in the case that she's not present—a key.* The iron key had been delivered in a sealed box to the doorstep of Coxton & Co. The widow was less than forthcoming about why the maid might not be there to greet us on the evening of our arrival. *There's been an uncomfortable feeling in the house as of late,* she wrote, *a change in the air. We do not feel haunted, Mr. Coxton. Rather, there is a sense of abandonment. Morton is no longer here with us. He was such a dignified husband and master...*

"We should wait until dark to leave the carriage," Violet said, allowing the curtain to fall back across the window. "Chris shouldn't be out where these people can see."

I glanced over at Christopher X, who didn't seem to be the least bit bothered by the hour. His large, powerful body hung limp against the carriage seat, and he snored with the sort of abandon that comes only to men in the deepest of carefree slumber. The linen bag Christopher wore over his head fluttered as he exhaled. Violet was correct, of course. Not everyone reacted kindly when they saw such a strange figure. If I didn't have the chance to relay the story about the fire and the orphans, people were likely to think that some contagious disease afflicted our friend.

"The street's empty," I said. "And at any rate, Mr. Tremmond was specific about the hour of commencement."

"Mr. Tremmond is dead, as I understand it," Violet said.

"His money spends as well as the living's."

Violet slipped a cigarette from her silver case.

"Must you?" I said.

"I think you know the answer to that," she replied. "Let's just get this over with."

I reached out to tap Christopher's oversized knee.

He sat up, nearly striking his head on the carriage ceiling and making a loud snorting sound. Christopher fumbled with his linen mask, adjusting it so he could peer at me with a gold-rimmed eye. The eye was stunning in the evening light, brown at the center with edges of burnished gold.

"Henry," he said, "the hour is late."

"Not so late, old friend," I said.

"It's six o'clock," Violet said. "And we are in the land of the *status quo*. So behave yourself when we're outside, Chris. Or we're all likely to get burned at the stake."

"Violet's already in a mood," I said.

Christopher gazed at her sympathetically.

"This isn't a *mood*," Violet replied. "It's what remains of my personality after spending so much time with the two of you."

I opened the carriage door as Christopher asked several questions about whether or not we were *actually* going to be burned by the citizens of Castle Crescent. A postbox stood near the entryway of Number 15, a decorative thing made of brushed metal, likely the sort that was meant to be wrapped in garland at Christmastime.

After knocking on the door and receiving no answer, I removed the iron key from my pocket along with one of my most treasured tools: a hand-held electric torch. Mrs. Tremmond had advised in her letter that we needn't bring any complicated accoutrement of ghost finding. Morton, her husband, requested only our presence. Yet, I couldn't resist bringing the torch or "flashlight," as it was known. It was a brass tube the size of a baton with a bulb in one end. The word "Reliable" was stamped into the tube near the switch. This phrase was, to some degree, false advertising, as the torch had often flickered and died at the most inopportune of times. Still, when I used it, I felt almost like Thomas Shadow with his various devices, including an ingenious electric pentagram. To live such an interesting fiction, I'd often thought, was preferable to living the life I'd been allotted.

"Are you going to tell us anything more about what's going on in there?" Violet asked, taking a final drag from her cigarette before flicking away the remains.

"I've already told you most of what I know."

"I know a lie when I heard it," Violet said.

"Henry does not lie, Violet," Christopher said. "Henry is good."

"Good is often a relative term," Violet replied.

Christopher turned to look at me. "Henry, are you good or not good at this moment?"

"Stop trying to make him uncomfortable, Violet. I need his skills tonight."

"You need your monkeys to perform, you mean," she said.

"I am not a monkey," Christopher said.

"Why so caustic?" I asked.

"Because if I'm not," Violet said., "who will be?"

I turned the iron key in the lock and opened the door, revealing an empty black foyer beyond. There were no switches on the wall. The house didn't look to be electrified, a fact that I considered odd, as the rest of the street appeared to be. I turned on my torch, and its pale beam illuminated dust motes in the air. Before us lay a long narrow hall and a steep staircase leading up to a second-floor landing. Both stairwell and hall bore the same wallpaper, an antique William Morris variety with a tangle of dark vines and fleshy-looking flowers in its design. The vines seemed to shift subtly as the beam of my torch played across them. A few scraps of newspaper lay about, but other than that, the foyer looked empty, as did the second-floor landing.

"It's abandoned," Violet said.

"Curious," I said, for this wasn't at all what I'd expected.

Violet picked up one of the pieces of crumpled newspaper from the floor and checked the date. "This is months old, Henry. Didn't you say the widow was living here?"

"I was under the impression—" I didn't have a chance to finish my thought. A scuttling came from the hall. The beam of my flashlight caught a large rodent moving along the floorboard.

"A rat!" Christopher said.

"A mouse, I should think," I said.

"I am more familiar with rats than you, Henry," he replied, a statement I could not argue with.

"An empty house, infested with rats, is it?" Violet said.

"Let's just get to work," I said, wondering if and when Morton Tremmond would attempt to contact me. The whole of what had been described in the letter sounded preposterous. But as a ghost finder, I'd learned not to discount even the most ridiculous ideas.

Christopher inhaled deeply through the mask.

"Picking up anything, old fellow?" I asked.

"Stew," he replied.

"Stew?"

"In the icebox. It smells as if the pot's gone bad. Unfortunate. I believe it was pheasant stew. With onions."

"Not particularly helpful, Chris."

"The chimney is unswept. There is a dead bird."

"Right. Nothing abnatural, then? No spirits?"

"No, Henry."

Violet removed her gloves. She ran her right hand through the air, moving her fingers almost as if strumming an invisible harp, and all the while muttering—*please should...please should.*

"Anyone home?" I called, shining my torch again down the long hall that appeared to open out onto the rest of the house.

There was no response.

I trained my torch on a large oil painting that hung crookedly near the stairs. It depicted a hare nibbling wildflowers in a sun-dappled field. The piece was poorly executed. Wide, awkward brushstrokes made the rabbit look overlarge, grotesque.

"I dreamed of rabbits, Henry," Christopher said, gazing at the painting.

"What experiences did the Widow Tremmond report?" Violet asked. "The return of her dead husband, I assume?"

"Not exactly," I said.

"Poltergeist?"

"No."

"Will-of-the-Wisp?"

"Violet."

She ceased the movement of her fingers. "What, then?"

"She reported nothing. No occurrence."

"So there's not even the *story* of a ghost? Christ, Henry."

"Do not take name of Christ in vain," Christopher said.

"Did you know him?" Violet snapped.

Christopher paused. "I do not recall."

"I'll take anyone's name in vain that I please," Violet said.

"There's a perfectly reasonable explanation for why we're here," I said.

"Well, let's hear it then."

"Morton Tremmond wishes to speak with me."

"The ghost that does not exist wants a word?" Violet asked. "And what nonexistent thing might he want to say?"

"I suppose we'll find out."

"Or not," Violet said.

"Yes," I replied. "Or—"

Christopher had stopped stock-still before the staircase. His muscles tensed beneath his suit, and his entire body canted forward as if on point. I'd seen him adopt just such a stance during the Case of the Wailing Boy as well as when we'd chased down a supposed sighting of Spring-Heeled Jack in Southwark. I shined my lamp across the broad expanse of Christopher's back. He took deep breaths, inflating and deflating his linen mask.

"What is it, Chris?"

He didn't respond.

"An abnatural?"

"Something more..." he said.

"You're going to have to be specific, I'm afraid."

"Strange forces..." he said.

A clattering sound came from the second floor. This time it sounded like something much larger than a rat.

"Hello?" I called. "Is someone up there?"

I heard the clear sound of footsteps then.

Christopher began to ascend the stairs.

"Hold on," I called. "We don't know if it's safe."

But Christopher had already disappeared into the darkness of the landing.

Violet shrugged. "This is what you get for not giving us enough information, you know."

"Come on," I said.

The ugly vines in the wallpaper seemed to shift as we ascended.

We found Christopher in an empty second-floor hall, standing on-point again, staring into the darkness.

"What is it?" I said.

"A figure," he replied. "A woman. I could not see her well." He lifted his hand to point toward the dark end of the hall. "The smell is stronger here."

I shone my flashlight into the cobwebbed hall. No one had walked there for a long time, by the look of it. I suddenly wondered if the Widow Tremmond had been telling the truth about her reason for hiring Coxton & Co. Perhaps she'd read about us in *The Strand* and invited us to an empty house as part of some ruse. Christopher set off again. The heavy sound of his footfalls moved quickly down an adjoining hall. Violet and I followed. The second hall was narrower than the first, likely leading to a servant's quarters. We arrived finally at a small room tucked away at the end of the corridor. This room was not empty. It was, in fact, overfull and in a state of great disarray, resembling some kind of burrow, cluttered with dirty plates and maps of London. There were rumpled clothes and magazines too—one of them, I noticed, was the issue of *The Strand* in which Coxton & Co. had been featured. Someone (or multiple someones) had been living here, but not living well. Christopher stood at the center of the room, studying the walls.

"A door," he said, pointing.

There was indeed a door, or rather a panel fitted snugly into the wall. Opening the panel revealed a sort of narrow servants' passage. Such passages were common enough in manor-style houses. They allowed for the discreet movement of a butler or maidservant. Christopher ducked as he moved into the low passage ahead. I'd rarely seen him so intent.

I shone my electric lamp first to the north and then to the south, seeing nothing but more cobwebs. "Chris, please."

"Something's wrong here," Violet whispered. "We need to regroup, Henry. Let's go back to the street."

I hesitated long enough for Christopher to turn a corner up ahead. Then my electric torch stuttered and went out.

Violet and I followed Christopher in the dark, listening for the sound of his footfalls. Halfway down the corridor, a loud clanging rang out behind me, and I turned to see that Violet and I had been separated by what appeared to be a latticed metal gate. She stood behind the gate, looking as surprised as I felt.

I put my hands on its bars and attempted to move it, but it was locked in place. "Maybe it was spring-loaded?" I said.

"Please should the gate open?" Violet whispered.

But the gate didn't budge.

"I'll retrace my steps," she said. "Let's meet in the outer hall."

I knew that if there was anyone to worry about, it was Christopher. Violet's ability made her strong. She could take care of herself. Christopher, on the other hand, was far more susceptible to the dangers of the outside world. And so I allowed Violet to turn around and walk the other way, moving back toward the burrow-like maid's quarters. I walked ahead, rounding a corner in the passageway and discovering another open panel. Through it, I entered a double room that had likely once served as some kind of library and reading parlor, though both rooms were now depopulated of books, and a layer of dust covered the empty oaken shelves. Through a doorway, I saw the figure Christopher had been searching for. She had a pinched square face and wore a black bonnet on her head. The woman whispered something to Christopher that appeared to hold him enrapt.

"Chris," I said. "Come away."

But he didn't move.

The woman turned to look at me. Then, as I watched, she gave Christopher what sounded like a command in another language, Italian perhaps.

Christopher, as if obeying, reached up and put one hand on the mask he wore.

"No!" I called.

Yet he could not be stopped. Christopher was removing the sack that obscured his features.

The event seemed to unfold in slow time. As it did, I felt as though I was somehow in two places at once. I was in the empty library at the Tremmond house, watching in horror as my friend revealed his true nature to the woman in the black bonnet. Simultaneously, I stood at the white kitchen door of Coxton & Co. at the very moment when I'd first encountered Christopher X.

I'd been nearly a year into my tenure as a ghost finder then. This was before I'd discovered Violet, but after I'd met Mrs. Hastur. I'd heard some noise that morning at the white kitchen door, a kind of rhythmic scratching. Mrs. Hastur herself stirred a pot on the stove.

"Are there children in the alley again?" I asked, irritated. For the week prior, I'd caught several ruffians making mischief.

"I should hope not, Mr. Coxton," Mrs. Hastur said, adding salt to her stew. "You gave them quite a talking to, didn't you?"

I opened the white door, poking my head into the alley, intending to tell the children to go home. But what I saw staring back at me was not a child. At first, my mind could not properly comprehend the thing. I felt disoriented, then nauseous. For I was confronted by some confusion in category. Body parts were insensibly mashed against one another. And from the look on the creature's face—the fire in its wicked golden eyes—I understood the beast wanted to bring me harm.

I slammed the white alley door and leaned my back against it, finding I could neither speak nor breathe.

Mrs. Hastur carefully laid a wooden spoon in the porcelain tray. Her features spoke a certain calm. "Whatever is the matter, Mr. Coxton?"

I dug my fingernails into the grain of the white door. I'd stand like that forever in order to ensure that the impossible and terrifying thing from outside could never find its way *inside*.

"Perhaps I should have a look," Mrs. Hastur said.

"No! We will not open this door again."

"I've never seen you in quite such a state," Mrs. Hastur said.

"It was like a man. Naked. Covered in filth."

Her dark eyes widened. "Perhaps it's a patient escaped from Bethlehem Royal, sir?"

I shook my head. "It only looked like a man at first, Mrs. Hastur. Then I saw—I saw its face."

"Face, sir?"

"Not like a man's face."

"What, then?"

As I searched for the words, a sound came from behind the door that made my blood feel like ice. The soft rhythmic scratching had started up again.

"It appears to want—" Mrs. Hastur said.

But before she could finish her thought, a great slamming sound came from the alley. The white door shook on its hinges. I clutched at the door as a man lost on a churning sea might clutch a raft.

"Oh dear," Mrs. Hastur said.

The slamming continued. The beast, massive as it was, would soon break the door down. Once inside, it would murder both Mrs. Hastur and me and then suck the flesh from our bones. The last thing I'd see would be the satisfaction in its terrible gold eyes.

"If you'll just stand out of the way, Mr. Coxton, I'll have a word with whoever is out there."

"Have you lost your senses?" I said.

Mrs. Hastur placed one hand firmly on the doorknob and the other on my shoulder. "Mr. Coxton, please."

In the end, I don't know how she managed to peel my body off the door. I was utterly petrified, frozen in place. But Mrs. Hastur had been with me for nearly a year. I trusted her. Her presence bred a certain confidence. Whatever the case, I finally did move and without hesitation, my housemaid opened the door and allowed the thing from the alley—the great foul-smelling, dirt-covered thing—to barrel through into the kitchen and fall to the floor.

Mrs. Hastur looked at the beast with keen interest. I believe that I myself was screaming. A faint blue light flickered in Mrs. Hastur's eyes. "Now then," she said to the thing that held her in its golden gaze, somehow enrapt, somehow calmed. "You really must learn how to behave."

In Tremmond library, I found myself, once again, terrified. Not of Christopher X this time, but of what the world might do to him. For when his mask came off, he became, once more, a confusion of categories. What was revealed as he lifted his mask in the library was the closest held secret of Coxton & Co., dearer than Violet's abnatural gifts or my own history aboard the merchant ship in my youth. Christopher's features, unmasked, were what had caused the flower girl in Mayfair to doubt her own sanity not more than three weeks prior. For his head was not a human head. It was covered in short wiry black hair, from scalp to face. Instead of a mouth he had a muzzle, long and narrow, full of wickedly sharp teeth. His velvet ears stood erect atop his skull. And his golden eyes shone like lamps. I'd reasoned once that his profile looked something like that of a pharaoh hound. But, in truth, it was stranger still. Otherworldly, though from what world, I could not imagine. All that I knew for certain was that his dog-like face was nothing to be feared. It had taken me a good deal of time to understand this. But once I had, I could see great beauty there.

I moved to enter the second room where Christopher and the tall woman stood, but before I could reach them, a door slammed shut between us, this one of paneled wood. I pounded on the door with an open hand, and then from behind me, a male voice: "No need for all that."

I turned and saw a sinewy-looking young man with careful blue eyes and rust-colored eyebrows. He wore a wide-brimmed black hat and black braces. He was handsome, yes, but he was also pointing an antique musket at me.

"What's this?" I said.

"You need to come with me, Mr. Coxton."

"How do you know my name? Have we met?"

"This way," he said, gesturing down the hall with the barrel of his gun.

"But who are you?"

"I'm called Brother James."

"Brother?"

"Just come along now," he said. "Don't turn this into a problem."

CHRISTOPHER X

"MONSTER," SISTER ROSE said. "Sweet monster."

We peered at her in the library room from behind our linen mask. The bones of her face were sharp and white. She looked sick to us. And she smelled of burning too. Just as Violet sometimes smelled of burning. We did not understand this woman's presence. We had been with Henry. We had sensed a power. And now this woman had appeared with her smile and her words that sounded kind but were not kind. "Why have you come here?" we asked.

"This is where I belong," Sister Rose said.

"Do you intend to torment me further as you did in the alley?"

"I'm here to *help* you," she said.

"I do not need help." We were stronger than she was. We could break her bones, devour her if necessary. Yet, there was something in the way she gazed at us. As if she herself was hungry.

"You're lost in this city," Sister Rose said. "You've forgotten your purpose. You must realize that."

"I assist Henry Coxton."

She showed her many teeth.

"Henry is good," we said.

"Trust me when I say you are meant for more."

"What more?"

She looked pleased by our confusion. "In time."

"You do not speak clearly."

"I have a gift for you. One that will make everything sensible again."

Henry had given us gifts at Christmastime: a tin of salted meats, fresh white collars for our shirts, a book for drawing pictures. We knew this woman would give us no such pleasant things.

"It's a gift you've been waiting for," she continued. "A secret that only I know. The New Lord won't like it one bit that I've given you the gift. I'm supposed to attend to Violet. But that can wait. In this case, I'll do as I please."

"I do not want a gift from you."

"Oh, this one you'll want."

We felt like running to find Henry. Perhaps he could help make sense of all this. Henry made sense of so many things. But then the woman spoke again. "Don't be weak. It doesn't become a soldier."

We broadened our shoulders, standing as tall as we could muster. "What is this gift?"

"You've been written about," she said. "You are a *storied* beast. And your arrival here was—anticipated. I understand the spell that's been cast over you. And more than that, I know how to break the spell."

We bristled. "I am under no spell."

"Is there some other reason that you've forgotten your past?" Sister Rose asked. "Some other reason why you behave as a bloodhound for a mortal man?"

We paused, unsure.

"All I have to do to make you remember," Sister Rose said, "is speak your true name to you."

"I know my name well enough."

Sister Rose took a step toward us. She was not afraid. "Christopher is the name *they* gave you."

Not "they," but Henry. He had given us the name, in honor of Saint Christopher. Henry said the name had belonged to a giant who carried Jesus Christ across a river. Some said the giant had a face like ours. *Perhaps Saint Christopher was an old relative*, Henry had said. And we liked the name because we liked Henry.

"*Christopher*," she said. "Such a pitiful sound. Your true name is tethered to the stars."

At that moment, the scent of power that we'd detected in the foyer wafted toward us once more. The source of it was in some room near the library. The scent made us dizzy. We wanted to go to it. And yet we did not know why it had such pull. "What smell is that?" we said.

"Smell?" Sister Rose asked.

"Something old."

"Wouldn't you rather hear your true name? Wouldn't you rather learn your purpose?"

"You do not know my name or my purpose."

"Oh, but I do."

We were tired of her games. "Speak it, then. Speak what you guess to be my name."

Sister Rose opened her mouth.

We felt dizzy, filled with the scent that drifted toward us from the other room.

The woman's bloodless lips formed a single word.

The room tilted.

We watched Sister's Rose's tongue. Her many teeth. We strained to listen to her voice. But we could not hear. It was as if the smell in the library had become a great buzzing sound that filled our head. The sound grew louder still, spreading until it vibrated our entire body, making our skin feel as if it was going to split.

This is what remembering feels like.

And then, we were no longer in the library room. We were no longer anywhere in London. We stood in what appeared to be the great desert of a foreign land. The sky was white. The sand, white. A great wall rose before us, made of charred wood and stone. The sun bore down. Flies circled, landing on our skin. We did not wear our linen mask or our suit of English clothes. Instead we wore a rough cloth fastened about our waist. Our chest was bare. Around our right arm, we wore a hammered copper band. Scorched bones were set into the wall. Skulls stood atop the posts. Empty eye sockets stared down at us.

This is Death's wall. This is where Death keeps his prizes.

The black gate began to open. The gate too was covered in bones. We did not want to see what lay behind the gate. We feared the sight more than anything we'd ever feared before. But we found we could not turn away. We had to see.

There, just inside the charnel gate, was a terrible scene: a man hung naked, nailed with his hands above his head on a tall pike. His legs were broken. Blood, blackened by the sun, streaked his torso. The man's face was swollen with death. His features, sun-spoiled. Flies crawled upon his flesh, drinking the dead man's tears.

We knew this man.

We'd met him long ago.

Mercurius. He was called Mercurius.

As we thought this name, the dead man's head impossibly began to shift. He lifted his chin, opening his mouth. Broken teeth hung from blood-black gums. He stared down at us with silvery eyes. Flies crept from the cavity of his mouth. More flies crawled in the dead man's nose and on his tongue. Shining bodies. Bright wings.

Reprobus, the crucified man said.

His voice was like a great swarm.

Reprobus, he said again.

The word tunneled inside our head, back through our own history.

This man—this Mercurius—flexed his rotting fingers

All is fallen, Mercurius said. *Prepare.*

VIOLET ASQUITH

ALL OF IT wrong. And all at once.

The grate slammed shut in the dim-lit corridor of Number 15 Castle Crescent, separating me from Henry. I turned toward the servant's quarters and noticed a hall I hadn't seen before, a dark stone corridor with rounded arch. Was it possible some hidden door had sprung open when the grate shut? The image of a complicated mousetrap came to mind, pulleys and springs moving in quick succession, leading an unsuspecting creature toward its death.

Henry stumbled away in the darkness, moving toward Christopher and whatever mysterious figure our friend pursued. I almost called out, but I knew that Christopher likely needed more protection than Henry or me. So instead, I returned my attention to the cobwebbed threshold that had so recently appeared. The opening of the second hall was narrow, yet wide enough for me to fit through. The corridor seemed a kind of afterthought, leading toward some barely visible room that was perhaps meant to store an overflow of household goods. Movement caught my eye at the back of the passage. And briefly, I convinced myself I'd seen a figure in the small room there, someone standing in the shadows, watching.

"Hello?" I said, advancing carefully, boots crunching on plaster debris. The only light here came from the faintly illuminated main passage. I raised my hands, palms facing out. If any trouble came, I'd use my talent to defend myself. "Is someone there?" The air remained still, silent. Only when I'd entered the circular room at the end of the passage, a room that was almost entirely dark, did I realize it wouldn't be possible for someone to conceal themselves there. The room was cramped. Not a proper room at all, in fact, but more of a vestibule. If someone stood in that space, I surely would have run directly into him or her.

Having assured myself that no one lurked in the storage chamber, I turned to leave. At that moment, a panel slid across the doorway through which I'd come, blocking my exit, sealing me in darkness.

Mousetrap, I thought again. *Now you're caught.*

Panic fluttered in my chest. Whether the panel had been moved by some mechanism or by an unseen hand, I didn't know. The only thing I was sure of was that I was locked in the dark, all alone. And I had to get out.

I extended my hand toward the closed panel, attempting to focus every ounce of my talent. "Please should the door open?"

The panel didn't budge.

"Please should the door make way?"

Still nothing.

I cursed. "Please might the panel slide? Please might the door— Christ—please might the blasted door do anything at all?" I pushed against the unmoving panel and felt another twinge of fear. Whoever had sealed me in this room had done a careful job. I pounded my palm against the panel then. "Henry?" I called. "Are you out there?"

There was no answer.

I slid my hands against the cold stone wall and began to feel my way through the dark, searching for another opening or some object I could use to batter against the door. But, as far as I could tell, the rough bricks of the wall were unadorned.

"Steady," I whispered. For if my ability wouldn't cooperate, I'd have to reason my way out of this room.

You've grown so weak, child, Father said, voice rising up from memories. *Helpless as a moth in a lantern case.*

"And you're dead," I replied. "At least I'm better off than that."

It was then that something even more incredible occurred. Though I felt no physical barrier in the darkness before me, my hands inexplicably ceased their exploration, and I found I could move them no further. I'd met with some resistance, and yet at the same time, I could feel no physical object before me. It was almost as if my talent was behaving in a manner directly opposite of what I was accustomed. Instead of me moving the world, the world was suddenly moving me. The very air before me had turned solid.

I listened intently, but could hear only the sound of my own breath. I attempted to press one hand forward again. Still, the hand wouldn't move. Then, from a distance, Henry's voice. He shouted for Christopher to stop and sounded terribly distressed.

"Henry?" I called, turning in the dark. "What's wrong?"

I don't know how long I waited, listening for some further clue as to what was happening to my friends. But, sometime later, I heard another panel open on my right-hand side. Then came the sound of a woman's voice. "No use calling out," she said.

"Who's there?" I asked blindly. "Who speaks?"

A match flame flickered. Before me, a face floated. The sharp angle of the cheeks and the broadness of the forehead made the face look almost like a funeral mask. It was the woman in the black bonnet. The woman who'd been pursuing me for weeks. She was pallid now, sapped of some vital energy.

"How—" I said, feeling at once angry and frightened.

The woman's match flame went out, plunging us into darkness once more.

I thought back to the black carriage that I'd seen in the courtyard, my own dead father's carriage. The woman had boarded it as if it belonged to her.

"Her highness wouldn't recognize any such as me," the woman said in the darkness.

"Highness?"

"She who comes from the great house. The girl with dark hair and wintery eyes."

"Do you mean Nethersea Hall? You *are* from the village, then."

"I am not from the *village*," the woman said sharply. She lit another match, and her face blazed into existence once more. Lines appeared at the sides of her mouth and on her forehead, an expression of deep-rooted anger. She spoke her next words through her teeth. "Look at me as I stand here."

"I *am* looking."

The woman smiled. "I too am from the great house. From Nethersea Hall."

I shook my head. "It was only Father and Mother," I said, wondering if she was mad. "There were the servants too. But no one else."

"Arrogance has made you blind," the woman said.

"I don't understand. I'm here with my associates. We're searching for an abnatural."

"You're here because I brought you."

"Tell me your name. Is it Tremmond?"

"Not Tremmond..."

"You caused the doors in the hall to move, didn't you?" I said. "Just as you untied the ropes on Bachelor Street. You're somehow the same as me. You have my ability."

"*Your* ability. Everything belongs to you, doesn't it, Violet? *Your* father and *your* mother. Your house."

"They are all mine," I said. "Much as I despise them."

"And you never considered—" The woman stopped, emotion getting the best of her.

"Considered what?"

"That you might not have been the first one. That there may have been *another* child. You never saw signs?"

Another?

I thought back to Nethersea Hall. Ancient house, filled with ancient relics: dusty dresses and worn-out frocks, a hand mirror and a hairbrush that might have once belonged to a child. I'd always assumed they were the property of some ancestor. I hadn't dared ask Father.

"Speak plainly," I said.

"You were not Father's first experiment. A sister came before you."

I fell silent. A sister? That wasn't possible. Surely I would have known. "But—why did I never meet you?"

"Father couldn't have you distracted from your task. From the dark mirror. I am what you might call his *failed* experiment. My name is Rose."

"Rose," I whispered. The name echoed in my memory. Had I heard it spoken before? Perhaps Mother, in her ravings, had even called me Rose once by mistake.

"Two flowers," she said. "Rose and Violet, Violet and Rose, both wanting the love of the gardener."

"Yet you wear the black bonnet," I said.

"Father sent me to the village, exiled me after it became evident that I could not commune with his dark mirror. He waited until it was clear that Mother was with child once again, of course."

"Sister," I said. The word felt strange in my mouth.

"You must have been so happy," Rose said, "to have Father all to yourself."

"No—"

"He was a man of vision, meant to rescue us all from torment. But you put an end to that, didn't you Violet? You were selfish."

"You don't understand."

"Don't tell me what I do and do not understand," she said. "I've spent years in study. I stole a book from Father. I learned things he would never have wanted me to know. Why do you think your powers have been waning? It's because I too am now connected to the mirror. But it wasn't until the New Lord came that—"

"New Lord?" I asked, fear twisting in my stomach.

"The heir to Father's kingdom. A man who understands the mirror."

"No one understands the mirror," I said. "The mirror—"

"The New Lord came to me in Nethersea Village. He explained what we must do. He trained me, helped me better my abilities. My acts still make me weak. You can see that I am sick. But I'll grow stronger still."

"You mustn't listen to this New Lord, Rose," I said. "I'm sorry I didn't know you as a child. I'm sorry Father treated you poorly. But you must understand—the magicians, all of them—they are dangerous."

"The woman I was forced to call mother," Rose said, "she was not kind. She treated me little better than one of her animals. Yet she allowed me to go out onto the street when Father's fine carriage descended from the great house. I loved the way the sun glinted off the carriage's glass windows. I loved the way his lordship kept the black horses groomed. I remembered riding in that carriage myself once. Time and again, I saw your face in the carriage window. Your ivory skin. Your silken hair. And I would think: how lucky she is, my sister. How lucky indeed. For I knew, of course, that you were my sister. And I knew you must be powerful too. You must have pleased Father in ways I could not." Rose paused. "Then there was a day when I grew bold. I thought I would speak to you. I thought I would tell you who I was. Ask you how it was to be in the great house still. I gathered my courage. I ran toward your carriage."

"You—" I said. For I remembered this moment, a wan girl in a black bonnet rushing toward Father's carriage.

"Do you recall what you did that day when I tried to speak to you?" Rose asked.

"I was a frightened child. I didn't understand the village or why Father took me there."

"You *recoiled*," Rose said, "as if I was some barking dog."

"I had my own pain," I said.

"I felt so ashamed. I thought you must have deserved your life. Just as I deserved mine. Somehow, you were better than me."

"It wasn't like that, Rose."

"You had *everything*," she said. "You had the attentions of his lordship."

"Attentions? Is that what you would call it?"

"And you threw all of it away. Every bit. Because you were a spoiled thing. Because you were callow. You took his lordship away from Nethersea. Even as he promised to help the people of the village, to help even me."

"What do you mean by 'help?'" I asked.

"If we served him," she said. "That was the covenant. It had always been the covenant since the coming of the Black Death."

"Rose," I said. "You don't know what it was to live in that house with him in those final days. Father was not a kind man. He served only himself."

"How dare you?" I could hear the sweep of her dress in the darkness as she moved toward me. "You will see. Father will help us still. And he will understand now which of his daughters has served him better. Which of his daughters truly deserved his attentions."

"Father is dead."

At that, Rose lit another match.

She stood quite close to me. For a moment, I thought she intended to set me on fire. But there was, in fact, a tallow candle in a wall sconce behind me. She lit the candle, illuminating the room. For the first time, I saw my surroundings clearly. And I wished the awful space would go black again. For there before me in the alcove was the very thing that had ruled over my childhood. The dreadful thing that had enchanted me, giving me my powers.

The magician's glass.

I'd shattered it so many years ago, broken it into three pieces. And yet, somehow, it had come back. Two shards of it hung on the wall before me, fitted together like pieces of a puzzle. The third piece was missing still.

I stood before the broken mirror, unable to speak.

"Look," Rose said. "See."

"What have you done?"

"We understand the mirror now. The New Lord has discovered how to unleash its power. To awaken what he calls its ancient technologies."

I backed away from the thing. Still, I could see myself reflected in the mirror's depths. The room was so small. I could not escape the mirror's gaze.

I felt as if I was a little girl again, pale and shaking. I heard Father's voice: *Look, Violet. Look until the mirror sees. Look until it knows you.*

"Please might the mirror fall?" I whispered in the stone alcove. "Please might it break?

The mirror did not fall. It did not break.

Rose laughed.

I closed my eyes, but still I could see the mirror. Dark and shining. Full of poisonous allure. I opened my eyes again.

And I stared into the black mirror.

It, in turn, stared into me.

ħEꟁRᴜ ꞬOXTOꟁ

A LACEWORK OF brown water stains spread across the ceiling and down the peeling yellow wallpaper of the room where Brother James took me. The stains seemed a hand-written message, a code no longer discernible. All meaning was obscured in the Tremmond house. Confusion knew no bounds.

With the barrel of his antique musket, Brother James gestured toward a wooden chair in the center of the room. "If you'll just sit, Mr. Coxton."

"I don't understand." I felt cold, covered in sweat.

"Just need to take a seat."

"Look," I said, "James, is it?"

"It is."

"I'm a ghost finder by trade."

"We are aware of that."

"Well, I don't mean you any harm. My associates and I are here at the request of a Mrs. Eldora Tremmond, the lady of the house. You can contact her. We aren't trespassing, if that's what you think."

"I don't believe you to be trespassing," Brother James said.

"I need to find my friends. I'm worried that they're—"

"I can't let you go, Mr. Coxton," Brother James said, and I wondered if I heard the slightest note of remorse in his voice. "The chair, please. Just do as I say."

I considered bolting from the room. But I was all too aware that the Brown Bess, an old military-style gun, fired a scatter shot. The small lead beads would likely hit me even if Brother James didn't have perfect aim. Slowly, I lowered myself into the chair, trying to think what Phillip Langford might advise in a moment like this.

Brother James moved to the far end of the empty room and adopted a wide stance. Despite my fear, I studied him, looking for some clue that might set me free. He wore clothes of a country fashion: wide black hat, farmer's braces, rough-looking black trousers. The whole of it almost seemed a kind of costume, much like the garments of the woman who'd been speaking to Christopher in the library. He was strong-looking, as if he worked the land.

Sinews in his forearms flexed as he lifted the musket into position, pointing it at me.

He used his thumb to pull back the hammer of the flintlock.

"Wait!" I said.

He looked up, eyes clear and sharp.

"You don't actually intend to shoot me, do you?"

"Stay very still, Mr. Coxton."

"But for what *reason*?" This entire mess seemed so absurd. We'd been on a ghost finding expedition, attempting to make contact with a dead man, and now I was apparently waiting to become a dead man myself. "What crime do you think I've committed?"

"It isn't about what you've done," Brother James said. "It's about what you *might* do."

"Might?" I said. "But I don't intend to do anything. I've already told you, I'm a ghost finder."

"Yes, we know a great many things about you."

"Who?" I asked. "And what else do you know?"

Brother James furrowed his brow. "I know about what happened on board the merchant ship, the *Daedalus*, for instance."

"You know about *that*?" I asked, honestly flummoxed. "How could you know such a thing?"

"You met a young man called Paser, Egyptian-born," Brother James said. "You cared for him. Like Achilles cared for Patroclus."

"Yes, but—"

"And you lost him. You believe that the other men, the sailors aboard the *Daedalus*, had something to do with it."

"If you care enough to know all of this, why would you want to shoot me?"

Brother James lowered his musket. "I don't want to shoot you, Mr. Coxton. But the New Lord has ordered it. So you must remain very still."

"New Lord? Who is this New Lord?"

"Bringer of salvation," Brother James said. "Slayer of death." He raised the musket once more, locating me in its sights. "Now, don't shift about."

"Stop!"

"I'm not even supposed to talk with you, Mr. Coxton. I've already said too much."

"You're going to kill me without even letting me know why?"

At that, Brother James pulled the trigger, and a thunderous report shook the room as black smoke spilled from the gun. I found myself suddenly on the floor with the chair on top of me, a high-pitched whine ringing in my ears. I knew I'd been shot. I must have been. Filled up with the musket's lead. I'd suddenly been made a ghost, and I'd haunt this house that had no spirits. But even as I thought this, I realized I was still able to move my limbs. I experienced no pain. I struggled to disengage myself from the chair.

Brother James stood on the opposite side of the room, peering at me through the smoke. "You moved, Mr. Coxton. I asked you not to move."

I half-crawled, half-ran for the door.

"Don't run," Brother James called. "That will only make things worse."

"Violet!" I yelled stumbling down the hall, running back toward the library. "Christopher!" No bullet had entered me, and I didn't want to give Brother James a second chance.

The library room was empty. Christopher's mask lay on the floor like some wrinkled piece of flesh. I grabbed the mask and held it tightly, as it was the only thing that made sense in this house of terrors. The passageway where I'd left Violet was empty too. I prayed my friends had exited the Tremmond house, made their way to safety. I too had to leave the house before Brother James reloaded his musket. And so, with that, I ran for the stairs, the foyer, and the street beyond.

CHRISTOPHER X

OUR HEAD, FULL of black flies, a maddening sound, the rise and fall. Winged bodies crawling upon the very surface of our brain, biting into soft tissue, wanting to burrow deeper. We pressed our hands against the hollows of our skull and howled as we blundered down the stairs. What house was this? Why had we come? We half-remembered a library. The woman. She must have been a witch. The house was a witch's snare. And she had conjured the man in the desert. *All is fallen, Reprobus. Prepare.*

Reprobus.

The name put a crack inside us. Black memories threatened to bubble forth.

Flies inside our skull again, blotting out thoughts.

All that mattered was escape.

We threw open the door of the house and stumbled out into a yellow fog that smelled of sulfur, the rot of the upper air. Our suit clung too tight. Fabrics squeezed our chest, restraining the movement of our arms. We pulled at the jacket, tearing buttons, letting them fall to the street. We ripped the stiff white collar from our throat, tossing it to the gutter. We hurried from the house, away from the witch and the library and images she'd conjured. We smelled the blood of slaughterhouses, the caustic vapors of tanneries. Piss in the streets and piles of dung. London was a wretched cage.

Then, some twenty yards ahead, a figure turned to look at us. A boy, no more than ten years of age, brown hair standing in unkempt whorls. He was tall for a child, long limbed. In his hand, he carried what appeared to be a letter, and he made his way through the fog toward a pillar-box on the corner. His parents must have sent him out, trusting their son would be safe, protected by the watchful eye of neighbors.

We slipped into the shadows and watched.

The boy heard our movements. He peered through the curtain of yellow fog.

All is fallen, Reprobus.

Our muscles tightened. The boy remained still.

The hunt was a game.

Who would move first?

The wind shifted, lifting tendrils of fog. We were revealed. The boy saw our shape. He stepped backward and opened his mouth. Such fear in his eyes. He saw us now. We, who were born of a nightmare. We, who had lived as a nightmare. And now this unsuspecting boy had fallen into our own dark dream. We could see the boy's teeth, his tongue. He looked as if he was going to sing. But, instead of singing, the boy began to scream. The highest of terrified shrieks. The sound surprised us. Our ears stiffened. The sound echoed. It made the flies grow wild.

We launched ourselves at the boy, feet barely touching cobblestone. With great force, we snatched the child up by one fragile arm. We raised him into the air, letting his feeble legs kick. He screamed again, a high and mewling wail. We squeezed his throat to stop his screams. Screams would bring men from the houses. But we did not squeeze hard enough to break the boy's neck. We wanted him alive. It was better when they were alive.

The boy dangled, weightless.

We gazed into his eyes, our face reflected there. Bright and golden eyes. Long muzzle covered in bristling hair. Saliva dripped from our jaw. When we had joined Coxton & Co., we had attempted to deny our nature. We wanted to be like Henry. To be loved by Henry. But no more of that.

All is fallen.

Every thought now of death. Every thought of blood.

Prepare.

We were hungry. We had been hungry for such a long time. We had acted not like ourselves. We wore an English suit. We lived in an English house.

We could smell the boy's liver. His beating heart. His twisted guts. He'd eaten chickpea soup and a crust of bread for dinner. He'd drunk a glass of his father's wine. We could smell the wine on his breath.

All is fallen.

We could almost taste the boy.

We drew him to our mouth. He made a squealing noise. An animal that knew its death had come. We opened our jaws.

"You there!" a man shouted from the fog. "Release that child!"

We strained to see.

The man wore a gray suit. He carried an umbrella and a leather case. His face was chalk white. His expression said that something as terrible as us could not exist. Not on his street. Or in his world.

"Wolf!" he called. "Constable, come quickly! There's some kind of animal!"

We released the boy from our grasp. He fell, striking the stone walk. We heard a bone crack in his leg. The boy began to scream, clutching at himself. We launched our body toward the black alley, the man still shouting behind us.

We hurried down alleyways, having learned London's patterns long ago, long before we met Henry and Violet and Mrs. Hastur. We'd stalked secrets and tunnels. And now we stumbled through the maze once more, scraping shoulders against moss-covered bricks, tearing holes in our English suit. A woman in a dank vestibule called out to us. She wore a low-cut dress and black stockings. She must have thought we were drunk. She'd mistaken us for a man who might want her sex. But when she saw our face, she too began to scream.

We wanted to devour her. Yet we knew we could not pause.

Danger pressed from behind. We rode its crest. Rushing past hidden saloons and decrepit shanties, Tarot houses and rooms for the sick.

All is fallen.

It was near the end of the alley that we saw *him* again—the dead man from the desert, Mercurius. He shimmered there, as if trapped beneath water. He'd descended from his pole. Bloodied hands hung at his sides.

75

His face was black and swollen, covered in shining flies. Maggots curled in pink flesh. The man's eyes were white, clouded with death. Still, he watched.

We shook our head furiously. Trying to make the vision depart. But Mercurius stepped toward us, hands raised. We saw moonlight streaming through holes in his palms.

We ran again, away from horrors we did not understand. We were close to Coxton & Co. Close to the home Henry had made for us. We had a moment to pause, to question. What would Henry think of what we'd done to the boy? The havoc we had caused? We were not wearing our mask. The mask that Henry had given us. He would be so angry. He would tell us what a wrong thing we had done. Yet Henry could not imagine all that we were capable of. We had not done as much as we wanted to do.

Reprobus, prepare.

We emerged in a familiar alley off Bachelor Street where there hung the tarnished brass plaque with the words Henry had once read to us: *Coxton & Co. Est. 1901.* Home. Finally, home. The red bricks of the house made the flies settle in our mind. The confusion of the street was behind us. And yet, even here, in this safest of places, something had gone wrong. For the white door that led to the kitchen appeared ajar. A line of the darkness appeared at its crisp border. Mrs. Hastur would never have left the door open. For her, every hasp was fastened, every button done.

We approached, sniffing for some clue, nudging the door, first with our hand and then with our nose. We smelled onions in the pantry, lye above the sink. We glanced behind us, worried that the fly-ravaged spirit, Mercurius, might have followed.

We entered the kitchen. No stew simmered there. The stove smelled cold, another fact that worried us. Mrs. Hastur's stove was always lit.

We moved down the long hall, sniffing for intruders. It was only when we got a good whiff of the air near the closed cellar door near the foyer that our blood turned to ice. For we smelled hollyhocks and ivy and the tang of human musk. Men from the country. They'd been here in Henry's house. Men who smelled like the witch in the library, the witch called Sister Rose.

When we reached Henry's offices, we saw what the men from the country had done. Our home was in shambles. Ransacked. Papers lay scattered across the hardwood, trampled by boots. The leather chair where clients sat and met with us was overturned. Henry's implements of magic had been torn from their cabinets. They lay broken on the floor.

"Mrs. Hastur!" we called. Now, we could hear the flies again. If something had happened to our old friend who tucked us in at night and told us stories, we thought we would kill everyone in the English city. We would tear down every English building. The streets themselves would bleed. "Mrs. Hastur, are you here? Make yourself known."

The house remained silent.

We searched for some explanation. Why had these men from the country come? Why had they disturbed our quiet living space?

A moan then from the staircase.

Mrs. Hastur was at the top of the stair. Her hair had been ripped from its pins and lay in long gray curls about her shoulders. A reddish welt ran down the right side of her face. Her usually cheerful expression was a mask of fear.

"Mrs. Hastur? What has happened?"

She gripped the banister. "Oh, Christopher, I think I've made a mistake." She moved uneasily, favoring her leg on the right. We thought she might fall. Might further injure herself. We rushed up the steps to help her, reaching out our arms. She drew back when she saw our state. "What in Heaven's name?"

Our suit, covered in alley muck, hung in ribbons. We were ashamed. Mrs. Hastur looked at us now as if we were some dangerous thing. "There was great trouble, Mrs. Hastur. The Tremmond house. A woman in the library. I was—not myself."

"Your *eyes*," she said.

We closed our eyes. We knew they were wild. Full of our old instincts.

"And your suit."

"I am sorry, Mrs. Hastur ."

"Where is Henry? And Violet?"

We shook our head. We did not know. "Tell me what happened. Why is the house ruined? And what error have you made?"

"I need to speak to Henry."

"He is not here," we said too sharply. "You must speak to me."

Mrs. Hastur leaned against the banister, covering her face with one hand.

"I am sorry," we said, for how could have spoken sharply to someone who was like our mother? "I am sorry, Mrs. Hastur. I did not mean to speak to you in such a way."

She reached out to touch the fur upon our face. She stroked us gently. "It's not your fault. I can tell it's not your fault, my dear Christopher."

"Please, tell me what happened."

"Three men," Mrs. Hastur said, "in black hats. They came to the door. They asked for Mr. Coxton. They told me he had something that belonged to them. When I said he wasn't home, they pushed the door open. I fell." She reached up to touch the welt on her face. "They spent nearly an hour searching the house."

We growled.

Mrs. Hastur shook her head. "You must control yourself."

"What does Henry have that belongs to these men?"

"I'm not sure."

"And the error? You said that you made an error."

"I can't tell you what the mistake is, Christopher. But, well, all of this, the entire situation, is much worse than I originally understood."

It was then that we heard a sound at the front door. Our hackles rose. The intruders had returned. We would punish them for what they had done to Henry's house, for what they had done to Mrs. Hastur. "Stand behind me, Mrs. Hastur. Stand behind me now."

She did as we asked, and we turned to face the door. We did not want our friend to see the blood we would spill. We did not want her to know how we could rip a man apart muscle by muscle, bone by bone. But when the door opened, it was not a man from the country who entered. It was Henry Coxton himself, clutching our mask in his hand.

"My God," he said, gazing up at us as we stood on the stairs and then at his offices. "Christopher, my God." He paused. "Where's Violet?"

"I believed she was with you, Henry," we said.

"Mrs. Hastur," Henry said. "Are you all right?"

"Oh, Mr. Coxton," Mrs. Hastur said, emerging from behind me.

"Can you see Violet? Can you see where she is?"

"I'm shaken," Mrs. Hastur said.

"Please. You must try."

Mrs. Hastur closed her eyes. She smelled so strange when she performed her act of seeing, like the sky itself. The room rippled. Finally, Mrs. Hastur opened her eyes, appearing confused.

"She's not here, Henry," Mrs. Hastur said.

"What do you mean?" he asked. "Not here in the house? Not here in London?"

Mrs. Hastur shook her head. "No, I mean—Violet, she's not here in the world. It seems she's nowhere at all."

VIOLET ASQUITH

MY REFLECTION. FRACTURED in shards of black obsidian.

Sister Rose, my murky double, hung behind me like some specter. "Closer," she whispered. "The mirror wants you closer."

"You cannot know what it wants," I said. For no matter how phantasmal Rose might appear, she did not speak for the mirror. No one could. "How did you find these pieces?"

"You underestimate my cleverness. Father always underestimated me as well."

"A clever person would have left the mirror alone. I broke it into pieces for a reason."

"You think you're so mighty with your friends and your abilities and your London," she said.

"None of us are mighty in the eye of the mirror."

"The New Lord understands—"

"Stop talking about this *New* Lord," I said. "The self-proclaimed magicians are a group of arrogant, foolish men. The sooner you recognize that, the safer we're all going to be."

"The New Lord rescued me from the village," Rose said. "Took me into his care. You cannot imagine how I suffered."

"At least the village was quiet and safe." I gestured toward Father's dark mirror. "Standing before this thing, day after day, trying to unlock secrets that could not be unlocked for a man who'd gone half-mad, *that* is suffering, Rose."

"You served a greater plan."

"I was Father's tool."

"You never respected him," she said, as if she hadn't heard me. "In the end, you did such terrible things, unforgivable acts. But all of that will be remedied now. Closer, Violet. The New Lord says you must be close."

I turned to look at the broken glass once more. A memory from childhood unfolded like the petals of a dark flower. I walked with Father over the cold and muddied paths in the bleak gardens at Nethersea Hall. I was so small. It was all I could do to keep up with his rugged strides. I believed Father was remarkable then. Cloaked and bearded, leonine in his grandeur. He wore three rings on his right hand: two of brass and one of gold. They were magician's rings, the ornaments of a sage. I trusted his proclamations and loved him so completely. More than anything, I wanted Father to love me in return.

If I tarried in the garden, the sound of Father's voice echoed from the sickly flowers and the withered vines, even from the ruined mouths of pagan statuary. "Violet, are you with me?" the voice said. And without hesitation, I would say: "Yes, Father, always." Then I'd run to him and place my small hand in his. We'd continue to walk as he spoke soliloquies about the mirror. "The Egyptians called it 'Eye of Osiris,'" he said. "Rotting green god of Death, yet I do not believe they forged the glass. Its true provenance is lost to time. But the mirror's emergence into history comes most certainly when it was discovered in the reeds of the Nile by the soldiers of Amenhotep. Those men went mad from looking at it."

"Mad?" I said.

"They were not prepared to receive its storehouse of knowledge."

"The mirror contains knowledge?"

Had I been older, I might have recognized that Father had no answer for my query. He understood so little about the thing that fascinated him.

"There are those who believe the mirror will one day allow us to commune with a cosmic intelligence," he continued. "The intelligence— be it angelic or some other more obscure divinity—will reveal knowledge lost to humanity since the age of the prophet Enoch. And there are still others who say the mirror will become a scrying stone. Visions are to be granted, an understanding of the spiritual dimensions. The arcane technology that lies dormant inside the mirror today was somehow still active, at least in part, when the soldiers of Amenhotep discovered it. Those weak-minded fools learned nothing, of course. They returned the mirror to the waters of the Nile. And there it slept, waiting."

"You hope to wake the mirror, then?" I asked.

"When the key is turned," Father said, "great understanding will come to us. There will be no more suffering, Violet. Perhaps no more death. Man will be master of creation, as before the Fall of Adam."

"But what is the key?"

"What indeed," Father replied, pulling his mantle of ermine against the damp cold of the garden.

* * *

Father's branch of the family line had grown queer over the years. Money dwindled and philosophies rose from ruined fortune. As a young man, Father delved into the Black Arts, presiding over a group of like-minded adepts, a cabal who thought they could change their own fates by learning antique secrets. At equinox and solstice, they arrived in lampless carriages and met together in a chamber beneath Nethersea Hall. Father made them privy to the mirror, and together they studied the thing. Mother, already fragile, spoke of Father's prowess. She lingered on the white divan of her tower room, cooing and praising his lordship. She said, "Violet, you must always be true to him. You are his hope for salvation."

Early in our dealings with the dark mirror, Father confided he was not the powerful magician everyone believed. All his studies in the Black Arts had come to naught. He possessed no special power. He'd never performed a conjuring. "Of course, no man is ever as strong as he pretends," he said. "But if you serve your purpose well, Violet, I can perhaps become something of the man I've imagined."

"I'll help you," I said. "I promise."

He patted me gently. "You are a fine girl."

I smiled. He loved me. I knew he did.

Yet despite my best intentions, making a man into what he'd imagined himself to be proved far too daunting a task for a child. I stood for months, then for years, in the mirror's Western Tower, staring at my own reflection in the black glass, waiting for a revelation. I recited incantations. Father drew symbols on my skin in ash. I drank countless foul elixirs that made me ill for days. One of them caused a temporary blindness. Another evoked fits of screaming. And when none of this had the desired effect, Father's rituals grew even more extreme. I was forced to kill a rabbit as a kind of sacrifice. He had some idea that putting the blood of the freshly dead animal on the mirror would enliven the glass. The poor field rabbit, soft and brown, wriggled in my hands, attempting escape. I had some difficulty breaking its skin with the blade Father had given me, and after I'd finally punctured the flesh, the rabbit began to howl. The animal scratched at me, attempting in vain to free itself. Hot blood ran down my fingers and onto my dress. I wept as I pushed the knife deeper, if nothing else just to silence the animal. The rabbit cried and then shuddered. And when it was finally dead, when my hands were covered in blood, the mirror still had not changed. It hung on the wall, nothing more than a black and silent stone. I dropped the knife and held the rabbit to my chest like a broken doll. I turned to look at Father and said through gritted teeth, "I will not do that again." He nodded, looking pale, and then he walked from the tower room.

I was tormented by our rituals, yes. But somehow Father seemed even more so. For it soon became clear to him that I would not wake the mirror. I was not to be its priestess. And because of this, he grew distant, sometimes even cruel. I didn't know then, of course, that he'd already enacted such rituals once before with my sister, Rose. That he'd abandoned her in the village.

Father spoke to me with increasing rarity. He stopped taking me on walks in the garden. Instead, he walked alone, muttering to the white peacocks. The creatures watched him with watery pink eyes, calling out in their odd cat-like voices.

I felt that I had failed. I felt that I was nothing.

* * *

Now, inside the Tremmond house, I stood before the glass once more, gazing into the shadows of its black and haunted plane. The tiny alcove was reflected there, and Sister Rose in her dark bonnet, holding the flickering candle. I saw my own corseted suit-dress and my pale, almost translucent, skin. I examined the crack in the mirror, remembering the day the glass had fallen from its mount upon the wall. *Please should the mirror rescue me?* I'd said. *Please should the mirror use its hand?* I took a step closer, studying the way Rose's candle flame shone in the polished surface. Darkness devoured the light. The closer I drew, the more the mirror seemed to thrum.

"How long have you been planning this?" I asked Rose.

"It is a culmination of our work," she replied.

"Why did you come to taunt me these last weeks? Surely, that wasn't wise."

"I couldn't help myself," Rose said. "I wanted to see your life as it is. As it was."

"Was?"

"Yes," Rose said.

"You must realize I can destroy the mirror."

"You might break it," Rose said. "But nothing will ever destroy it."

I took another step closer to the thing, feeling the pull of it. As I looked deeper into the mirror, Rose seemed far less important, as did the plans of the so-called New Lord. "Why now?" I said, knowing that magicians were fascinated by calendars, markers of time.

"We have found a way to make the mirror *restless*," Rose replied.

I worried, for a moment, that she might speak the truth. Perhaps that's why my own talent had waned. The mirror drew energy back into itself.

"Just a few more steps," she said. "It's gears—they're turning, Violet. Can't you feel it?"

Her words sounded as if they were spoken from some great distance.

"What exactly do you think the mirror will do? Open like a mouth? Announce some secret?"

Rose made no reply. I was very close to the mirror now. And I realized I could no longer see her reflected behind me in the black glass. The light of her candle was gone. And I felt as if my boots were no longer planted firmly on the ground. It was as if I floated in the slippery fluid of the mirror's eye. And when I turned to look behind me, I discovered Rose had left the alcove. The door to the little storage room stood open. I was alone. I looked back at the dark mirror. It stared blankly at me.

"Henry?" I called.

My voice echoed oddly in the room—odd because the room was so small, there should have been no echo. I walked down the narrow hall that led to the main artery of the secret passage. The hall had changed in some subtle way, though I could not describe precisely how.

"Christopher?" My voice sounded too loud in my ears.

I exited the secret passage and moved into what appeared to be a library cleared of its books. From there, I went to the foyer. It felt like so long ago that the three of us had all stood together in that room. Finding no one, I left the Tremmond house through the front door and moved down the nighttime street of Castle Crescent. The sky above looked strange. Not black exactly, but rather a flat gray. There were no stars.

Halfway down the street, I stopped. Something was wrong. The street appeared deserted, entirely so. There were no longer any candles in the houses. No arc lamps had been lit. It couldn't be much past eight o'clock in the evening. Yet silence ruled Castle Crescent, such a silence as I had never known in London. I heard no voice in the distance, nor horse's hoof, nor the whine of an electric motorcar.

I walked on. But, soon enough, I paused once again, for the sound of my own boot heels was impossibly loud. I told myself I'd halted because I was worried the sound might draw attention. Yet, it was something more than that. My own footfalls had, in fact, sounded unnatural in the dead silence of this place. And that fact frightened me.

Quickly, I unfastened my boot buckles, slipping the boots off and carrying them in my hand. The cobbles beneath my stocking feet were neither warm nor cold. It was as if no life had ever touched this place. This was the London I knew, and yet it was not that place at all. Everything I loved about my city, the bustle and the life—the features that made London so different from Nethersea—had been drained.

I decided, in that moment, to return to Coxton and Co. Henry would help me make sense of this. And even if he couldn't, it would be good to at least see his face.

Yet the further I walked, the more I began to doubt that I would find Henry at all. For why would he be here if no one else was?

I moved toward the center of the city, toward Piccadilly. Still, I saw no human and no animal. Then, finally, a sound came just as I reached the bookman's stalls on Holywell. A kind of hushed sigh, quite loud in the dead silence of the street.

"Steady, Violet," I whispered.

My voice was nearly like a scream.

The sighing floated toward me once more.

I hurried along, barefoot, striving to remain as quiet possible. But my heart beat too hard in my chest. I could hear its throb.

Finally, I turned to look behind me down the cobbled thoroughfare. And in the far distance, I saw a figure, though the lack of light from streetlamps made it difficult to discern the figure's precise form. It appeared to be a human body, yet it did not stand on two legs. Instead, the figure crawled on its hands and knees, slouching toward me. It came slowly, but with a relentless sense of purpose. The figure's head swayed as if searching. I heard it sigh once again (for it was this creature that sighed). The sigh was the sound of yearning. The creature was filled with want. In all my time with Henry, all my hunting of abnaturals, I'd never seen or heard anything so frightening.

I thought that if I could just reach Coxton & Co., if I could make it home, I would find safety. Because even in this strange, silent city where I now found myself, I still had a home, didn't I? A safe place that Henry Coxton had made for me.

When I reached Bachelor Street, barefoot and striding, the sigh, for the briefest moment, became a voice. And what a strange voice it was. Airy. Filled with the silvery tones of another world.

Violet, are you with me?

I did not respond.

Are you with me? the voice said again. *Are you with me?*

These words were the same as those Father had spoken long ago in the garden.

And I wanted to call out, to tell the voice that I would never follow anyone again. Yet, I could not open my mouth. I could not speak in all that silence. So instead, I ran. Fleeing toward the safety of home.

ħЄПRY ÇOXTOП

COXTON & CO. stood in shambles, and the frightened expression on Mrs. Hastur's face indicated she understood what had happened no better than I. On top of all this, Christopher appeared to have devolved. He looked nearly prehistoric, gold eyes nearly as wild as when I'd first encountered him in the alley. His suit was torn, and his rough fur showed through. Worst of all, his spectacular face was entirely exposed, and likely had been for his entire race through the city. I thought of the man I'd overheard on Castle Crescent explaining to a constable what he'd seen: *Monstrously deformed, sir. Slavering jaws. Like that of a wolf. He would have murdered the child if I hadn't—*

"Three intruders," Mrs. Hastur said. "Black hats, Mr. Coxton.

"Men from the country," Christopher added.

"Searching for something," Mrs. Hastur said. "They believed you have an object that belonged to them."

I bent down to pick up the broken fragment of a Coptic vase, one of Phillip Langford's occult antiquities. These men, dressed like Brother James by sound of it, had been interested in one of the relics. But which one? It was impossible to know.

"The Tremmond house," I said, "the whole case, Mrs. Hastur, was some kind of ruse. A way to separate us."

"For what purpose?" she asked.

I shook my head, trying to imagine a way to proceed. "The woman in the library," I said to Christopher. "You recognized her?"

He bowed his head. "She came to look at me in the alley last week when I was catching rats. She told me her name was Sister Rose. I am sorry I did not tell you."

"Were you wearing your mask in the alley?"

"I was not."

"And this woman—this Sister Rose—she wasn't afraid?"

"She was not."

"So she must have had some prior knowledge of you?"

"I believe she did," Christopher replied.

"And what did she say to you in the library? It sounded like a word in some foreign tongue."

"I am afraid I cannot tell you that, Henry."

"Now isn't the time to be hiding things, Chris. We are all in some danger, I believe. Especially Violet."

"I do not want to put Violet in danger," Christopher said.

"Then you must be forthcoming. What word did the woman speak to you?"

"My name," he said. "The woman told me my true name. The one I had before you called me Christopher."

Of all the things he could have said, I certainly hadn't been expecting this. "How could anyone know that? We don't even know where you came from."

Christopher shook his head. "Sister Rose said she learned it in a book, Henry."

"Well, what was the name?"

"I do not want to repeat it," he said.

"Why not?"

"Because the name brings back the past."

"Whose past?"

"My own," Christopher said.

"Mr. Coxton," Mrs. Hastur interrupted. "Perhaps we shouldn't press poor Christopher too much right now. I'll have a word with him after you've decided what course of action to take."

Mrs. Hastur was right, of course. Christopher had been shaken to his very bones by what had happened in the Tremmond house. Pressing him on the subject would likely have no positive effect. And it wouldn't help us find Violet either. "Was there anything else, Chris? Any other clue this woman gave you as to her plot?"

"She said she knows our secrets, Henry. I believe she is some variety of witch. She had a smell of the abnatural."

I took a breath. We weren't dealing with anything as clear-cut as a witch. "I'm going back to the house to look for Violet."

"I will help you," Christopher said.

"You'll do no such thing. Every constable in London is searching for someone of your description after what you did on Castle Crescent."

He looked pained. "The boy."

"From what I heard, you shattered the bones in his leg. What's got into you?"

"The past, Henry," Christopher said.

I shook my head, not fully understanding, but also knowing there was no time to explore further. "Stay with Mrs. Hastur. Protect the house. And wait for Violet, should she return."

"Henry—"

"You will obey me in this matter."

"Yes," he said. "I am sorry."

I softened. "We'll pull through this, old friend. If we work together." I turned to Mrs. Hastur. "Send word to Phillip Langford. Tell him I must speak with him. It's a matter of great urgency. He might have some idea what artifact these men in black hats would be interested in. And, if not, he can at least suggest the best course of action. We need his experience in this matter."

"Of course, Mr. Coxton."

I turned to leave.

"Sir," Mrs. Hastur said. "There is perhaps something else I should tell you."

"I promise we'll talk tonight, Mrs. Hastur," I said. "Lock the doors after I am gone. Lock them well."

* * *

I hailed a hansom cab and began my journey through fog-damp streets back to Number 15 Castle Crescent, hoping beyond hope that I'd find Violet Asquith there. Perhaps she was locked in some room or trapped behind a gate I'd previously overlooked. I wished I had a pistol to defend myself in case Brother James still lurked about, but being a ghost finder, I'd never found the need for a firearm.

My intention was to ascertain as much information as possible about Violet's whereabouts, and then I would travel to Phillip's manse in Mayfair. He had a way of putting things straight in my mind, and as this was one of the most confounding situations I'd ever encountered, I needed him more than ever.

Upon arriving at the darkened Tremmond house, I entered through the unlocked front door and stood for a moment, listening. The house was silent. Brother James and Sister Rose had likely departed. I turned on my electric torch, which appeared to be in working condition once again, and made my way through the large empty rooms on the ground floor, searching for any sign of Violet. On the second floor, the secret passage we'd used to make our way from the servant's quarters to the library was empty. A door with a curved arch led off from the main passage, but the door appeared firmly sealed and looked as though it had been for some time.

I made my way back down the stairs, feeling at a loss. That's when I encountered a man dressed in workman's clothes standing in the frame of the open front door. I shined my lamp in his weathered face, glad to see he didn't wear a wide black hat. The man raised a hand to shade his eyes, squinting. "Hey!" he said. "Enough now."

"What's your business here?" I said.

"I'd ask the same of you. Douse your light, sir."

I lowered the lamp.

"My name is Tom Price," he said. "I'm caretaker for several of the houses on Castle Crescent. I heard there was some trouble. Someone tried to harm a child on the street. I came to make sure the homes weren't being tampered with. You wouldn't know anything about the trouble, would you?"

"No," I said. "I'm Henry Coxton of Coxton & Co. I'm a ghost finder by trade."

"Ghosts?" Tom Price said, interested. "My own mother saw spirits. Her hair turned white after one bad evening. One of her teeth fell out."

"Things of that sort have been known to happen," I said, not wanting to get caught up in such a conversation.

"Do you think you might require some assistance in your ghost finding this evening, Mr. Coxton? I'm a man of some good mettle."

"I'm sure you are," I said. "But I must press on alone, I'm afraid. You said the house was a rental property?"

"That's right. I saw the door standing wide and I thought—well—I've always had a strange feeling about Number 15. Something's not right in this place."

"I was retained by the mistress of the house, a Mrs. Eldora Tremmond," I said.

"Tremmond?"

"She claimed to have been living in the house with her husband, Morton, and their maid Lucy until Morton Tremmond very recently passed away."

"I haven't heard a story like that," Tom Price said. "The last people who lived in this house were called Waverly, and that was some two or three years ago. The people before that"—he paused—"they were called Kline."

"So the house has gone unrented for some time?"

"Oh, the house is rented, sure enough. But the renter does not wish to live at the property, as I understand. Can't say as I blame him."

"Who is the renter?" I said. "Do you have a name?"

"I'm not privy to information of that sort. You'd be wanting Mr. Yarrow, the man who handles leases."

"Can you tell me where to find this Mr. Yarrow?"

"At his firm, sir. Yarrow and Yarrow, on Gainsford Street. He might be late at work this evening. Mr. Yarrow is one for such things."

"Thank you, Mr. Price," I said.

"And the ghosts? Did you find any sign of such things here?"

"I did not," I replied as I passed by him in the doorway. "Number 15 isn't haunted, Mr. Price. But there may be worse things afoot."

CHRISTOPHER X

OUR PURPOSE WAS to guard the house. To protect Mrs. Hastur and Henry's belongings. And though we would comply with Henry's wishes, we wanted to go into the streets. We felt compelled to search for Violet. She was our friend. She had helped us through many difficulties. For soon after Henry had first discovered us in the alley, we began to feel that Coxton & Co. was a kind of prison. We wanted to return to the shadows. To hunt our rats. Yet Henry said we could not be seen. He did not even want us to go on investigations. And so we had stayed inside for weeks, pacing like a caged creature. On one such occasion, Violet had come to sit with us. We were in Henry's gymnasium on the second floor of the house, where we went to lift barbells and swing the medicine ball. Henry kept a gymnasium because he had been a sailor in his youth. He remained interested in the strength of the body. We had not felt like talking that day—to Mrs. Hastur, to Violet, to anyone. We wanted to be left alone. Yet Violet remained with us in the small gymnasium, sitting on a chair in the corner, smoking one of her cigarettes. The scent of it burned our nose.

"Christopher," she said, exhaling brown smoke. "I think it's time we had a talk."

"I do not want to talk," we said, lying on our back and lifting Henry's barbells. "I have an ache in my head."

"I rather doubt that someone of your constitution gets headaches," Violet said.

It was true. We did not have an ache in our head, nor did we even know what that might feel like. We had learned the complaint from Mrs. Hastur. When she had an ache in her head, she would lie down in a darkened room. Henry instructed us to leave Mrs. Hastur alone and not ask for food on such days.

"I do not actually have an ache in my head," we said.

"I didn't think so." Violet tapped the edge of her cigarette on a silver ashtray she held in one hand. "And that's the sort of thing I wanted to talk with you about."

"Aches of the head?"

"No. The fact that you and I, we are different," she replied. "And not different in the way that Henry is."

"How is Henry different?"

Violet cleared her throat. "Never mind that."

We sat up from the bench and put the barbells on the floor. Lifting barbells had no true effect for us. Our body did not change. The activity merely helped to alleviate some of our boredom.

"Tell me, Violet."

"He is"—she paused—"what some would call an invert."

We tilted our head.

"It's not really Henry's problem," Violet said. "It's just that other people don't want to talk about what he is. It's not palatable to them. Do you understand?"

"No, Violet."

"Henry prefers the company of men. And the preference causes him great anxiety, I think."

We blinked, considering. "I prefer the company of you and Henry and Mrs. Hastur."

She examined the tip of her cigarette. We hoped she did not snap at us. But this subject seemed too important not to pursue. "This isn't really what I came to talk to you about."

"Violet, I would very much like to know more. Henry has been good to me."

She sighed. "He prefers the company of men in a way that is not merely familial or even social."

We sat waiting for more.

"You don't understand indirect reference, do you, Chris?" Violet said finally.

"I do not think I do."

"Think of it this way—Henry appreciates what one might call 'male beauty.'"

"All of you are interesting to look at," we said.

"Henry *desires* men, Christopher. He wants to have congress with them. To make the beast with two backs."

Our eyes widened. "Is that an abnatural?"

"Do you know what amorous congress is?"

We nodded.

Now it was Violet's turn to look surprised. "Have you *had* amorous congress?"

"I do not recall."

"Right," Violet said. "Your amnesia. How precisely do you know what such congress is?"

"I saw people making amorous congress in an alley. I asked Henry about it."

Violet shook her head. "This house is so very strange."

"What is strange about it?"

"Never mind. Look, as I was saying, you and I are different. And not in the way that Henry is different. We are both abnatural in our own right. And I want you to understand that I appreciate that fact, and that I would do anything in my power to help you. To make sure you are safe. Because you are a good fellow, Chris. I've spent most of my life taking care of only myself. And I wouldn't mind taking care of someone else for a while."

"You think I am someone worth caring for?" we said.

"I do."

We felt a sting in our eye at this. We reached up to wipe a certain dampness away.

"Are you crying?"

We shook our head. We never cried. We were thinking about all the things Violet did not know about us. And all the things we likely did not even know about ourselves. "You are a good fellow too, Violet," we said.

"Every once in a great while, I try to be," she replied.

* * *

We had promised solidarity. And we felt ashamed for staying in the house when Violet was outside, possibly in danger. It was likely she needed our help. The men from the country and the woman called Sister Rose could be pursuing her. Yet we were also aware that we had to obey Henry. He had taken such a serious tone with us in the foyer. And, in truth, we were still not feeling entirely ourselves. The sound of the flies remained in our ears, fainter now. But still there. There was also the memory of the dead man from long ago: Mercurius. He had appeared to us in a London alleyway. He could return at any time. If we went out, it was possible we might have another episode. We might smell blood. Our jaw would ache. We would feel the urge to harm someone as we'd wanted to harm the boy on Castle Crescent.

"I will search the house for intruders, Mrs. Hastur," we said.

Our old friend pushed gray hair from her brow and looked at us with care. "I don't think that's necessary, Christopher."

We found that Englishmen often liked to argue a point even if the point did not need to be argued. We were not very good at arguing. It was so easy to get wrapped up in confusing details. And we did not much care for details. So instead, we'd made a habit of repeating our own point, unchanged, until the Englishmen gave up.

"But do as you must," Mrs. Hastur said. "I'll—" She looked around at the mess the men from the country had left in the office. "I'll start tidying things up, I suppose."

We left her there in the foyer and proceeded with our investigation. Coxton & Co. was of three levels. On the topmost level were our sleeping quarters, as well as Henry's gymnasium and a kind of velvet dressing room where Violet kept her perfumes and ointments. On the main floor there was a smoking parlor, a formal parlor, Mrs. Hastur's kitchen, and, of course, Henry's offices where he met with prospective clients. Finally, there was the cellar. Members of Coxton & Co. rarely went into the cellar, though it did contain some of Henry's more interesting artifacts, including several purported books of magic written in poison ink, the tusk of an unknown prehistoric beast, and a large Egyptian sarcophagus.

We made our way through the third story first, checking behind draperies and inside wardrobe cabinets. We wanted to make sure the men from the country were not hiding there. We searched with our eyes, but, more importantly, we searched with our nose. We opened the door to Henry's pinewood wardrobe and found nothing inside but his gray suits, all in a row. The suits smelled like Henry—lemon soap and a mild cologne. We felt bad for all that we had done after the events at the Tremmond house. We had possibly compromised the firm by revealing ourselves. A sketch of us might appear in the newspaper once again. We touched the arm of one of Henry's empty suits and said, "I am sorry, Henry. I will work to make this better."

It was then that a voice came from the hall, startling us. Mrs. Hastur whispered our name. She was searching for us. She appeared in the doorway then, putting a finger to her lips. We knew this gesture. It meant we should remain silent.

"What is wrong?" we asked, attempting a whisper, though our throat was not good at whispering.

Mrs. Hastur appeared to tremble. We did not like to see her frightened. "I was sweeping near the cellar door," she said. "And I heard a noise from below."

Our ears swiveled, listening.

"What sort of noise?" We forgot to lower our voice. This caused Mrs. Hastur to put her finger to her lips once again.

"A rustle of movement."

"Rats come into the cellar, Mrs. Hastur. Especially after a heavy rain."

She shook her head. "This wasn't any sort of rat."

We raised ourselves up to full height, swelling our chest. Mrs. Hastur might be frightened of sounds in the cellar, but we were not. Instead, we felt excited by the prospect that the men from the country—the very men who had torn apart Henry's house and injured Mrs. Hastur—were still hiding there. If they were in the cellar, we could punish them. Henry could not become angry because he had told us to protect the house. He would likely even tell us we were good.

"Mrs. Hastur, you will wait here in Henry's bedroom," we said. "Lock the door and do not come out."

This sounded like a very good thing to say.

Like something Henry himself might say.

Mrs. Hastur put her hand on her arm. "Do be careful, Christopher. These men, they have a terrible look about them. And they are unpredictable. Even I can't predict—" She trailed off then, listening.

We turned to move down the hall.

"Christopher," Mrs. Hastur said.

We looked back at her.

"There's something I should tell you," she said, "before you go."

"What is it?"

"It's difficult to put into words. But you see—the things that are happening now, I knew they would happen."

"You knew that men from the country would harm the house?"

"I had a sense of it, yes. But I didn't realize the degree of trouble they would cause."

"I do not understand, Mrs. Hastur. To what degree is trouble occurring?"

She pursed her lips. "Maybe it's better if I just say this—Violet and Henry are strong, Christopher. But they are not as strong as you."

"Of course they are not. No Englishman is."

"At some point, in the near future, you are likely going to realize you have a job to do. And when you realize what that job is, I want you to do it without question."

"Can you tell me what the job is?"

"I can't. That's not how this works. I can only put you in the *position* to understand the job. Just know that Henry and Violet, they are your friends. No matter what anyone says to you. You'll do that for me, won't you? You'll protect them because they are your friends."

"You are my friend as well, Mrs. Hastur."

She nodded. "And I always will be."

We stepped into the hall, and Mrs. Hastur closed the door behind us. We heard the sound of the lock as we descended to the foyer. Soon after we arrived there, we heard the noise that Mrs. Hastur had described. A faint creaking. A rustle. Perhaps the sound was nothing. But perhaps—

We sniffed the air. We detected a faint musk. We'd believed it was a residual scent upon first entering the house. But now we could not be certain.

We looked toward the painted cellar door. The door was closed. We opened the door. The scent of musk floated up from the darkness. The cellar was not electrified. But such things did not matter to us. Unlike the Englishmen, we could see in the dark.

We put our foot on the first stair, and we could already taste blood. We could feel soft organs between our teeth. We wanted a reason to harm someone. We hoped for it.

The cellar was heaped with various collections. We saw the stone sarcophagus. We saw the poisoned books. The smell of musk was very strong here. Then in one corner of the cellar, something shifted, and we believed it was a man.

As we approached, we realized it was a not a man at all. It was instead, one of Henry's artifacts, a pale sheet, perhaps a shroud for burial. A breeze coming through a half-open cellar window caused the movement. The window, we knew, should not be open. Mrs. Hastur did not leave windows open.

It appeared as though someone had tried to force the window open the rest of the way, but they had given up. The window was now stuck in its casement.

Just then, we heard movement on the other side of the cellar. We turned and, from the shadows, there emerged a pale lean figure. He wore a wide black hat and black suspenders. He smelled like one of the men from the country. In his hand, he held something that looked like a wooden pipe.

"The dog has come," the man said.

We knew he referred to us, though we were certainly not a dog.

Another man, shorter and broader, emerged from a different corner of the cellar. He too held a length of wood. We realized the wood was actually a gun. Quite an odd-looking gun. But we were not afraid of guns.

We bared our teeth. "This is the house of Henry Coxton and Mr. Phillip Langford," we said. "Why have you come here?"

The lean man appeared calm. Like Sister Rose, the sight of our face did not trouble him. "We have new orders," he said.

"Orders of what nature?"

The lean man grinned. "Sister Rose made a mistake. And the New Lord told us to come take care of the dog."

"I am not a dog."

The lean man stepped toward us, brandishing his gun.

We tensed our muscles, preparing to launch ourselves at him. But then we heard a sound on the stair. A sound that made our heart stop.

"Christopher, are you all right?" It was Mrs. Hastur's voice. Mrs. Hastur was on the stairs.

"Mrs. Hastur," we called, "do not come down here!"

But it was too late.

Mrs. Hastur appeared atop the stair in her rumpled gray uniform. Unlike us, she could not see in the dark. She could not tell what was happening in the cellar. One of the men in black hats, the shorter and broader of the two, swiveled and, without hesitation, he fired his gun.

The air of the cellar filled with a black and searing smoke. Through the smoke, we saw Mrs. Hastur, the front of her uniform covered in blood. She looked startled, then pained. She stood atop the stair for only a moment longer. Then she toppled forward, falling. She struck stair after stair on her descent until she landed heavily at the bottom.

The tall, lean man spoke harshly: "Brother Athol, we weren't told to kill anyone. Why did you shoot the old woman?"

"It was an accident, Brother Simon," Brother Athol said.

We crept toward the stairs as the two men spoke.

We needed to see Mrs. Hastur.

The men from the country stopped their talk. They watched us. We did not care if they watched us.

Mrs. Hastur lay with one leg folded under her body, the other leg extended. There was a great deal of blood. And, for the first time, we did not care for the smell of it. Mrs. Hastur's face, her kindly face, no longer bore its healthy reddish glow. Her flesh was white. There was still fear on her face. Fear and pain and surprise. There were many holes in Mrs. Hastur's chest. Many holes where pieces of metal had gone. Her neck and chest were covered in blood. Her arms were thrown out at her sides, as if she might hug us. But we knew she would never hug us again.

We heard the men from the country approach. They wore heavy boots.

"At least it's distracted him," the one called Brother Athol said.

"True enough," Brother Simon said.

The men were close. Close to Mrs. Hastur's body.

We bared our teeth.

Brother Simon did not hesitate. He raised the butt of his gun and struck us above our left eye. Bright pain flashed. We felt dizzy. Then the one called Brother Athol struck us on the top of our skull with his own gun. We were driven backward, falling over the body of Mrs. Hastur.

"Again," Brother Simon said.

And Brother Athol struck us again. Then more times. He did not stop striking us.

VIOLET ASQUITH

I RAN BAREFOOT through silent London streets, and the shambling thing followed, making its needful, mewling sounds. The figure no longer crawled on hands and knees, but rather shuffled with a broken gait. I could not see its face. The body was bent, misshapen, and the flesh was the same odd gray color as the sky. The voice was like a strange appendage, a cold hand, searching for me along empty streets. I crossed Hawthorne, then Maggot's Court, and I tried to picture the cheerful fireplace in our offices at Coxton & Co., the way the orange light played across the walls. I thought of the smell of Mrs. Hastur's stews and Christopher's charmingly oversized brown suits. I imagined the wreath we hung at Christmastime. If there was anywhere that could provide safety and solace, it was that place and those people.

And yet, the more I saw of this altered London, the more Coxton and Co. felt like an impossibility. For the city before me appeared to be nothing more than a painted façade. Every piece of brick and mortar, drained of vitality, as if the structures themselves were reflected dimly in Father's dark glass. Had the mirror done this? Did Sister Rose and her so-called New Lord truly know how to amplify its power?

A voice rose. This time the sound seemed not come from the pursuant creature, but from every brick and every pane of window glass: *Violet, are you with me?*

You're dead. I thought. *And you'll remain dead.*

But even as I thought this, I questioned whether the voice did indeed belong to Father or even the ghost of Father.

For I sensed something alien in its tone. As if some Other was attempting to reconstruct Father's voice.

I nearly stumbled on a cobblestone, and then turned to look once more at the awful shambling form, wanting to ensure it had not gained any ground. But the street behind me was empty. The creature, no longer there.

Seeing the thing had been awful, yes, but *not* seeing it felt nearly unbearable. For if I couldn't locate the gray form, that meant it could be anywhere. Perhaps the beast had found some shortcut and was even closer now. I tried to tell myself that I'd simply outrun it. But even as I attempted to convince myself of this, I caught movement out of the corner of my eye. The vague flicker of a shadow in an alleyway.

I wanted to cry out, but stifled the urge. Sound would draw attention.

Then, from the alley came a hurtling form. I realized that this was not the shambling figure, but rather a man, white-haired and dressed in a tailored suit.

"Sir!" I called, my voice echoing. Sound was a sickness in this place. A blight that spread.

The man hurried away, and I followed. He was quick, and he appeared to know the streets well. I worried I might lose him. Then, halfway down Barlow Street, he fell, landing on hands and knees, panting for breath. His skin appeared dry, hands and face red and peeling. His fingernails were overlong and woody.

"Please," I said. "I don't mean you any harm."

"You—" he said. "You look like the *beast.*"

This comment struck me as mad. What beast did he mean? Certainly, I didn't look like the bent gray thing that had shambled after me. "My name is Violet Asquith. If you'll come with me, I believe I know a place we might be safe."

"You are not the beast?" the old man said.

"No. I'm a woman. Just as you are a man."

"Water," the old man said. "Please."

"There should be both water and food," I said, thinking of Mrs. Hastur's pantry, hoping beyond hope that Mrs. Hastur still existed.

The old man made a feeble attempt to stand. I helped him, wondering how long he'd been here in this empty city.

Together we walked in silence. Thankfully, the gray creature didn't return. And I wondered again what the old man had meant when he said I looked like the beast. I glanced down at my own hand and reminded myself that I'd seen my face reflected in the dark mirror not more than half an hour ago. I was myself, certainly.

Coxton & Co. appeared then, rising before the cobbled walk of Bachelor Street—brickwork a reddish-gray, windows black and staring. My hopes fell at the sight of my dear old home, because I realized that Coxton & Co. too looked like a painted façade. There was no life. No sense of what it once had been. Still, I had to go inside. There was no other recourse. I needed to discover if my friends were there. I prayed I would find them. I wanted all of us to be safe.

I found the door unlocked and stepped into the foyer that was also silent and drained of life. I led the old man to the sofa near the unlit fireplace in Henry's office.

"I've been in so many empty houses here," he whispered.

"Rest, "I said. "I'll look for water."

"Madam." He reached out with one dry, scabbed hand. His face appeared skeletal in the dim light. "Do not abandon me."

"Only for a moment," I said.

I left the old man there on the sofa and entered the foyer. Coxton & Co. had all the feelings and conditions of a dream. Yet I was not dreaming. I was quite sure of that.

"Henry?" My voice echoed through the rooms of the empty house.

Henry was not here. Nor was Christopher. Nor Mrs. Hastur. I suddenly had a sense that my friends were in some other place, the real Coxton & Co., wherever that might be. And I was here in this false replica, this doll's house, with no understanding of how to get home.

I moved to sit on the stairs that led to the second floor, and I put my face in my hands.

Father's mirror was responsible for this somehow. It must have been. This was what Sister Rose and her New Lord intended. I thought again of my long-ago final moments with the black glass in the East Tower at Nethersea Hall when the child who looked back at me from the dark mirror suddenly no longer appeared to be precisely the same as me. The shift was subtle, yet definite. One moment, I'd been looking at my own dull reflection, the same image I stared at each day in my tower room, and the next moment, I looked at what I felt was some other girl. There were no physical differences between myself and the child that I came to think of as "Mirror Violet." Her hair was smooth and black, parted in the same fashion as mine. Her cheekbones were high and pale. Her eyes looked tired, just as my own eyes looked tired. And yet, something about the essence of the reflection had altered. I could not quite name the difference, though.

I remembered rubbing my face and then leaning toward the mirror to get a better look. I gazed into Mirror Violet's gray eyes (the color of those eyes—due to the mirror's own shade—was darker than my own). Mirror Violet leaned forward to look at me as well, inspecting my face just as I inspected hers. Again, I was entirely aware that there were no physical differences between the two of us. Yet from a close proximity, I had an even stronger sense that I looked at another entity, a separate being. There was something in the girl's gaze, a faint expression that made me think Mirror Violet had taken a cold interest in me. She lived in a darker world than I, a world behind the surface of the mirror. This girl breathed the strange air in that other place.

When I blinked, Mirror Violet blinked too. When I moved my hand, she moved her own. And yet, all of it, every action, seemed like play-acting on her part. Mirror Violet was purposefully mimicking me, all the while studying me coldly. I paused and told myself again there could be no truth to what I perceived. This reflected girl *was* me, just as I was her. And yet, the more I examined Mirror Violet, this duplicate, the more my questions multiplied.

On that afternoon when I first recognized her difference, I glanced toward the doorway of the Western Tower to make sure Father had not returned. He often approached surreptitiously, to ensure I still did his bidding. When I saw the doorway was empty, I turned back to Mirror Violet and whispered: "Are you real, then?"

The girl on the other side of the glass whispered the same words to me. Our lips moved in unison. We shared a single voice. And yet, it seemed to me that she asked a question of her own. Mirror Violet wanted to know if *I* was real. And if I was, perhaps she had some use for me.

"Yes," I said. "Yes, I am real."

Mirror Violet said the same.

"Prove to me you're not a reflection," I said. "Make some sign."

After speaking, I realized Mirror Violet had made the same request of me. She too wanted a sign. So I raised my hand, putting three fingers in the air.

Mirror Violet made the same gesture simultaneously.

I squinted at her, frustrated. "If you do everything in just the same manner as me. I won't believe you're real. You're behaving just as a mirror would behave. Don't you see?"

Mirror Violet paused at this, though I admit I too paused. Then, before anything more could occur, I felt a presence at the door. I turned to see Father, the dark tendrils of his hair hanging about his waxen face. False tears leaked from his eyes.

"You *speak* to it?" he said loudly. "I did not tell you to speak to it."

I shrank in fear. Father had never struck me, but I had the sense he would if he deemed such an act necessary. And certainly this perceived transgression had rankled him in some way I could not fully understand.

"I—I was tired, Father."

He glanced at the dark mirror. "Did something change in it? Is there some difference?"

I shook my head. "I promise you I was only tired."

"If you're lying to me—"

"I never would."

"You waste my time. You're wasting *everyone's* time."

"Father—"

"Get out of my sight. Go to your bed."

I did as he asked, thinking of Mirror Violet. Thinking about how I might test her, and worrying all the while that I had simply gone mad from staring into Father's dark glass for too long.

It was the next day, when I was alone with the mirror once again, that I moved even closer to the girl, nearly pressing my nose against the glass. Mirror Violet, in turn, came closer to me. She did not shift in any manner distinct from my own, and yet her essence, still, was different: cold yet intrigued. Ever so watchful. I felt relieved by this. Glad I had not imagined that difference on the previous afternoon.

I smiled at her to show Mirror Violet that I was kind.

She smiled in return.

"Are you pleased to see me?" I whispered. "I want you to know, I'm very glad to see you. I thought about you all night long. And I've been wondering something." I paused, trying to find the right way to ask the question that needed to be asked. "Please don't think I'm being cruel, but I must know this—are you actually a girl or do you only *look* like a girl?"

Mirror Violet stared at me. There was something haughty in her expression.

"Understand," I said, "I'm not asking the same question I asked you yesterday. I believe you are real. But I don't know what sort of—what sort of matter you're made of. Are you flesh. Or stone? Or something else?"

I had, in fact, been thinking of something Mother once said to me, a phrase from one of her mad rambles in the Eastern Tower. Father had forced Mother to undergo certain magical rituals during her pregnancy, and these experiments had left her in a place that was less than rational. Yet her words had seemed far more apt than anything Father had ever told me about the dark glass. She said: "The mirror has a taste for our world, Violet. All mirrors do. But this one is ever so hungry."

* * *

"I'm sorry Father sent me away yesterday," I whispered to the dark glass in the Western Tower. "But please, won't you give me some sign that you are real, that you might be my friend?"

Mirror Violet hesitated.

I wasn't going to say any more. I wanted her to speak of her own volition.

But she only watched me carefully.

Then, just as I was ready to turn away, something happened. This time, it wasn't some slight difference in the reflected figure. No. This time, what changed was something inside of *me*. I felt different. Some mechanism turned—not inside the mirror—but in the gears and pulleys of my very soul.

I took a startled breath, feeling suddenly stronger. No more the little girl that Father could control. "Please—" I whispered for the first time, "Please should the mirror show me—"

And with that, Father's great table that stood behind me, covered in books and scrolls, toppled over. It made a tremendous crash, scattering bottles of ink and breaking glass vials.

I turned to look at the table. I heard Father on the stairs. But I realized I was not afraid.

"Thank you," I whispered to the glass. "Thank you, my friend."

ħEΠRУ ᴄOXᴛOΠ

YARROW AND YARROW emerged from the fog, ghostly electric lamplight flickering behind its wooden shutters. I ascended the front step and raised the brass doorknocker, taking note of the placard to my right: *Edgar and Morgan Yarrow, Imports and Sundry*. My initial bout of rapping went unanswered, so I moved to the front-facing window and peered through the shutter slats. There, at a high counting house desk, was a gnomish figure, dressed in a starched collared suit, spectacles perched on his bald pate. His chin dipped as though he studied the ledger before him, but his rhythmic breathing led me to believe he was actually drowsing.

I hesitated before knocking on the window glass, worried that if I awoke this diminutive gentleman, the surprise would cause him to topple from his high seat. But I needed information as to the identity of the renter of Number 15, and according to the caretaker, Tom Price, this Mr. Yarrow was the only one who might be able to give me such details.

I removed one of my leather gloves and tapped on the shutter, lightly at first and then with greater force. The man stirred and, without opening his eyes, began to move the pen over his ledger. I wondered what sort of dream numbers he might be noting, and how they would look to him when he awoke. Soon enough, the ink pen slowed, and Mr. Yarrow grew still once more, as if he was some automaton whose cogs had wound down.

Using the palm of my hand, I banged on the shutter, causing wood to rattle. This time, the presumed Mr. Yarrow opened his eyes with a start. He sat up, peered about the room as if he expected to see someone there, and then finally looked toward the window. A perplexed expression appeared on his face, and I realized that he likely couldn't see me clearly, either because of the shutters' obstruction or perhaps because his eyeglasses were perched atop his head. I made a gesture (rather broadly) indicating that I required his attention. He seemed to understand and lowered the glasses.

I gestured toward the door, indicating that the gentleman should come speak to me there. Mr. Yarrow nodded as if to say, yes, that was, of course, the best plan of action. He dismounted from his high stool with great effort and made his way toward the door. When he opened it, he stood gazing up at me, for I was a good deal the taller than he. Finally, he said: "Mr. Borely?"

"No, sir. Coxton."

"Coxton?" he said, brow wrinkled.

"Henry Coxton. And you are Mr. Yarrow?"

"Edgar Yarrow. Yarrow, the younger. I don't believe we have an appointment. You are here to see my brother, perhaps?"

"I'm not particular in that regard," I said. "I'm—"

"*Coxton.* I have heard of a Coxton."

"I'm a ghost finder. My name has been in the papers and in an issue of *The Strand.*"

Edgar Yarrow furrowed his brow. "No. I'm sure that wasn't it. But how convenient this is. You should come in."

"I—"

"Do have a cigar with me."

"Oh, I don't smoke cigars."

"Everyone smokes cigars here, Mr. Cox—what was it?"

"Coxton," I said.

Edgar Yarrow nodded. "My brother Morgan used to tell the story of how, when King Edward took the throne, his first words were 'Gentlemen, you may smoke!' Victoria didn't allow such things. Yet, every modern Englishman smokes cigars, Mr. Coxton."

Before I knew precisely was happening, I was standing the offices of Yarrow and Yarrow beneath the pale electric light with a lit cigar held between my fingers. I didn't intend to put the thing in my mouth, and I also doubted that Edgar Yarrow would notice. He appeared rather preoccupied.

"If it's my brother Morgan you've come for," Edgar Yarrow said, "I'm afraid—well—he's been missing for nearly a month. And, because of certain recent events, I fear the worst."

"I'm sorry to hear that."

Edgar Yarrow allowed foul cigar smoke to float from his small, thin-lipped mouth. "How much do you charge for your services?"

"I'm not here in my official capacity. I'm looking for information."

"I have not slept well since Morgan passed on," Edgar Yarrow said.

"I thought you said he disappeared, Mr. Yarrow."

"Death and disappearance. They are so much the same after a time. Only with the disappeared, mourning feels like a hollow thing."

I thought of Violet. Her own absence certainly presented me with a hollow feeling.

"That's why you caught me sleeping, Mr. Coxman."

"Coxton."

"I don't know how it is with your other clients, but I am quite often under the impression that Morgan—my dear Morgan—has not left our offices at all. His body is gone but his spirit remains. Something invisible walks my bedchamber after I've doused the lamp."

I leaned forward slightly, interested despite myself.

"I hear the creak of footsteps," Edgar Yarrow said. "The faint smell of cigars hangs in the air."

I looked at the smoke that drifted lazily toward the ceiling from Edgar Yarrow's cigar and thought that there was likely always such a smell when he was present. My guess was that there was nothing abnatural about the phantom scent.

"So you believe this visitant to be your brother?" I said, thinking I could close his story off with a few more questions and then move on to my own inquiry.

"I do not *believe*. I am quite certain. There is a room here at our offices—Morgan's own room—where I often feel such a terrible draft. Shall I show you, Mr. Coxton?"

I rolled the cigar between my fingers. "I'm amenable to returning on another day. But I'm afraid I have business that is quite pressing this evening."

Yarrow squinted at me.

"I come in regards to a certain house. Number 15 Castle Crescent."

I waited for some reaction. But there was no sense of recognition on Edgar Yarrow's face.

"My services were procured by one Mrs. Eldora Tremmond. Widow of the late Morton Tremmond. She claimed to reside at Number 15, but when my associates and I arrived there this evening, we found the house quite abandoned."

"I recognize the street's name," Edgar Yarrow said.

I felt relieved.

"But I'm afraid the business of leasing was entirely under the auspices of my brother. And Morgan's papers remain in—in great disorder."

I took a breath. I refused to come to nothing here. A great deal rested on this information. If someone other than Morton and Eldora Tremmond were indeed renting Number 15, I needed to discover as much information about the renter as I could. "But do you think, Mr. Yarrow, that, with a bit of searching, you might be able to discover who has rented the house on Castle Crescent?"

Edgar Yarrow paused. "May I show you the room where I felt the draft, Mr. Coxton? It's also where my brother's papers are kept. You might find it illuminating."

I nodded.

Mr. Yarrow lit a candle and placed it in a brass holder. I followed him up a dark and winding stair, listening as he told his tale. "My brother and I are in the business of handling imports, you know. Objects of some great rarity. And very recently—not more than six months ago—we handled a particularly confounding delivery. Various parties were involved: a man of some good standing here in London, a young woman in less good standing, and then another Englishman who'd been living in India for a time. He claimed to be a sorcerer or some foolish thing. Such a story should be expected, I suppose, from a man who chooses to live amongst the heat and black flies. I don't know much more about the specifics of the delivery, you understand. My brother, in fact, destroyed all records of this particular shipment before he disappeared. But I do know that the man of good standing and the young woman were at odds. There was some disagreement about how the item in question should be handled. Some notion about how *dangerous* the thing was. It was clear that they themselves wanted little contact with it at the time. My brother, Morgan, finally grew exhausted by the whole affair. Perhaps his interest was piqued too. Morgan was a man of great curiosity, you see. And so he opened the crate that contained the item. What he found buried there in the packing straw was quite absurd, he said. It should not have caused such consternation."

"What was it?" I asked.

"A broken shard of stone," Mr. Yarrow said. "Black and reflective. But otherwise unremarkable."

I didn't understand why Mr. Yarrow was telling me this story. I thought it likely had something to do with the case he wanted me to take up—the disappearance (or perhaps death) of his brother and the subsequent haunting.

"You may have noticed my surprise when I saw you at the window tonight," Yarrow said.

"I did."

"I'm sure my reaction made me look something of an old fool. But when I saw you there, I thought you were one of *them*."

"Them?" I asked.

"Those who finally came to collect the black stone. They were scoundrels with odd country accents who wore wide-brimmed black hats."

"Black hats?" I said, feeling a chill.

I followed Edgar Yarrow down a long narrow hall. The doors on either side of us were closed.

"Morgan was a sensitive sort," he said. "And by sensitive, I mean he had what they once called 'second sight.' He could locate missing objects, he sometimes heard voices, that sort of thing. Our mother was much the same. And when Morgan sat with the shard of black stone for a time—

the thing he began calling a *mirror*—well, he grew quite obsessed. He believed the stone had some special property, and he said he wanted to keep it, to study it. I told him that wasn't right. It didn't belong to us. We'd received the stone for delivery, and so we must deliver it. But Morgan, as usual, did as he pleased. He stayed up late with his stone, doing research in old books. And, then one morning, Morgan did not come down to our breakfast."

My shoulders and neck had grown tense as Edgar Yarrow spoke. I thought of the men in black hats who'd finally come to retrieve the stone. I wondered if one of them had rust-colored hair and a cleft in his chin.

"I came upstairs that morning," Edgar Yarrow continued. "I went to look for Morgan in his office room where he kept all of his papers." He used a key to open a door at the end of the hall while I waited. "And I found this, Mr. Coxton."

Beyond the door stood a room filled with high wooden cabinets. Some work had been done to organize the place; papers were piled here and there. But for the most part, the room was in an astonishing state of disarray. Many of the documents were shredded. There were deep scratches in the wooden cabinets. It looked like someone had gone mad inside the office.

"My brother," Edgar Yarrow said, "never liked a mess, Mr. Coxton. He was so particular. In this room I've felt a draft of cold air over and over again. And I cannot help but think—I cannot help but think that Morgan believes he left some business unfinished."

"And the stone?" I said.

"The men in black hats took it away. They said I was never to speak of it to anyone. But, of course, here I am speaking to you, Mr. Coxton."

* * *

I left Yarrow and Yarrow, feeling greatly confused.

Edgar Yarrow had agreed to attempt to find the name of the renter of Number 15 amongst his brother's papers. And I, in exchange, would return to Yarrow and Yarrow as soon as I was able to help him investigate the cold in his brother's office and the odd sensation in his own bedroom.

I pulled up the collar of my coat against the damp of the London night, hoping that Violet had somehow already found her way back to Coxton & Co. But the more I learned about this case, the less I thought that likely. There was only one person who I trusted to advise me on complicated matters such as these, and that was my recently hermited mentor, the great occult detective, Philip Langford. I hailed a horse-drawn hansom cab and we were off toward Hart Street on Hanover Square, where I hoped to find Philip awake and willing to speak.

CHRISTOPHER X

WE AWOKE TRAPPED inside Henry's Egyptian sarcophagus. We knew the smell of that box, bitumen and fleshless bone. Heavy chains bound us. This was the work of the men from the country. They'd killed Mrs. Hastur and then beaten us until we could no longer raise our fists to fight. We were stronger than they were. But we had allowed them to best us. For what did it matter? We had loved Mrs. Hastur. We loved her more than anyone. She had taken care of us from the very start. She'd never feared us. She taught us how to wear our English clothes and how to use a knife and fork. She told us stories. And now she was dead. We had not rescued her. So what did it matter if we fought?

We heard voices outside the sarcophagus, the sharp tones of Sister Rose. "You think a few chains will bind him?" she said.

"The New Lord told us to chain him," replied a male voice, Brother Simon. He was the man who had chastised Brother Athol for shooting Mrs. Hastur.

"The New Lord," Sister Rose continued, "is just that, Brother Simon. *New*. Certainly, he is wise. And certainly, he guides us when things are dire. But he too can make mistakes."

"Do you not trust him?" Brother Simon asked.

"I'm not talking about *trust*," Sister Rose said. "I'm talking about knowledge. I knew the true Lord Asquith. I spent years with him. And he taught me much. There are things I understand—things the New Lord cannot possibly foresee."

"So you know the plan better than the New Lord himself because of the time you spent in a tower?" Brother Simon asked.

"The New Lord thinks you're dangerous, Sister Rose," another male voice said. It was Brother Athol, the man who'd shot Mrs. Hastur.

"Brother Athol, you will not speak," Brother Simon said.

"Dangerous?" Sister Rose said. "*I* am dangerous?"

"The New Lord believes you made a mistake at the Tremmond house," Brother Simon said. "A mistake that must now be corrected."

"You overstep, Brother Simon," Sister Rose said. "Do you actually believe that I haven't already spoken to the New Lord?"

"You talked to him?" Brother Athol sounded surprised.

"Of course I did. I met with him directly."

"And what did the New Lord say?"

"He told me to come here and take over this job because he knew that both of you would bungle things, just as Brother James bungled things with Henry Coxton."

"That was unfortunate, to be sure," Brother Simon said.

"Yes," Sister Rose said. "And now, you two have put Coxton's monster, his most formidable ally, in a box." She kicked the side of the sarcophagus, causing us to flinch. "You put chains around him, believing those chains would hold such a beast. Don't you realize he could snap your necks with a twitch of his finger?"

"*You* are the one who attempted to drive him mad," Brother Simon said, "with whatever words you spoke to him in the Tremmond library. You clearly understand the dog in ways the New Lord does not. The New Lord himself has told me that the creature remains a confusion. He does not know how or even *if* this so-called Christopher fits in with the greater plan. You're being secretive, Sister Rose. You should not withhold information from the New Lord."

Sister Rose did not speak again for some time. Then finally, in a calmer voice, she said, "I am not secretive. I'm doing what's necessary. I'm the daughter of Lord Asquith, protector of our village. You must trust me."

"We obey the New Lord. All of us."

"Of course," she said. "And that is why I have come to tell you what the New Lord has instructed."

"He said to drop the dog in the river," Brother Simon replied. "Drown him and be done with it."

"The New Lord has changed his mind."

"Why should we believe you?"

"If you need further indication—here is the New Lord's fiat."

We heard the rustle of paper.

"That *is* his signature," Brother Simon said. "But this letter is written in Latin."

"The New Lord always writes in Latin!" Sister Rose said.

"He says to leave the dog with you?"

"Coxton's monster," Sister Rose said, "is to be left in my care. You two have already done enough damage. I can't believe you killed the domestic."

"Brother Athol has been reprimanded," Brother Simon said.

"If I have anything to say about it, he'll be made a eunuch," Sister Rose replied. "Now go. Both of you. Get out of here."

"But what will you do with the dog?"

Sister Rose sighed. "I don't have to tell you the details of my plans, Brother Simon. In the New Lord's army, you are a soldier, and I am a general. The New Lord himself recognizes my worth even if he doesn't always comprehend my manner."

At that, we heard heavy footsteps on the stairs. Sister Rose then paced around the sarcophagus in silence for a time, strumming her fingers against its lid. "Are you awake, monster?" she asked.

At first we thought we would not answer her. Why bother to say anything? But we realized we could get no information if we did not speak. And the things she had said to Brother James and Brother Athol interested us. "Yes," we said, finally. "I am awake."

"Very good." She continued to strum her fingers against the stone lid of the sarcophagus. "And have you had time to reflect on the gift I gave you?"

"I did not like it," we said.

"So few people appreciate gifts that are necessary. They think they know what they need. The New Lord thinks he knows. But that simply isn't true. *I* know what is necessary."

"Let me out of the box."

Sister Rose sighed. "I do find you amusing. Your voice. Your simple turns of phrase. But you are not meant to be an object of derision. You are so much grander than that."

"How could you know what I am meant for?"

"Because my father, Lord Asquith, was a truly learned man. Far more a master than the New Lord. He didn't reveal everything to me, of course. He believed too much information would distort my thinking."

"You do seem distorted," we said.

Sister Rose slapped her palm against the sarcophagus lid. "You mustn't talk to me like that. I am on your side, monster. I learned about you in the book I stole from Father, the Grimoire. I know how to return you to your proper state—your cosmic state."

"I do not know what you mean."

"Your name," she said. "That was only the beginning. What effect did it have on you?"

"I saw a man," we said. We did not see a purpose in hiding this information from Sister Rose. It was possible she could even help us understand what we had seen. "A man who had been slain in the desert. He hung from a pole."

"A memory," Sister Rose said. "Yes, you see? That's good. You want to have more memories, don't you?"

"No."

"But if you don't have memories, you will never know your purpose. Isn't that true?"

"I suppose it is," we said, though we felt guarded. We thought of what the last memory had done to us—the boy on Castle Crescent, our running mad through the streets.

"I can give you more memories," Sister Rose said. "Henry Coxton kept you a prisoner. You were his dog. His fool. He did not allow you to explore your full potential. He made you a ridiculous ghost finder. But I— I will show you how to become your truest self."

"What is it you want exactly?"

"What I want," Sister Rose said, "and what you want as well—though you don't know it yet—is for you to fulfill your destiny and slay Violet Asquith."

Our eyes widened in the darkness of the sarcophagus. "I would *never* harm Violet. She is my friend."

"You will kill Violet Asquith because it is what you were sent here to do," Sister Rose said. "It is, in fact, your duty. And you will act out your duty. There is no other purpose for you."

We could not respond. We had seen madwomen in the street. They dressed in rags. They lived in filth and wailed. Sister Rose was different than them. But she was mad nonetheless. Especially if she thought we would hurt Violet. We had already lost our own Mrs. Hastur. We would not lose Violet as well. Next, Sister Rose would try to tell us that we were supposed to harm Henry too.

"Tell me precisely what you mean," we said. "Say it plainly."

"I don't have to tell you. I can show you."

"Show us how?"

"Your name," she said. "When I speak it once more, you will know."

"Do not," we said, struggling against our chains in the darkness of the sarcophagus. We did not want the flies to return. The flies that bit our brain. We did not want to see the dead man.

"It is necessary," Sister Rose said. "It is written."

"No," we said.

"Time to remember, monster," Sister Rose said softly. "Time to learn."

VIOLET ASQUITH

I SAT IN Henry's leather chair, or a chair that looked very much like Henry's. A frail gray light that indicated neither day nor evening streamed through the tall windows. The white-haired gentleman I'd discovered in the street lay curled upon the sofa, knees drawn nearly to his chest. His eyes were closed, his chapped lips parted. I was sorry I had to wake him, but there was no other choice. If he had information about this place, I needed it. "Sir," I whispered. He stirred only enough to place one trembling hand over his eyes, as if even the milky gray light was too much. I moved to touch his shoulder, but before I could, he started awake and scrambled abruptly into a sitting position. He looked like some frightened animal, gazing at me with bloodshot eyes.

"*You*," he said.

"Violet Asquith," I reminded him. "And your name?"

The white-haired man sat breathing in an intentional manner, trying to convince himself, perhaps, that there was no immediate danger. "Morgan—Morgan Yarrow."

"And how did you come to be here in this place, Mr. Yarrow?"

He shook his head. "Difficult to say. Difficult to *know*. Not through any rational means. My brother and I, we receive shipments. Delicate items sent from abroad, often of great value. In one such deployment there was—did you find water, Miss Asquith?"

I'd searched for food and water in Mrs. Hastur's pantry but found nothing. It was as if the entire house was a disused theater set. "Not yet," I said.

He shook his head. "You won't find anything. Soon, you'll be like me. All bones."

"How long have you been here?"

He ran his fingers through his thin white hair. "Days? Months?"

I doubted it had been as long as months. Certainly Morgan Yarrow could not have survived that long without sustenance. "Please go on with your story."

"Why should I?" he asked, placing his feeble hand over his eyes again. "We're both going to die. You must have realized that by now."

"I don't intend to die here, Mr. Yarrow. Finish telling me what you know."

"The shipment in question was from a man in India who called himself a mage. The crate was to be delivered to another man in London, a wealthy sort—a gentleman. The lid of the box was painted with an odd symbol, three jagged blue lines lying one above the next. That's what first caught my eye, I suppose. I was intrigued. I thought I recognized the picture. As a dealer of antiquities, I've become something of an amateur symbologist. With some research, I discovered the drawing was meant to be a hieroglyph, representing the Egyptian god Nun. Are you familiar with Nun, Miss Asquith?"

"I'm not."

"I suppose to call it a god is somewhat misleading. Nun is not a proper personage, you see. Rather, it is the dark liquid sea from which all creation sprang. Nun is said to exist still at the boundaries of our world. And one day—according to the magician priests of Egypt—the waters of Nun will rise again. Chaos will consume order. Creation will be made to disappear."

"And what was inside this box?" I asked.

"It seemed ridiculous at first," Morgan Yarrow said. "The hieroglyph on the outside of the box was so intriguing, and yet, what I found inside, packed carefully in straw, was not even a true relic. It was nothing more than a piece of stone, a black shard. Polished. Reflective. I thought it might be obsidian. But—but I was wrong."

I restrained myself from sitting forward. I didn't want to further agitate Morgan Yarrow. "*Obsidian*, did you say?"

"That's right," he replied. "Volcanic rock."

He had likely received one of the shards of the dark mirror. The pieces must have been dispersed after Father died. Mother, I'd heard, had taken her own life, leaping from the Eastern Tower. I had not mourned her. I'd willed myself not to. She had, after all, left me in the hands of Father for my entire childhood. She must have had a moment of clarity prior to her leap. She'd seen to the disposal of the shards, or at least their separation.

"The more time I spent with the curious delivery," Morgan Yarrow said, "the more fascinated I became. For I began to realize it was not merely a stone. It had certain unique properties."

"What sort of properties, Mr. Yarrow?"

"There was a *resonance*," he replied. "I felt vibrations—even when I was in my bedroom, late at night—the rock seemed to call for me."

"Tell me more."

"I considered its origins. Likely not Egyptian, despite the hieroglyph. I thought it might be Aztec, something similar to the mirror John Dee once used in the court of Queen Elizabeth. He employed a sort of dark mirror as a scrying stone in order to commune with what he called angels. Dee took down all kinds of transcriptions from the heavens. But in the end, the mirror wasn't that. No, it wasn't that at all." He paused and said again: "Did you find water? Please tell me you did, Miss Asquith."

"I'll keep searching, Mr. Yarrow. I promise. But first I want to make sure I'm following your tale. My own father had contact with this dark mirror, you see."

Edgar Yarrow put his hand lightly on his brow. "Does London still exist, Miss Asquith?" he said. "*Our* London."

"It does. I've just come from there. Do you know what this place is, this silent city?"

"I've thought about this long and hard, Miss Asquith, and—I honestly believe we've been swallowed. We're in a sort of belly."

"*Belly?*"

"The thing that walks the streets," Morgan Yarrow said. "The crying thing. I've taken to calling it the *soul* of the mirror. And this plane where we find ourselves, it is the surface on which the soul might move. It will have both of us soon, I think. We've been making so much noise."

"What do you mean when you say the mirror has a soul, Mr. Yarrow?" I'd begun to fear that everything he'd told me was a symptom rather than a truth. "How can an object have a soul?"

Morgan Yarrow made another odd laughing grimace. "So many secrets, Miss Asquith. But it's all so obvious too. I'm what some would call a sensitive. As a child, I heard voices. Ghosts in the churchyard. Phantoms in the cellar. After my own mother died, she came to my room one last time to tuck me into bed. Her hands were cold like the grave. So I've seen spirits, you understand. And when I began to spend more time with this stone—"

"Yes?"

Morgan Yarrow closed his eyes. "The man in London who was to receive the shipment, he didn't come to collect the stone himself. It was as if he did not want direct contact with the thing. Instead, I was instructed to begin a correspondence with a young woman. From our letters, I gathered she was, in some way, at odds with the man. I think she wanted the stone for herself. She was a sensitive too."

Sister Rose, I thought. Morgan Yarrow was talking about Sister Rose and the New Lord. "But the mirror shard itself," I said. "You told me you realized it was neither a scrying stone nor a portal. So what is it?"

"The man in London who was initially to receive the shipment," Morgan Yarrow said. "He was adamant that I not open the box. By that time I'd already done so, of course, but I didn't tell the gentleman. This Phillip Langford—he was some sort of antiquary himself."

"I'm sorry," I said, unable to believe what I'd just heard. "What did you say was the name of the man who was to receive the stone?"

"*Langford*," Morgan Yarrow said. "Phillip Langford. He's a known occultist in London. I've done work for many such men. Most of them are harmless fops, you understand. They merely have a particular affinity for antiques."

I suddenly could not breathe. "Phillip Langford was to receive the stone? And this young woman—was her name Rose?"

"That's right," Morgan Yarrow said.

"They worked together? You're sure of this?"

Morgan Yarrow nodded. "To acquire the stone."

I sat very still. Henry's mentor, a man I myself had spoken to time and again—the kindly and eccentric Phillip Langford—he was the so-called New Lord. He had taken my father's place. And he'd somehow set all of this in motion. Langford was the right age, of course, in his early sixties. He could have been one of the magicians who'd come to Nethersea Hall in those long-ago days. He might have been in that number of men who'd made experiments on the dark mirror. And yet—what did this mean for Coxton & Co.? What did it mean for Henry? I suddenly worried for my friend. He was out there somewhere in the real London, and he had no idea that his most trusted advisor was actually the New Lord.

"Mr. Yarrow," I said, "it's imperative that you tell me what you discovered about the dark mirror. If it isn't a scrying stone, then what—"

Before I could continue, I heard it: the hushing sound, the needful sigh. Like a cold hand reaching. The sound didn't come from the street outside. It was inside Coxton & Co., coming from somewhere near the back of the house.

"My God." I turned toward the office door.

"You see?" Morgan Yarrow said. "It follows us—the thing that walks. It pursues."

"Come, Mr. Yarrow," I said standing from Henry's chair. "We have to get away from here."

"There is no *away*," he said. "Don't you understand that? There is nowhere but here, Miss Asquith."

I grabbed his hand and pulled him up from the couch. Morgan Yarrow was fragile and so terribly dry.

Are you with me, Violet? The whispering again. Not Father's voice. I was sure of that now. It was an airy tone. A reproduction.

I guided the old man out of the office and into the foyer. I heard the sighing once more. At the end of the hall that led toward the kitchen, I saw the form, bent and gray, moving toward us. I could not make out its features still. They seemed, in fact, to shift and change before my eyes. In some ways, the form didn't look like a distinct entity at all. It appeared to be part of the very fabric of the hall. A distortion of my own perception.

Are you with me, Violet? Are you with—?

Before I knew what was happening, Morgan Yarrow had pulled away and was running up the stairs to the second floor of Coxton & Co.

"Stop!" I called. We needed to go outside, to make our way down the street and find another hiding place.

But Morgan Yarrow did not pause.

I ran after him. The form, ever shifting, continued its odd, shambling progress.

Yarrow had run into Henry's bedchamber, a room that overlooked Bachelor Street. I rushed inside as well, shutting the door after us. "Help me bar the door," I said. I pointed at the imposing pine cabinet where Henry stored his suits.

Morgan Yarrow shook his head. "It doesn't matter now," he said. "It's all of one piece. All of it. We are inside it, Miss Asquith. The mirror, it isn't a stone or a portal—it's a living thing. Not a mythic figure, no. It doesn't fit into any sort of story. It's an organism, ancient, petrified. My sensitivity allowed me to apprehend its spirit...its dreaming ghost. The organism has been asleep for ages, since the beginning of time perhaps. And now it wants—it wants more than anything to awake. And to feed."

"An *organism*?" I said. "You believe the mirror is a living thing?"

Morgan Yarrow nodded. "A sleeping creature from another place that has always dreamed of our world. It wants so very badly to be part of it. The dark mirror stirs now. It will awaken. The only way to escape would be to somehow how murder it. For, if it lives, surely it can be killed. But you would have to find a weakness—"

I heard a pounding then. Something battered against the bedroom door. The moaning grew louder too. Such a hungry sound.

"The window." I went to Henry's bedroom window and wrenched it open, looking out at the two-story drop to Bachelor Street below. "We have to jump, Mr. Yarrow."

I turned from the window to look at him. Morgan Yarrow stood at the center of the room, staring at the bedroom door as the thing beyond—the thing he said was the mirror's soul—continued to pound. "I am tired of running," he said without looking at me. "I have been running for so long. I'll keep its attentions. Go, Miss Asquith. Do what you can. If *anything* can be done."

I leapt from the window just as the door crashed open. I landed on the walk below, rolling my ankle but not breaking a bone. From the open window, I heard Morgan Yarrow's screams. The sound of them echoed throughout all of London.

ΗΕΝRΥ COXTON

"HENRY, MY *BOY*," Philip Langford said, clasping my hand in his. He'd answered the door in a wine-dark dressing gown, hair disheveled by sleep. His kind eyes and eloquent manner made me feel instantly more at ease. My own father had abandoned me in Warwickshire when I was very young. And Phillip had, for all purposes, taken his place. I found I simply wanted to fall into his arms.

"What hour is it?" he asked. "And what's the matter? You look positively harrowed."

"I'm so sorry. I need—"

"Never apologize for coming here. My door is open to you. You know that well enough." He backed away from the threshold, allowing me to step inside. "The chill is simply terrible, isn't it? One might mistake this for January. And you're not even wearing your coat! Come sit by the fire."

He led me to his study that was full of the bric-a-brac of his years of collecting, skulls and talismans and weapons of every sort. I sat in one of his comfortable leather chairs by the low-burning fire. The fragrant smell of oak logs further comforted me. On a table beside my chair was an oddity I had not seen before—an ivory-handled dagger with a rather cruel-looking curved black blade. I glanced at the thing, wondering what the blade might be made of. Stone, perhaps? At any rate, I thought it should be sheathed. It looked dangerous.

Phillip put his hand on the top of my head, stroking my hair for a moment. His touch felt safe. Things would be all right now that he was involved. I should have come to him sooner.

"Now, tell me, my boy," he said.

"I hardly know where to begin."

"At the beginning, Henry."

"We took a new case," I said. "The investigation of a house at the request of a woman named Eldora Tremmond."

"Go on."

"The spirit of her dead husband was to communicate with me. But when we arrived, Phillip, we realized, well, it wasn't a case at all. The house wasn't inhabited. It was set up as some sort of trap. A carefully laid thing."

"A trap?" Phillip said, sitting across from me in a wingback leather chair. "But who would want to trap you, Henry? You don't have any enemies."

"It was a trap nonetheless. An empty house. The three of us were separated. Doors and grates moved of their own accord."

"Violet's handiwork?"

"Not Violet, no. Some other force."

"Do continue."

"Christopher removed his mask," I said. "He wreaked havoc on the street. He's been *seen*, Phillip. The police will be looking for him."

"Oh dear," Langford said. "That's not good."

"I left him at the house with Mrs. Hastur. She'll take care of him. But worse than that, Violet's disappeared. I can't find her anywhere."

"Disappeared?

"Someone's sacked the offices too. Coxton & Co. is torn to pieces."

"All of this in one night?"

I nodded. "They were searching for something. There's some notion about the pieces of a mirror, a dark mirror."

"An occult object," Phillip said.

"I believe so, yes. But how did you know?"

"Dark mirrors are traditionally used to aid a person with seeing far distances or even through time. There are stories too of communications with beings of the astral plane via such a glass."

"I wanted to ask you," I said, "is there anything in the house, anything you've given me, that might cause someone to come after us? Or even want to harm us?"

"No, Henry," Phillip said, sounding sure. "I've always been quite careful with what I store at Coxton & Co."

"Yes, you've always taken good care of us."

"I think of that boy on the ship—the *Daedalus*—the boy you were so fond of."

"Paser?" I said, imagining my old friend's dark eyes, the sweet taste of his lips.

"The world has been so cruel to you. You seemed a luckless thing when I met you. But all you needed was a kind hand."

"Yes. That's right."

"What was the first thing I said to you when I met you outside that tavern so long ago?"

"You asked me...if you could help me to stand." I felt tears in my eyes. It was so good to sit with Phillip.

"I didn't see an invert when I looked at you. I didn't see a drunk. I saw a good man. A *strong* chap. I knew all of that mess with the *Daedalus*, with the Egyptian boy, I knew all of it could be put behind you. You were the sort of person who could take the reins. You'd become my pupil. And you'd learn. You've done just that, haven't you, Henry? You've turned it all around."

"I suppose I have," I said. "But it's really been because of the help of Violet and Christopher—their abilities—that's why the firm's gotten recognition."

"Violet and Christopher, spectacular though they are, would be nothing without someone to lead them. A kind hand. You see? Someone to help them to stand."

It was true. All so very true.

"Now, tell me, my boy, where did you last see Violet Asquith?"

"At the house on Castle Crescent. Number 15. But she's not there anymore, Phillip. The caretaker said there'd never been a Tremmond at the house. And I forgot to tell you, there's a woman too. She has an odd way of dressing, country-like. She wears a black bonnet. There's a whole group of them that follow her—men in black hats. She's been taunting us.

She's the reason Christopher took off his mask and ran through the streets."

Phillip sighed. "Sounds like we might have some sort of fringe group on our hands. Have you contacted the authorities?"

"I thought that would make Christopher and Violet vulnerable."

"Very good," Langford said. "We'll work this out in our own way, I promise you. The next step, though, is for me to fix you a drink, dear boy."

"But Violet."

"She's a strong girl," Phillip said. "Much stronger than either of us. She'll be fine." He moved toward the cabinet where he stored his rum. When his back was turned, I looked again at the ivory-handled dagger that sat on the end table. Such an odd blade. Its surface reflected my own face. I thought of Violet. And I thought of Paser too, the horror of what had happened to him on board the *Daedalus*. Paser and I had been found out. The other sailors knew we were unspeakables. And then, the storm had come. They'd taken that opportunity to do away with him. Paser was an Egyptian. The sailors on board the ship barely thought of him as human. I was an Englishman. They couldn't harm me. Instead, they would watch me suffer.

"Just one more moment, Henry," Phillip said, his back still turned. "I'm looking for an old Spanish rum I've been saving for a special occasion."

"Can I help you?"

"Oh no, no," he said. "Just try to relax."

Yes, I thought. I had to relax. "If we could only locate this woman in the black bonnet who's been taunting us," I said, "I believe we could find Violet. The woman will know something about the whole thing. She must."

"That's very likely true," he said, handing me a glass of honey-colored rum. I took a sip immediately. I wanted to feel the warmth of it, the calm. I remembered my days at the Prince Alfred.

I tasted bitterness at the back of my throat. "It has a distinct flavor."

"Something new," Phillip said, "from an area near Motril, on the southern coast."

I took another sip. "We should start at the Tremmond house. There could be some clue I've missed. You'll come with me, won't you, Phillip?"

"Of course I will, my boy."

My eyelids felt heavy. I hadn't realized how tired I was until I sat down in Phillip's leather chair. "I've been out all night."

"You must be exhausted."

I took another sip of rum.

"Perhaps you should rest," Phillip said. "I'll wake you once I've dressed. How does that sound?"

It no longer felt like I was merely tired. It was as though gravity had become twice as strong. I couldn't move my legs, couldn't even lift the glass to my mouth. And then I realized the rum was slipping from my hand, falling to the rug.

"Oh, Phillip—" I said, feeling embarrassed, even as my eyes closed. "I'm—" But my lips would no longer move.

"Quite all right, Henry." Phillip's voice, echoing in darkness. "We all make mistakes. Even me."

CHRISTOPHER X

WE FELL FROM the sky, plummeting through rays of a blazing sun. The desert spun below, a bright surface. Wind ripped at us. Then, with incredible force, we struck the earth and were driven beneath the sand. We could not breathe. We could not see. We struggled to pull ourselves up toward the rim of the crater. We used the strength of our arms and pushed with our legs. Then, finally, we were free.

This was a memory.

We were inside a memory.

We lay naked on the sand, bloodied. Our wounds reminded us of our purpose. We were a soldier. We were meant to be torn and battered. We were meant to protect the barrier. The heat of the desert pressed on us like a hand. We could smell this world. The world of men. A fire burned in the distance. Someone cooked meat.

We knew our aim. We knew our purpose.

At one time, there had been many of us, many soldiers. We all worked to protect the barrier.

Now, so few remained.

Still, we were all of one mind. Our bodies went where we were needed. We fell from the sky.

And we were needed here.

We set off toward the fire, traveling as the sun began to set. We gazed at the pillar of white smoke that rose toward the stars. We approached. We found the campsite. There was a tent made of animal hide. A man in rags squatted by the fire. He was thin, his hair long and tangled. He wore an amulet around his neck, a white stone in a knot of old leather.

"Magician," we called to him. We spoke in a language he could understand. The soldiers knew many languages.

The man glanced up from his cooking. Humans always looked so fragile, so frightened. The man realized he could not run, for there was nowhere in the vast empty desert to hide. From the look in his eyes, we thought he recognized us. Perhaps he had known we would come. Magicians told stories of our kind, stories of the soldiers who protected the barrier.

The man squatted, clutching his amulet, gazing at us. Finally, he said, "God."

"No," we said.

"What, then?"

"A soldier," we replied.

"Of what army?" he said.

We did not answer.

"Mercurius," he said, finally. "That is what I'm called."

"We do not need your name," we said. "Show us where it is. The object."

"Object?"

"Lies will not help you," we said.

"Do you mean the dark mirror?"

"Mirror, yes," we said. "Show us."

The magician scrambled toward a long post that rose from the sand some distance from the fire. He began to dig. He had buried the object. "You say you are a soldier," he said. "But what do you guard?"

"You do not need to know."

"But I wish to understand."

"That is the problem," we said.

Mercurius' hands were covered in sand. He sat back, looking at the hole he'd made, confused. "I buried it here. I marked the place with a post. I don't know what happened. I have not left the camp. No one could have taken it."

"It moves," we said.

"Moves? But—"

We inhaled, taking in air, searching for the object. We thought we could smell it, like ashes. "It has not moved far. It is not so strong. Both of us must dig."

And so we set about our work, digging in the sand, looking for the object the magician called a dark mirror. While we dug, the magician asked more questions. "You are of some race? Your people have some city?"

"A race, yes," we said. "But there is no city."

"Once we find the mirror," he said, "I will pay homage to you. I have never been in the presence of one so—"

"We will not be worshipped."

"But," the magician said, "such a divinity must be—"

"We are not divine," we said, still digging. "When we are needed, we fall."

"There must be some intelligence," Mercurius said. "Someone who sees when you are needed. Someone who sends you."

"Such questions are not ours to ask," we said. But even as we said this, we paused at our digging. Mercurius had caused us to think. Thinking was not good for soldiers such as us. But sometimes we could not help ourselves. "How did you come to be in possession of the object?"

"It called to me," Mercurius said. "I was in the ranks of Cassander, general of Alexander. The mirror called me to the desert. It has allowed me to do the most marvelous things. I can move objects with my mind. I can levitate."

"That is how it begins," we said. "But it does not end there."

"What do you mean?"

"The object gives. But it intends to take."

Then, we touched something hard beneath the sand. We felt it wriggle between our fingers. It moved like a serpent, attempting escape. We grasped the object's edge and held firm. We pulled. This action was difficult, even for us. Finally, we pulled it from the earth and laid it before us. It was a small black disk. Smooth and shining. It reflected the light of the magician's fire.

Mercurius came to look at the object.

"We will carry it away," we said.

"You will destroy it?"

"It cannot be destroyed."

"What, then?"

"We will carry it away. Its existence is not the problem. The problem," we said, "is the magician. For it is a magician who will one day wake this dreaming thing."

"I don't understand."

"You," we said. "The magician is what must be destroyed."

"No." Mercurius backed away, placing his hands around his white amulet. It was a useless charm. "I wasn't going to do anything with the mirror. I only found it. It spoke to me. It gave me strength."

"That is what it does. It calls to men. And men are foolish."

"But I intended to get rid of it. That's why I buried it, you see?"

"We do not see."

"Mercy," Mercurius said, shaking the talisman. "You seem like a merciful god."

"We are neither merciful nor a god."

"But you must understand—I am different. Different than those magicians who you have met before."

"The object wants to awaken. It wants to devour. It knows that all magicians are the same."

"Mercy," Mercurius said again. "Oh, please."

We put our hand around the magician's neck. We lifted him. His sandaled feet dangled above the earth. "Your death will be swift. That is mercy enough."

Before we twisted the magician's neck, he spoke. He uttered a phrase. We knew there had been words. The mouth of the magician had moved. And yet, we did not understand the words he had spoken. *All is fallen. Reprobus, prepare.* There was suddenly a buzzing in our ears. A pain inside our head. We snapped the magician's neck, just as we intended. His tongue slipped from between his lips. His body hung limp.

We turned to look at the meat the magician had been cooking. It was covered in black and crawling flies. Our ears too were full of flies. They were all around us. Flies inside our body. Flies inside our head. The magician had cast some spell. We realized this, but it was too late. We swatted at the flies that now surrounded us. We tried to avoid their biting mouths. We forgot about the mirror as we swatted. We forgot about our people and our past. We forgot why we were there in the desert. We pulled out the iron spikes holding the magician's tent. We used them to nail his body to the pole. He would act as a sign. Beware this place. Beware the black glass. We were so full of flies. They devoured our memory, faster and faster. Soon, they devoured all of us.

VIOLET ASQUITH

A WEAKNESS. I had to find a weakness. And yet such a feat seemed impossible as I fled the harrowing screams of Morgan Yarrow. The creature had had taken him. Now, it would come for me. Certainly it would. I felt helpless beneath the flat gray sky that was not like a sky at all. The cobbles beneath my feet had an eerie look about them too, colorless and without true dimension. I considered all that I'd learned from poor Mr. Yarrow—Father's mirror was not a scrying stone or a portal. It was an organism. Some sort of alien life, petrified. Mother had once intuited a similar idea from the vantage of her mad aerie: *Your father's mirror has a taste for our world, Violet, just as all mirrors do. But this one, I think, is particularly hungry.*

Sister Rose and Phillip Langford had drawn me into a snare. They'd transported me here, wherever *here* might be. It was possible, as Morgan Yarrow had said, that we were somehow caught inside the mirror's dreaming soul. And if that was so, I knew there must be some limit to the organism's consciousness. If the creature could dream, there was an edge to its reverie, a boundary between sleep and waking. Between reflection and the object itself.

My job, then, was to find that edge, to discover the boundary and cross over it.

I paused. The buildings around me on Bachelor Street (the silversmith and the grim Hotel Walford) were silent. The mirror desired matter, yes, and therefore it had dreamed of matter. A whole city full of it. A faulty model. For the mirror had not been able to populate its city with souls. There were no people here. No lives. This was a dead place, a landscape imagined by a thing that was not human, that could never be human.

The creature's sigh rose in the distance. A low voice, partly sated, but still wanting more. And suddenly I realized there was only one thing in this dead city that did not seem to truly belong. One thing that flickered and appeared confused. It was the figure itself. The moaning, needful form. If there was an edge, that was likely where I'd find it. The creature itself was the boundary.

I turned back toward Coxton & Co., understanding what I had to do. I could no longer run. The only way back to my world, the only way out of the mirror, was through the imperfection, through the creature's own desiring body.

I passed down the barren street, back toward Coxton and Co. The front door was locked, of course. I'd locked it myself. I pulled a loose bar from the iron fence that surrounded the building. Then, I struck the large window at the front parlor. The shattering was loud and would certainly draw the attention of the creature. I continued to batter against the window, striking at it until all the glass was cleared. Then, I crawled into the parlor and stood breathless amongst the glittering shards, knowing I'd need to work out my plan as I went along. There was no time now to worry about specifics.

"Where are you?" I called.

A hiss came from upstairs. A rustle of movement.

The figure was still there in Henry's bedchamber, where I'd left it with Morgan Yarrow. I moved up the stairs, holding my dress so the hem didn't get tangled in my boots. The oaken door had been torn from its hinges. And there, in the center of the room, was the figure. Only it did not look anything like what I'd expected. It was not some gray and formless monster. It was a child—a girl of no more than eight or nine years of age, with black hair and gray eyes. Here before me then was Mirror Violet, the girl who had stood inside the glass in the Western Tower so long ago. She who had gazed at me with alien eyes. Mirror Violet knelt over the body of Morgan Yarrow. The old man was dead, though it was unclear precisely how she'd killed him. She peered at his face, his open dead eyes. She appeared to study the dark mirror of his irises, as if perhaps she could come to some understanding of what it was to be human through them.

When she heard me at the door, her head jerked up, and she turned her attention toward me. There was such wanting in the expression on her face. So much desire. She opened her mouth and made the sighing sound. Then she held out her arms, the gesture of a child to a mother. I went to her, knowing what had to be done. She was the only way back to London—to Henry, to Christopher, to Mrs. Hastur. I had to warn them about Phillip Langford, to protect my friends and my city.

Here, in this version of Coxton & Co., there was no longer a surface that separated me from Mirror Violet. I could touch her now. And she could touch me. *If only the mirror had arms,* I'd once thought, *it could reach for me. If only the mirror had hands, it could hold me as Mother and Father refused to hold me.* I knelt before the girl and opened my own arms. She came forward and pressed herself inside my embrace.

As soon as I touched Mirror Violet, however, I realized she was nothing like a child. She was cold and formless, her edges not as firm as they appeared to be. It was as if I was attempting to put my arms around a cold, dark sea. Mirror Violet began to flicker, changing. Father's haggard face appeared inside hers, a man's visage pressing up through the flesh of a child. *Are you with me, Violet?* he asked. *Violet, are you with me?* The mirror had seen Father and me. Captured our reflections. It knew us so well that it could *be* us. Father's massive arms were around me then, squeezing. I felt the vastness of him. And within him I could feel the immensity, the inhumanity, of the organism that was the mirror. It surrounded me. Surrounded everything. I put my fingers then around Father's neck, pressing. The tips of my fingers punctured his skin. Something like blood ran down my hands, my arms. The substance was like blood, yes, but it was black, the color of the mirror. Suddenly, I held Mirror Violet once more. My fingers were inside the girl's neck. I knew I could not stop, could not allow myself to be fooled. I pulled Mirror Violet's throat apart, ripping her strange flesh. The expression on her face was one of strange ecstasy. I tore into myself. My own childhood. And as I did this, I realized this was somehow what it wanted. This was what the mirror had desired all along. The girl was everywhere at once, somehow growing in power. Yet, I found I could not cease. I had to finish what I'd begun.

ħEnRy COXTON

I AWOKE, PAIN in my head like a blade. My hands were bound. My ankles, tied. I was no longer in the home of Phillip Langford. Instead, I found myself sitting in a wooden chair in a high-ceilinged warehouse. Dark birds fluttered in the rafters. Moonlight streamed through tall windows. Before me, in another wooden chair, sat a man I recognized, a square-jawed figure with rust-colored stubble, wearing a wide-brimmed black hat. A musket lay across his lap. Apparently Brother James, who'd attempted to shoot me in the Tremmond house, had returned to finish the job.

"Mr. Coxton," he said.

In my delirium, I found it difficult to interpret his tone. Was it one of coldness? Or might there be some hint of remorse? I attempted to speak, but my tongue was too heavy. My head, packed with cotton. I couldn't remember what had happened in the moments before I'd lost consciousness. How had I come to be in this place? "Phillip—" I said finally. "Where?" For what had this man—this killer—done with my mentor?

"He needn't concern you," Brother James replied.

I closed my eyes. The world threatened to slip away. But Brother James' voice cut through the darkness. "Come back. I need to speak with you."

I opened my eyes, still thinking about Phillip. When had I last seen him? Had Brother James taken me from his house? Hopefully my friend had been able to make it away to safety.

"Are you awake, Henry? Do you mind if I call you that?"

I squinted. Brother James's wide-brimmed hat was tilted back on his head so I could see his bluish eyes.

"I'm afraid you're in a lot of trouble," he said.

"How—"

"All of us have a job to do," Brother James said, "the New Lord, Sister Rose, myself. You and your group, you have jobs to do as well. But instead of doing those jobs, you're causing all sorts of disruptions. You're not following the plan."

"Plan—"

"I'm going to be honest with you. And if you'll listen, you might make it out of this in one piece. But if you don't listen, you're going to end up dead. Do you understand?"

"You tried to kill me."

"I've been shooting grouse all my life, Henry. I can fell a bird at two hundred feet. So I certainly could have shot you in the head at ten paces. But I didn't. Sister Rose was in the house. And it was important she believed I at least *tried* to shoot you. She isn't very good about following instructions herself most of the time. She thinks only her own reasons matter. But we all have our motivations, don't we?"

I ground my teeth. "What are your *motivations?*"

He shook his head. "That's where things get difficult. I serve the New Lord, but not because I believe in what he's doing. I'm not like the rest. I grew up differently, you see. My mother let me go walking in the forest. I used to swim in the old pond. I played games with invisible boys, playmates of my own invention. Maybe that's what changed me. Something as simple as that. But still I serve him because, well, because he's made certain threats."

"Threats against what?"

"I can't tell you. But you should understand that when I met you in the Tremmond house, I already knew all sorts of things about you. I'd studied you."

"Why would you study me?"

Brother James looked down at his rifle. "I'm not from London. I'm not good with words. But I know about Paser and the *Daedalus*. I know how the two of you felt about each other. That's why I volunteered to tend to you at the Tremmond house. Because I knew I could avoid harming you."

"I don't follow."

Brother James took a breath. "I am *like* you, Henry."

"You are—" I said, but I found I couldn't finish the sentence, just as I'd never truly been able to finish the sentence for myself.

"But I'm also a part of the village," he said.

"Village?"

"A hamlet in the English countryside, where there is no one else like you or me. That's why I knew I had to meet you."

"In an abandoned house with a loaded gun."

"All that terrible business with Paser, him being thrown overboard during the storm. I wish I could have been there. I'm good in a fight. We have matches in the village to keep up our strength—boxing and that sort of thing."

"I'm still quite confused." I said. I didn't trust Brother James. But at least it didn't seem as though he was going to use the gun that lay across his lap any time soon. "Explain this village of yours further."

"It's a kind of fiefdom," he said, "of a great house, called Nethersea Hall. Lord Asquith, in his time, watched over us."

"Asquith?" I said. "Violet's father?" I'd heard her speak of him briefly on a few occasions. I knew that they had lived in the country and that he was now deceased. Both of Violet's parents had passed on, in fact.

"You know very little about your business partner," Brother James said. "She's not the woman you think she is. There are all sorts of goings on that you're not privy to, Henry."

"I'm beginning to realize that."

"As I said, the New Lord has made threats." Brother James closed his eyes. There in the moonlight, he looked like a melancholy painting. "There's no real reason to hurry through any of this. What's done is done."

"What do you mean?" I asked. "What's been done?"

He shifted the gun. "I'll tell you about the village. I can't see how that would hurt."

"All right. Tell me."

"Long ago, during the time of the plague, many people died in my village. Whole families were found gathered cold and breathless around their hearths. Husbands and wives perished in each other's arms. Children were found stiff in their beds. There was no time for prayer. Bodies were burned. The sky was always black with ash. It was during that desperate time that the council struck a deal with the lord at Nethersea. For he was said to be a dark magician who could control nature itself."

"Magician?"

Brother James offered a grim nod. "He would have been a distant ancestor of Lord Asquith, Violet's father. After the deal was struck, the village and the great hall were bound by a powerful oath. The lord at Nethersea helped to heal our people. Plague sores faded. The terrible, rasping cough subsided. But the lord at Nethersea said he could do even more with our help. That's why we wear the black hats. So we remember to serve the lord. To serve the greater good."

"And what is the greater good in this case?" I said.

"To stay the hand of death."

"So this lord of yours is trying to find some cure for plagues?"

Brother James shook his head. "The lord at Nethersea wants to cure all suffering. And, finally, to cure death itself."

I sat in silent bewilderment. "You must be kidding."

He shook his head.

"This entire farce," I said, "that's what it's about? Someone is trying to cure death?"

"It's not a farce, Henry."

"How in the world does that sound like something reasonable to you?"

"The lord at Nethersea keeps a dark mirror, a powerful magician's glass. I can't tell you about it. I don't know enough. Only the lord at Nethersea and Sister Rose are privy to such information. And Violet Asquith has some part in this too."

"Do you know where she is?" I asked.

"Yes. But the New Lord wouldn't want me to tell you."

144

"Who is this New Lord?"

"Henry," Brother James said.

"Can you at least untie me?"

"The New Lord said I was to keep you tied on account of the fact that last time you leapt from the chair. He thinks that's how you escaped. You leapt from the chair. I missed my target. And you'd already made it out of the house before I could reload my gun. He doesn't want me to miss my target again."

"But you're not going to shoot me."

"That's true."

"So there's no reason to keep me tied. I need to find Violet."

"You'll find her soon enough."

"James," I said. "Please."

He appeared to consider something. "If I untie you, do you think, well, do you think you would do something for me?"

"Name it," I said.

He rubbed his musket nervously. "A kiss."

I blinked. "You want me to *kiss* you?"

"I might never have such a chance again."

Somehow this request seemed less strange than most of the other things Brother James had said. He struck me as far less a threat than the one called Sister Rose. He might even be a help if I managed the situation correctly. And he was, in fact, quite handsome in a countryish way. Different than Paser. I thought of my beloved friend, the look in his dark eyes the last time I'd seen him.

"Untie me," I said.

Brother James put down his musket and came to kneel before me. He untied my boots and then, rather than moving behind me to untie my hands, he leaned forward, nearly hugging me. I realized he wasn't actually untying me. He was simply holding me like that, kneeling on the floor, arms around me.

"James," I said.

"Sorry," he said. "I suppose—I suppose I got carried away." He worked at the knot that bound my hands. As soon as he was done, I put both hands on his stubbled cheeks, lifted his face to mine and kissed him on his thin hard lips. He tasted of tobacco and bitter sweat. It had been years since I'd kissed anyone. And I confess that I lingered for a moment more than necessary.

"How did that feel?" I said when he'd pulled away.

Brother James had a rather stunned look on his face. "It felt like walking in the forest so long ago."

"Take me to Violet."

"Will you kiss me again if I do?"

"I might."

He grasped my hand. And like that, we were off.

CHRISTOPHER X

THE LID OF the sarcophagus lay at our feet. We had broken free of our chains. We were more powerful than any such implement. Our English suit hung in ribbons, a mere reminder of days when we did not know ourselves. We looked down at our large hands, our powerful arms. They were covered in the dust of Egyptian stone. We felt stronger than we had in ages. And more than that, we knew our aim and our purpose. We remembered the truth of our name: Reprobus, Dog of God, Guardian of the Barrier. We understood that, although Sister Rose was treacherous, she spoke the truth. We had to stop Violet. For she was not a telekinetic as Henry believed. She was one of the magicians. Perhaps the strongest there had ever been. We had to stop her before she awoke the object, the dark mirror. Mercurius himself had caused us to forget. He too had been powerful. But we remembered now. Yes, we remembered.

We turned from the sarcophagus, and there, at the foot of the cellar stair, was what we did not want to see. A vision we could hardly bear. The sight of it confused us. But we knew we must follow our aim. We must act. Even though our friend, Mrs. Hastur, lay there twisted and exposed. She lay there as if she had always lain at the bottom of the cellar stair. As if she had never been lively and loving and filled with care. Blood had dried on her gray uniform. Her body rested in a now sticky pool. The blood smelled like the death not only of Mrs. Hastur, but of all things. The end of our age in London. We would avenge her. We would not only stop Violet from what she was about to do. We would stop the men who had done this to our beloved friend.

We went to the body and knelt before it. We took Mrs. Hastur's hand in our own. Her flesh was cold. Her eyes open. We thought of all the men and women we had killed. All the blood that we had caused to run. Death had never moved us. It seemed a necessary thing. But this death was not necessary. Mrs. Hastur should be alive.

We thought of her stroking our head before she went to sleep, of the way she gave us chicken bones and told us stories of an invisible world. We paused. Had Mrs. Hastur somehow known about our true nature? Had she been trying to tell us something all along? We looked into her eyes again. It did not matter now what she had known. Mrs. Hastur could tell her stories no longer. Her voice would never fall upon our ears again. We lifted both her hands and placed them over her chest, crossing them in a reverent manner. Then we used our finger to carefully close her eyes. We did not press hard. We did want to hurt the eyes. They were beautiful to us. Mrs. Hastur was dead. But she was still beautiful to us. We bowed our head. We knew that Englishmen said prayers in the presence of death. But we did not know any prayers. And we did not know any gods. So instead, we spoke to Mrs. Hastur herself.

"I want you to know that I will always think of you, even if you cannot think of me," we said. We reached up and wiped something damp from the fur beneath our eye. Then we continued, "I know my aim now, Mrs. Hastur. I know my purpose. And you were right all along. I *am* good. I am meant to protect this world. Still, there are things I do not know. I do not know, for instance, where do souls go after death? There are still mysteries, you see. I wish you were here. I would ask you my questions. And though you would not likely give me a clear answer, I would still enjoy the sound of your answers. I very much appreciated your voice, Mrs. Hastur. I hear it sometimes in my dreams. It calls to me from the sky. Implores me to take action. Did I ever tell you that? I would stand very still in my dream, listening to the sound of your voice, not understanding."

We paused in our speech, wishing Mrs. Hastur would respond to us, but knowing she would not.

"I wish I knew what it was you wanted to tell me at the end," we said, "the reason you came down the cellar stairs. I told you to stay in Henry's bedroom. And still, you came down to the cellar. It must have been something important indeed that you wanted to tell me. I wonder if, perhaps, it was about Violet. I know what she is now, Mrs. Hastur. A powerful sort of magician. Perhaps the most powerful there has ever been. I did not understand that before. Violet is one who reaches far beyond the boundary. And I know what I must do to one such as her. It is going to be very difficult because I love Violet. But I know my aim, Mrs. Hastur. I know my purpose."

We paused, waiting, listening.

There was no response from Mrs. Hastur. Of course there wasn't.

"At any rate," we said, "thank you for all that you did. I am glad you do not have to see what will happen to Violet. You would not like it very much."

We stood, pulling a sheet off of an old oil painting that depicted a Roman market square, another piece in Henry's collection. We put the sheet over the body of Mrs. Hastur. Then, slowly, and with a great sense of purpose, we began to ascend the cellar stair.

VIOLET ASQUITH

THROUGH AND THROUGH and further through, swimming in a liquid dark that was not a mirror and certainly not a girl. After I'd pierced Mirror Violet's body, I found myself no longer in false London. Instead, I moved in a black fluid of some great density. In the sable distance, monolithic forms hovered, shadows so large, they were difficult to perceive outright. Difficult to even hold in my memory. As soon as I looked away, elements of their proportions slipped from my reckoning, as if they existed in dimensions too preposterous for my mind to comprehend. It was only when I gazed directly at the vast silhouettes (as one would peer at a dirigibles in a fog-ridden sky) that I could actually recall their terrors. The shapes may have been alien bodies or even organs of a *single* body. For some of them swelled and contracted like lungs. And others rippled and shone like coiled intestines. Behind them, they dragged somber tendrils through the bleak protoplasm, undulating stalks and branches that might have been some arterial matter. Between these hellish shapes was nothing but emptiness, a great void, the presence of which, at times, seemed to call to me, telling me I was small, as was all of humanity. We were infinitesimal compared to its greatness.

And then, in that dark matter, a faint and glimmer of light appeared, as if hope itself had manifested. I slipped onward through the substance, moving arms and legs, rising toward the light. The great bodies, thankfully, drew no closer. They appeared to have no regard for me.

Finally, I saw that the light was a kind of orifice. I was surrounded by the light then, passing through it and spilling, miraculously, onto the floor of the storage room in the Tremmond house.

I could tell immediately that this was my London. The eerie silence had abated. Colors were in full bloom. The dark mirror no longer hung on the wall behind me. All around me lay the liquid of what might once have been its body. The mirror was now nothing more than a series of thick amniotic puddles. And as I watched, even these puddles dissipated, like water evaporating in heat. The mirror was disappearing entirely from existence.

Coughing and gasping, I realized I had destroyed the wretched thing, just as I'd set out to do. I'd found its weakness. I'd dissolved its awful soul.

Then from the shadows of the candlelit room, the voice of Sister Rose: "Father's work is finally done." She leaned against a curved stone wall in her gray over-dress and black bonnet, smoking one of my black cigarettes and looking oddly serene for one who'd put so much stock in the dark mirror. All of her anger, all of her hatred, seemed to have disappeared.

"It's gone," I said. "I've defeated it."

"Oh, Violet," Rose said. "Still nothing more than a confused little girl."

I glanced back at the empty wall where the mirror had hung, confused.

"You've done your job," Rose said. "Done it marvelously, in fact."

"What job?"

"Do you think the New Lord would have sent you on a quest inside the mirror if he thought you could actually destroy it?"

"But it's gone," I said. "No one can make use of it anymore."

"*Two* pieces are gone. But there is a third piece, isn't there, Violet? This wasn't Father's entire mirror. We both know that well enough. And don't you feel it now?"

"Feel what?" I said. Yet even as I spoke, I realized there *was* something—a distant vibration. I looked toward the now open door of the secret room.

"Please should the door shut?" I whispered.

The door swung closed with sudden force.

My power had returned. "How?" I asked Sister Rose.

Still, the distant rumbling. The horrid tremor.

"We are stronger than ever," Rose said. "The spiritual clockwork has been activated. Your actions have unlocked the mirror's true potential."

"No..."

"Whatever you communed with was just the thing."

I thought about Morgan Yarrow's words: The mirror wasn't a scrying glass, and it wasn't a portal. It was an organism. Was it possible that somehow, through the violence of my act in false London, I had awakened the creature?

"The New Lord thanks you," Sister Rose said. She glanced up at the bricks near the ceiling of the small room and whispered something to them. Immediately, they shifted. Dust began to fall. "I *feel* so strong, Violet."

"Wait," I said. "Rose."

She whispered a few words more, and the first bricks began to fall. She turned toward the door of the room and lifted her hand. The door swung open. I heard the entire house creaking beyond the narrow hall, beams bending, bricks scraping.

"What are you doing?" I said.

"Killing you," Rose replied calmly. "I've always wanted to do that."

Without further warning, a wall of the secret room toppled, bricks spilling down upon bricks, striking my body. The pain was immediate. Rose raised her hands, fingers splayed, and suddenly she was floating some three feet off the ground. Her boots dangled above the now trembling floor.

"Goodbye, Violet," she said.

The wooden floor of the room spasmed and then, with immense force, exploded around me, throwing me toward the ceiling. I struck the hard surface, knocking the wind from my chest. I fell back onto the broken floorboards. One of them pierced my side. I screamed. The hall beyond the door was collapsing, dust now so thick I could not see.

"Please should the bricks stop falling?" I begged.

But it was too late. Gravity had taken over. The room continued to crumble. The house seemed to be caving in upon itself. All of it was coming down so quickly. All of it coming apart.

I crawled down toward the door of the secret room, but before I could reach it, what remained of the floor tilted like some surface in a house of horrors. I could not maintain my grip. I slid and fell through some broken chasm into darkness.

I landed then in another room below—a parlor of some sort. The walls of the parlor shuddered. A window exploded behind me. Floors rolled like ocean waves.

And then, a voice: "Violet!"

It was Henry, though I couldn't see him because of all the dust.

"Here!" I yelled. "I'm here!" Something exploded behind me. Debris rained down. One of my legs was suddenly trapped under a fall of masonry. "Hurry, Henry!"

Henry emerged from the dust, and behind him, one of the black-hatted men from the village. I recoiled, thinking this must be some further trap. But the man from the village bent to help Henry move bricks from my leg. At that moment, a great chunk of the ceiling fell down upon all of us. Henry and the man in the black hat were lost in rubble. I twisted, pushing to free myself, searching for my friend. And then through the curtain of dust came a giant form.

"Christopher!" I called.

"I am here," he said, pulling me out of the debris and throwing me over his shoulder.

"Henry," I said. "He's buried in here too." But Christopher did not pause. He moved through the falling rubble, carrying me. Once I was outside, I saw that the entire top of the Tremmond house was gone. All that remained was the jagged shell of the ground floor. A fire had started somewhere near the kitchen. Onlookers came from the neighboring houses on Castle Crescent to gape. Christopher laid me on the ground. I gazed up at him. There was such an odd look in the golden eyes that peered at me through his mask. They were filled with some emotion that I had never seen before. "Christopher, go find Henry!" I said. And at that, a section of the house exploded behind us. Onlookers scuttled back, letting out a cry.

HENRY COXTON

TURPENTINE AND TONIC, the moaning of the sick. I awoke to find myself in what appeared to be a hospital ward, long, gray and sterile. Perhaps one of the infamous injury halls at Great Ormond Street or Northampton General. A hazy, antiseptic light streamed in through the latticed windows, making the white-caped nurses who roamed the chamber look themselves like winsome specters. Narrow beds crowded the open room. Linen curtains formed partitions, making it difficult for me to see all aspects of the space. On a cot directly to my left lay an injured man whose hair had been burned away. He had no eyebrows, and on the top of his head, fire had left nothing but a pinkish, ragged scalp covered in painful-looking sores. One of the man's eyes was swollen shut. The other stared at me with a terrible vacancy.

"Sir," I whispered, my throat coated in a thick layer of dust. "Can you tell me we are?"

He made no response.

I thought of Violet and the falling house. I'd seen her body, limp in the dust. I'd rushed ahead. Timbers collapsed. Plaster rained down. Then darkness.

"What day is it?" I asked, reaching up to touch my left temple. It felt swollen and bruised.

The burned figure merely glared at me with his single open eye.

I prayed for some sign of my friends. But neither Violet nor Christopher nor James was anywhere in sight. I saw the falling Tremmond house once more. The second story of brick toppled with a great rush into the first. Window glass exploded onto the street. A column of fire and black smoke rose. I'd run directly into the maelstrom. James followed without hesitation, proving his mettle a second time after untying me in the warehouse. The house itself remained a mystery. The identity of the person who'd rented it was still unknown. I'd once believed it belonged to the widow called Eldora Tremmond, but according to what I'd learned from Edgar Yarrow—

I paused, finding I couldn't properly finish my thought. The name "Tremmond," though I'd heard it many times before, had suddenly lodged itself in my mind, as a bone might stick in a throat. Along with the name arrived a series of phrases: *Prominent forehead. Large, melancholy eyes. She had an air of death about her. As one who's seen too much of life.* The words appeared to rise from some psychic reservoir. And I had a vague sense they were in reference to Eldora Tremmond herself. Yet I had never seen the widow, of course, so I could not have made any such observation about her forehead or her melancholy air. No one else either had ever described her to me. And yet, here was this description: *Prominent forehead. Large, melancholy eyes.* I realized I could picture the words themselves, printed on a page in black and white. Was it possible that I had not been told about Eldora Tremmond at all but had somehow *read* about her?

I glanced to my right. My gray suit lay folded beneath my overcoat on a chair. On top of the pile was my book, *Thomas Shadow: The Ghost Finder*—the collection of adventure stories that Phillip Langford had given me early in my tenure. I kept it in my pocket in the same way that some men would carry a Bible. The book appeared to have been damaged during the incident at the Tremmond house, as the binding was broken and the leather cover had been nearly sliced in half. I wondered who had removed the tome from my pocket and laid it on top of my clothes in such a manner.

I extended my hand toward the book, wanting to examine its pages for reasons I did not quite understand. But I realized soon enough I could not reach it. And as I had a sense that it was vital I got hold of the thing, I pivoted in the bed, putting my feet on the cold tiles of the hospital floor and attempting to stand. My legs proved weaker than I expected, and without warning, I fell to the floor. Grabbing the edge of my coat, I toppled the whole pile of things down upon me.

I paused only for a moment and then began searching through the clothes for the now buried book. As my fingers brushed the leather binding, I heard the swift report of a nurse's shoes as she approached. "Mr. Coxton," she said in a high clear voice. "Have you hurt yourself?"

I lifted the broken leather volume and began to fumble through its pages, scanning words and phrases, trying to grasp something that hovered just beyond my reach. And then I came to the final story—the one entitled "Prefiguration of an End." I remembered the narrative well enough. Mr. Thomas Shadow, the ghost detective, was hired by an aging householder to investigate a series of accidents that had threatened her staff. For the most part, these were minor occurrences: a maid slipped in the kitchen on a puddle of water, an unruly horse nearly kicked the liveryman. Shadow was brought to the house due to reports of a dark figure that appeared just before each accident occurred. The "Prefiguration," as the figure was known, provided no direct warning to the victims. It only observed.

The nurse knelt beside me. She had a kind and heart-shaped face. "You read that book all night, Mr. Coxton. You insisted upon holding it, even though you seemed barely conscious."

"I was reading?" I said. For I had no memory of such an act. Nor did I recall the passage of any night at all.

"We finally pried the book from you in the early hours of the morning," the nurse continued. "But even then, with your eyes closed, you were hard pressed to give it up."

I read the first few sentences of "Prefiguration of an End": *It was evening when I arrived at the Tremmond house. Seven o'clock, and the street was dark as pitch. I rang the bell and was greeted, not by a servant, but by the lady of the house herself, Mrs. Eldora Tremmond. She had a prominent forehead and large melancholy eyes. There was an air of death about her, as one who had seen too much of life.*

I looked up at the nurse, no longer feeling quite inside my own body. I'd recognized the name "Tremmond" the first time I saw it written on the blue envelope. And now I realized where I'd seen it before. But what could it mean that Eldora Tremmond was part of a fiction—and not just any piece of fiction, but a character from a book I carried with me everywhere I went? I felt a wave of panic then. "My friends," I whispered hoarsely to the nurse, allowing *The Ghost Finder* to fall from my hand.

"Friends?" the nurse said.

"Two men," I said, having a vague notion that Christopher had arrived at the house after James and I entered. "And a woman. I must speak to them."

"You were brought here alone, sir," the nurse said, "by the ambulance."

I glanced down at book, wondering if my entire life was somehow a fiction. Had I imagined the fabulous individuals who populated my days? Violet and Christopher and now even James were the very people who made me feel that I was not merely some drunk lying in a puddle outside a tavern.

"You have to rest, Mr. Coxton," the nurse said. "And don't fret. While you were in your state of confusion, you told us who we should contact. We sent word to him directly."

"Who?" I said, not remembering.

"Mr. Phillip Langford, sir." She patted my hand. "I'm sure he'll be here soon."

I looked down at my copy of *The Ghost Finder*.

Phillip?

My own Phillip?

I thought of the odd bitter taste of the rum he'd served me when I'd come to him for help. James had removed me from Phillip's house with some apparent ease and taken me to the warehouse where he was to murder me at the orders of the New Lord. I remembered the kindness in Phillip's eyes as he'd told me we'd find Violet together. That everything would turn out all right in the end. It was as I began to struggle to stand from where I'd fallen on the floor—feeling a pain in my ribs and at the back of my head—that I heard Violet's voice, not in some memory or delusion, but in the hospital ward itself, echoing in the cold gray light: "Henry, thank God."

I turned with some difficulty and saw her striding across the wide expanse of the ward, black suit-dress covered in dust from the falling house. She was followed closely by Christopher and James. James' arm was tied in a white sling, and he no longer wore his black hat.

"Look there, Mr. Coxton," the nurse said. "Are those the friends you were talking about, sir?"

"They are," I said, trembling. "Truly, they are." I felt relieved, despite the fact that I'd just discovered that my most recent client had been lifted from the pages of a poorly-written adventure novel. At least, in fact, I was real. My friends were real. When the three of them arrived at my bedside, the nurse departed, saying the doctor would be coming soon.

Violet sat on the edge of the hard mattress and took my hand. "We thought we'd lost you," she said. "They sent us to Saint Catherine's, but you weren't there. It took three hospitals to find you, Henry."

"This book," I said, lifting *Thomas Shadow: The Ghost Finder*. But before I could say more, I fell into a coughing fit.

"Don't speak, Henry," Violet said. "Just listen. There's much you should know." She explained then that Sister Rose, the woman in the black bonnet, was her actual sister. Violet's father, Lord Asquith, had kept Sister Rose hidden. "Rose has something akin to my own power," she said.

"She's stronger than you now," James countered, looking rather stone-faced. "Nearly as strong as she always wanted to be."

Violet glanced at James with a certain distaste.

"You're all right? I asked him, pointing at the sling he wore.

He nodded. "All except for a twisted arm. I think you fell on it. You or a roof beam."

"And you, Christopher?" I said.

"I am well, Henry," Christopher said from beneath his mask. I thought I detected some trouble in his tone. "Bricks from a house cannot hurt me."

"Henry," Violet said, "I'm afraid I've done something terrible. Something that will change the direction of all this."

I turned to look at her.

"I've fallen right into the trap," she said. She explained Lord Asquith's black mirror. I recognized it as an object similar to the one Edgar Yarrow had described. Violet then recounted the story of the secret room in the Tremmond house, the feeling that she'd been inside the strange mirror's dream. That was where she'd met a man named Morgan Yarrow.

"You met *Morgan* Yarrow?" I asked, astonished. "Did he come back from that place with you?"

"He's dead," Violet replied. "Murdered by the mirror. And we're all in just as much danger, I think. The letter of solicitation from the Widow Tremmond, the investigation itself, all of it was a plot. I thought I was defeating the mirror from my childhood, my father's magic glass, but really I was—I was doing exactly what it wanted. I awakened it."

"Awakened?" I said. "But how can a mirror be awake or asleep?"

"Because it *isn't* a mirror," Violet said. "I think I understood that, on some level, even as a child."

"What, then?" I asked.

"An organism, Henry. Something that was petrified for ages. I still don't understand it entirely. But Rose believes she does, and that makes her all the more dangerous. We have to find her."

"I know where she's gone," James said.

We all turned to look at him, but before he could continue, we were interrupted by a physician in a white smock. He'd paused beside our group to gaze up at Christopher. "Shall I have a look at whatever's under that dressing, my good man?" he asked, indicating Christopher's mask.

We all said "no" almost in unison.

The doctor appeared rather taken aback.

"Thank you ever so much, doctor," Violet said. "But it's really just a bit of a rash. Nothing to concern yourself with."

The physician glanced again at Christopher with suspicion and then moved off toward other beds.

All of us turned again to look at James.

"Where is Sister Rose?" I asked.

James looked grim. "If I tell you, Henry—if I go this far in disrupting the New Lord's plan—I will be punished."

"He's been saying that all night," Violet said. "I told him I could make more bricks fall on his head than Sister Rose."

I pulled my hand gently away from Violet and reached for James. He took my hand in his.

"You can see this Sister Rose is unhinged," I said. "Whatever she's planned cannot be good, James."

He appeared to contemplate this. "But the New Lord—"

"Henry, there's something more I should tell you," Violet said.

"What more could there be?" I said.

"I don't pretend to understand all of this entirely," she said. "But you see the person behind all of this—the person the villagers call the New Lord—"

"Phillip," I said, barely able to believe his name was on my lips. Phillip had sent me on this mad chase. Phillip had tried to have me killed

Violet paused, surprised. "Morgan Yarrow told me as much," she said. "Brother James here has confirmed it. Phillip was a ghost finder here in London, yes, but he was much more than that. Likely, he was one of the magicians who came to Father's meetings in the bowels of Nethersea Hall. There were so many of them. They all wore hoods. I was sent to be with Mother when they came. I never saw their faces. One of those men could very well have taken over after Father was—deposed."

I heard the creaking of the Tremmond house in my mind, the breaking of its beams. I clutched the book, *Thomas Shadow: The Ghost Finder*. "If Phillip is the New Lord," I said, "then all of this—Coxton & Co.—"

"A plot," Violet said. "We've been involved in his plot for a long time. The magicians are careful men. They prepare elements as an alchemist would prepare an alembic."

"And my work?" I said. "It must have been part of this preparation."

"According to Brother James, they've been preparing for this event for years. They had to find a way to contain me while they studied the mirror. They tried several methods of extracting me from The Dragon—lovers, a woman who wanted to act as my mentor, even the purported owner of a more reputable theater. Nothing worked. I remained resilient. I wanted my independence. What they realized was, well, they realized I needed a friend."

I felt the hot sting of tears in my eyes. "Violet—" I said. "I did this to you. I lured into this. I told you I'd make everything well."

"It's not your fault," she said. "How could you have known?"

All of it was falling into place quickly now. The way Phillip Langford had scooped me up out of the gutter, deducing that I was an invert, an unspeakable. The way he'd groomed me to look a part, but had provided very little in the way of actual instruction. I knew Phillip's procedures for so-called ghost finding, yet, at the same time, I knew very little else about the ghosts I was supposed to search for. Instead of training me, he'd given me a book of fiction, because I was to *be* a fiction. Using the name Eldora Tremmond on the blue envelope had been a cruel joke. He'd told me once that I wasn't meant to ask whether or not ghosts actually existed. Instead, I had to look for the right question. I realized I knew the question now: Do ghosts matter? They didn't, of course. All of it had been a ruse. The only abnatural that mattered was Violet Asquith herself. They wanted someone to get close to her. Someone that she wouldn't find threatening.

I looked at James. "You knew about all this?" I said. "You knew and you didn't tell me?"

"The New Lord would have harmed my—my family," James said.

"Family?" I asked. "Your mother and father?"

"Henry," he said, squeezing my hand.

"And that's why you were ordered to shoot me? Because I was no longer of any use? My part of the plan was complete?"

James nodded.

"Was all of it a lie?" I asked. "Even the fact that you'd taken an interest in me?"

Violet glanced up at James. "An *interest?* You're an invert?"

"What interest does Brother James have in Henry?" Christopher asked.

James looked at me with compassion. "Henry, everything I've done, I've done it to protect you. And everything I said was—"

"He's one of them, Henry," Violet said. "The villagers at Nethersea are all in the grip of their death cult. They only see what their lord tells them to see. They can't be trusted. Not even the handsome ones."

"I want what's best," James said. "For a time, I admit, I followed the New Lord because I was afraid. I saw how he could hurt people. And now Sister Rose—"

"Rose is beyond reason," Violet said. "She wants to *be* Father. She wants to be the lord at Nethersea."

"So where is she?" I said. "Where is Sister Rose?"

"She's gone to find the final piece of the mirror," James said. "She told us that when it was finally active—when Violet had done her job—then she'd be able to tell us where the final piece was. She'd sense it. She'd lead the New Lord to it."

Violet stared at James in silence.

"Do know where the final piece of the dark mirror is, Violet?" I asked

She nodded.

"Where?" James asked.

"What if this is part of their plan, Henry?" Violet said. "Phillip Langford is obviously clever. What if this is his way of discovering where the mirror is?"

"I promise you," James said. "I no longer act on behalf of the New Lord. He told us he was attempting to rescue humankind from suffering, from death, but that was never true. He only wanted power."

"If you cross us," Violet said, "if you cross *me*, terrible things will befall you. Worse than anything the New Lord or Sister Rose could do."

"I won't," James said.

Violet took a breath. "The final piece of the mirror is still at Nethersea Hall. Mother wouldn't have found it. She wouldn't have been able to send it away as she did with the other pieces. It was hidden."

"Then we must all go there," I said.

Violet looked pale at the thought. "Back to Nethersea," she said.

"The mirror, as you say, is awake now," James said. "Things will be—"

At that moment, the nurse who'd spoken to me after I'd awakened reappeared. "More of your friends are here, sir," she said. "They said Phillip Langford sent them."

Cold water trickled down my spine.

"Right over there, sir," the nurse said, pointing.

I strained to look and saw that two men in black hats where striding toward us. One of them held a long black case that he was in the process of opening. I assumed it contained their muskets.

"What do we do?" I said, looking at James.

"We run, Henry. Quick and far."

CHRISTOPHER X

BROTHER SIMON AND Brother Athol, we smelled these men before we saw them. Hollyhocks and ivy, the scent of the country mixed with musk. Our hackles rose. Our lip curled. The men in black hats strode toward us, moving between sickbeds. Their manner was bold, foolishly so. The taller of the two, Brother Simon, took two muskets from a long case. He handed one of the weapons to Brother Athol. This was the very gun that had been used to murder Mrs. Hastur. We thought of her face, mouth open, eyes wide. The way her body tumbled down the stairs. We thought of her blood. We had not told Henry what had happened. For how could we? He too loved Mrs. Hastur. And Henry was already in so much pain.

Brother Simon and Brother Athol continued their approach. These men intended to harm Henry. We had learned they acted upon the order of Phillip Langford. Langford himself had never liked us. He told Henry that our presence did not serve the company. And now we did not like him either. We would not allow his soldiers to harm Henry. And we would punish them for what they had done to Mrs. Hastur.

We advanced.

From behind, we heard Henry's voice: "Chris, no. Not here."

But we did not listen.

Brother Athol slowed first. He saw that we did not fear him. Then Brother Simon slowed. Both finally ceased their advance. Several of the men and women in white—doctors and nurses of the hospital—had also stopped moving about the ward. They stood watching us. We did not care who watched. We knew what we must do.

We came to Brother Simon first. He raised his musket and fired. Pieces of metal, similar to those that had killed Mrs. Hastur, fell upon our chest. They stung, but nothing more.

When his weapon did not fell us, a look of fear spread across Brother Simon's face. We were glad to see this expression. We came to stand before him. Brother Simon opened his mouth to speak. Perhaps he wanted to reason with us now that he had not hurt us with his weapon. Without hesitation, we put our fingers in his mouth, grabbing hold of the lower part of his jaw. The human jaw was so delicate, nothing like our own powerful jaw. Brother Simon's eyes went wide as we held his mouth open. We curled our fingers around his lower front teeth, and then, with great force, we jerked downward in a swift motion. We heard a popping sound. We tore the lower jaw from Brother Simon's face. Blood sprayed onto our hand and our arm.

Brother Simon's eyes widened, as though he was not yet certain what had occurred. His upper teeth were now revealed. His tongue hung down toward his neck like the gobble of a turkey. Blood poured from the hole in the lower part of Brother Simon's face. We tossed his jaw to the floor. He stood staring at us for another moment. Then he looked at his lower jaw lying there on the floor, the ring of teeth, the ragged flesh, the protrusion of yellow bone. After that, Brother Simon began to scream. A high, gurgling cry. The sound pleased us. We smelled the freshness of Brother Simon's blood. We wanted to eat. But that would have to wait.

Others in the hospital ward had also begun to scream. People ran for doors. The sick fell from their beds and dragged themselves along the floor, forgetting their crutches and wheeled chairs. Brother Athol, the man who had murdered Mrs. Hastur, had turned to run while we were seeing to Brother Simon.

We moved toward the other man, Brother Athol.

A nurse stood in our way. She was, perhaps, Henry's nurse. We thought we remembered her face. We threw her to the floor. She too began to scream.

We stepped on the back of a crawling patient. We heard his spine snap.

Brother Athol turned and pointed his musket toward the sack that covered our face. "Back, devil!" he yelled. "Get back!"

Before he could fire, we grabbed the barrel of the gun and directed it away from us. Brother Athol fired. Shot scattered into the hospital wing, felling several nurses attempting to help a patient. We pulled the musket from Brother Athol's trembling hands. Then, we reached up and knocked his foolish black hat from his head. We stepped on the hat, crushing it with our foot. We wanted to show him the hat meant nothing. The symbols of man were nothing.

We grabbed Brother Athol by his short brown hair and jerked him toward us. He pleaded. We thought again of how he had shot Mrs. Hastur on the stairs. We spun his musket around in our right hand. We put the barrel of the gun in Brother Athol's mouth. Still, he tried to say the word "no." But speaking had become difficult for him because the barrel of the gun was pressed against his tongue.

We did not fire the gun. Instead, very slowly, we began to slide the barrel of the musket down Brother Athol's throat. He squealed as we had heard animals squeal when they were slaughtered. We slid the gun further down his throat. We slid it all the way down so the trigger touched Brother Athol's lower lip. Blood ran from his quivering mouth. The blood smelled good to us. We twisted the musket several times, churning Brother Athol's insides.

His eyes rolled to white. He was still alive. We could smell the life in him. We put our mouth very close to his ear so he would hear us above the din of the hospital ward. "You should not have done the things you did."

He made a muffled screech.

We reached up then and pulled the trigger of the musket. The lower part of Brother Athol's body exploded, spilling across the gray stone floor. We wiped blood and pieces of his flesh from our suit. Then, we let him fall dead at our feet.

We turned. Brother Simon still stood in the distance bleeding from the great hole where his jaw had been. He swayed, gurgling. We made our way toward him, tossing patients out of our way, considering what more we might do next. But before we could reach Brother Simon, one of the long white beds from the ward suddenly shot out in front of us and we fell over it. We landed painfully on our face. Just as tried to right ourselves, another bed shot forward and struck us with the force of a moving autobus.

No one had touched the beds.

Black flies swarmed in our skull.

Magic had moved the beds.

We sat up and saw Violet Asquith coming toward us, brow creased with anger. We put our hands against our ears, trying to block the sound of the flies. But we could still hear them. For they were inside us.

We had not harmed Violet at the Tremmond house. We had been too concerned for Henry. We had not harmed her during the night either. Still, we'd worried for Henry. But now the flies were inside of us again, biting at our brain. We remembered our past. We remembered our aim, our purpose.

Violet—daughter of the black magician called Lord Asquith and now a great magician herself—looked wild there in the hospital ward. Her dark hair hung down in tresses. We thought of Mercurius in the desert. We thought of how he had hidden the black mirror in the sand. Mercurius had not been as powerful as Violet Asquith. Violet had awakened the mirror. This act would do more harm to the boundary than had ever been done before.

The buzzing of flies grew louder still.

Violet was not one of us. She was, instead, one of them: those who crossed over the boundary.

In our mind, we saw our hand around the throat of Mercurius. We saw our fingers closing. The sharp twist to the right. We felt the breaking of his bones.

All the while, Violet stared at us with cold gray eyes.

We reached up our hand to remove our mask, revealing our gaping jaw, our jagged teeth.

Violet looked surprised that we were showing our teeth at her. It was good to surprise a magician.

We opened our mouth, tensed our muscles and then, we leapt.

VIOLET ASQUITH

I HAD ONLY a moment to react after Christopher launched his body at mine. "Please should—" I said. Then he struck me with a driving force such as I had never felt before, throwing me backward into a rack of surgical implements. Scalpels and scissors clattered across the floor. I rose to my knees, turning to see Christopher—nearly seven feet tall and wide as a freight car—barreling toward me once again. I pointed at a pile of needles scattered across the tiles. "Please should the needles fly?" I said. And upon my request, they rose from the ground like some swarm of metal insects. I turned again, just in time to see Christopher veer off his path to avoid the flying needles. This brief pause in the onslaught gave me enough time to get to my feet and run for the other end of the hospital ward. I pointed at beds as I moved, tossing them behind me without regard to where they landed. I had no idea what had gone wrong with Christopher. But I knew that he could kill me if he got his hands on me, and I couldn't allow that. For I was the only one who could stop Sister Rose. I had to make it to Nethersea.

I'd nearly reached the opposite end of the ward when I heard the pounding of Christopher's feet. He was charging. I looked about me, searching for something else to hurl.

Raising my hands, I pointed at one of the large leaded windows. "Please should the glass shatter?" I asked. The window's metal lattice twisted, causing a great creaking noise; and then, quite suddenly, every pane of glass in the high window broke and flew across the room at Christopher. He dropped to the ground, turning his face to protect his eyes. Great shards pierced his already shredded suit. I heard him howl.

"Please," I said, breathless, thinking, "please should the whole room help me?"

It was then that the beds, the breathing apparatuses, and every sort of instrument began to fly at Christopher. He attempted to stand but was driven backwards. Objects pummeled his body. Yet despite the storm of metal and glass, he tried to come for me. He flailed his arms, attempting to find some method of attack.

Eventually, I realized that neither I nor the objects of the hospital ward could hold him back. Christopher dove at me. His hands clutched my throat. His gold eyes were wide. Long strands of saliva hung from his jaw.

I heard Henry's voice then, roaring: "Stop this, Christopher! If you have ever listened to me, you will listen now!"

Yet Christopher's hands continued to squeeze. The whole of the room grew dim. Furniture fell from the air around us. And just as my eyes were about to close, I saw Brother James' body hit Christopher from the side, causing the great beast to momentarily loosen his grip. James scrambled up from the floor and threw himself at Christopher again. This time Christopher was ready, though. He grabbed James by the arm and made as if he would shatter him against floor.

"Stand down!" Henry roared, walking across the ward, hand pressed to his ribs.

Miraculously, Christopher did pause. He released Brother James. He looked at me and then at Henry, blinking, as if perhaps awakening.

"Violet?" Henry said, coming to kneel beside me. "Are you all right?"

I was shaken, bruised. "I'm fine. Or rather...I will be."

Henry turned on Christopher, filled with rage.

"Henry, I—" Christopher said. It was good to hear him speak again. For at least it might indicate a return of his sanity.

"You attacked unprovoked," Henry said. I'd never seen him so angry. "You could have killed Violet."

"Henry, I was only—"

"*Only*," Henry said. "You weren't *only* doing anything. You tried to kill our partner, our friend. And you exposed us—forced us to show ourselves to all of London. Just look at this place."

"Henry," I said, "do calm down."

But Henry didn't listen.

"I was mistaken," Henry said to Christopher. "*Mrs. Hastur* was mistaken. You should never have been brought into our house. You belonged in the alley."

"No, Henry, please," Christopher said, raising his hands like a child.

"Perhaps we should just discuss this rationally," I said.

"No more discussions," Henry said. I could see that he was not only angry—he was shaken to the center of his being. He looked like a man whose entire world had fallen apart. "Phillip Langford cannot be trusted," he said. "Christopher cannot be trusted. Nothing is as it seems." He pointed at Christopher. "I want you out of my sight. Get out of here before you harm anyone else."

"But where, Henry?" Christopher said. "Where would I go?"

"Do whatever ridiculous thing is in your head. You are no longer under the protection of Coxton & Co. You are no longer my concern."

Christopher lowered his head. His shoulders fell. "You told me we were family, Henry."

"I was wrong about many things," Henry replied.

Christopher began to walk away. His back, I saw, was full of broken window glass.

"Chris," I called.

He looked at me. Then he turned away, slinking toward the exit. I watched him go, still hardly believing what he had done to me and to the people at the hospital. Sirens rang beyond the door of the decimated ward.

ĦƐ∩Ŗƴ ꝖOXƮO∩

ON CROWDED EARLHAM Court, costermongers had paused at
selling their wares. Cabs and busses had ceased their transit. Everyone in
London, it seemed, wanted to gape at the hospital that billowed smoke
from its open windows. Stories circulated in the street about a monster.
Violet and James walked on either side of me, arms looped under my
own, providing support. My face was bruised, and I'd barely had time to
don my suit. Violet's black gown was still covered in dust, and her dark
hair had fallen from its pins. James's antiquated village clothing was torn
and bloodied. Yet, thankfully, no one in the street stopped to question us.
The whole thoroughfare was too much in chaos.

I could not force from my mind the image of Christopher destroying
those two men from Nethersea. He'd tossed aside nurses as if they were
so much garbage and crushed the spine of a crawling patient. He hadn't
managed to harm Violet or James, but certainly he'd intended to. The
image of Phillip Langford floated ghost-like toward me then. My beloved
mentor had been—for the entirety of our relationship—hell-bent on
deceiving me. Every lesson he'd taught me, every maxim he'd spoken, all
of it was a hollow thing. The self I'd built after returning to London from
the *Daedalus*—the self I'd believed was so strong—was, in fact, no self at
all. There was no Henry Coxton, Dark Detective. There was only Henry
the Shill, Henry the Dupe. And now, if I understood correctly, we were
about to face an abnatural occurrence like no other in the history of

humankind, the awakening of some petrified organism, a creature that did not belong in this world. How could I hope to ever help combat such a thing?

"I should go alone to Nethersea," Violet said, as if reading my troubled thoughts. Her skin was blanched, her expression strained. We'd emerged from yet another crowd headed toward the sirens at Saint Bartholomew's. "Facing Sister Rose and the mirror will be too dangerous. And you're in no condition, Henry."

"You'll need me," I said.

"But you'll be of no help."

I pressed one hand against a flash of pain in my ribs, attempting to gather my wits. I didn't feel strong, that much was true. But at least I could appear so for my friend. "I can be. And I will."

"How, Henry? How will you do anything in your current state?"

"For the first time in years," I replied, "I am, at least, standing on my own two feet. That must count for something." I removed the copy of *Thomas Shadow: The Ghost Finder* from the pocket of my coat and tossed it into the gutter.

"Your book?" Violet said.

"I'm writing a new one," I replied. I glanced at James. "Are you up for this?"

He nodded solemnly, looking like some noble, red-haired knight in the afternoon sun.

Violet surveyed him. "You're not duty-bound to us, James."

"I helped the New Lord bring all of this about," he said. "There are—other circumstances, but I believe I can resolve such things now."

"Do you understand what's meant to happen at Nethersea?" Violet asked James. "What precisely is the New Lord's plan?"

"I'm not privy to everything," he replied. "But from what I've gathered, there will be a kind of convergence at the great house. Some think a doorway will open on to some astral plane. Others believe that the mirror will become a divining glass. Occult knowledge will pass through it. Still others have predicted Lord Asquith himself will emerge from the mirror. He'll bring with him a newfound understanding from the land of the dead."

"It won't be any of that," Violet said. "The mirror is a creature, an organism. It has desires. It's been manipulating the magicians all along."

James didn't respond. Instead, he gazed at the street ahead.

"What is it?" I asked

"Villagers," he said. "From Nethersea."

James pushed us into an alley, and we watched as two young men in black hats moved toward St Bartholomew's. One of them wore a beard. The other was clean-shaven. Both had a troubled look in their eyes.

"How many of them are here in London?" I asked.

"Twenty or so," James said. "There are many more at Nethersea, of course. They'll be investigating what happened at the hospital. They'll realize you're alive, Henry."

"They think you killed me?"

James nodded. "I was hoping they would continue to believe that for a while longer."

"Why would Phillip be so intent on—"

"Because he wanted a pawn, a kind of prop," James said. "But he sees something more in you. A quality he believes might be dangerous."

This made my pride swell. Phillip Langford thought I was dangerous. He believed I might be someone to be reckoned with.

"There's to be some final ceremony at Nethersea Hall," James said. "The New Lord will—"

"We should call him Phillip Langford from now on," I said. "He's not the lord of anything."

James cleared his throat. "Phillip Langford, then. He will be at Nethersea for this rite. All of them will."

* * *

We went directly to the station at Birmingham New Street and were on a train to the country in no time at all. James left Violet and me in the burnished private car, as I told him I needed a glass of water. I'd begun to worry that my injury from the collapsing house might have been more severe than I first believed. My ribs continued to ache, and I felt periodically dizzy.

Violet leaned forward from her seat, peering at me with her sincere gray eyes as the train rocked to and fro. "You look like death, Henry. You don't have to do this. I'd never forgive myself if something happened to you."

"All of this is my fault," I said. "I *lured* you. I told you we were going to be ghost finders—of all things"

She sighed. "I would have left The Dragon eventually, you know. Honestly, I'm glad I left with you. We had a good run."

"I was so naïve."

"We all were," Violet replied. "Just make sure you're now fully disabused of your illusions."

"How do you mean?"

"Understand that Brother James is still dangerous. No matter how good he seems on the surface."

"He had a gun pointed at my head just a few days ago," I said. "I think I understand."

"I'm concerned because I can see you've begun to care for him. There's a new light in your eyes."

"What sort of light?"

"Your feelings—they are apparent."

"Violet—" I was going to argue, but found I could not. "It's difficult to find anyone like James...anyone at all."

"I appreciate what he did for me both at the Tremmond house and the hospital. But I want you to always remember he's from the *village*. I know those people much better than you. The men and women there, they are different. They've been trained like an army. And I assure you that we do not share a common reality with them."

"He rescued me. He protected me from Phillip's death sentence."

"You were hurt when you lost Paser on the *Daedalus*, Henry. Phillip Langford knows this. He'll use whatever means he must. If he's anything like my father, he'll even turn love into a weapon."

"We have no other choice at the moment," I said. "We have to trust James. He's our way into the village."

"But we can still be careful. And you don't have to fling yourself at him."

I bristled. "Are you jealous, Violet?"

She raised a dark eyebrow. "Of what?"

"Of James," I said. "Of the possibility that I might have met someone."

"Don't be ridiculous. It's just—"

"We're a family," I said.

She gazed at me. "You told Christopher the same thing."

"I've been thinking about him. Perhaps I was too rash. He'll likely return to Mrs. Hastur at the house, though. He'll be all right. We'll deal with all of this later."

The door of the train car opened and James entered. He held a glass of water toward me and said, "Train's quiet. It worries me."

"How do you mean?" I asked.

"The New Lord—Phillip Langford, I mean—he sees all. He likely knows what's happened. He's put all the pieces together. He'll be looking for us. And he'll want to punish us, Henry." He paused. "What exactly is our plan? To simply walk into Nethersea Hall?"

"I think we need a change of clothes first," Violet said.

"Clothes?" James said.

Violet pointed at his own accoutrements.

"You want to dress as villagers?" James said.

"That way no one will take notice of us. We can move about as we please. From there, we'll go to find the final piece of the mirror. I'll discover some way to destroy it."

"How?" James said.

"I haven't figured that out yet."

CHRISTOPHER X

WE STUMBLED DOWN blind alleyways, blood dripping onto cobblestones. No longer did we wear our linen mask. We put our hands over our face, covering our eyes, our jaw. We hoped that no one would see. We had believed we knew our purpose. And because of that, we had tried to kill Violet. Violet, who was our friend. She, who we'd once sworn to protect. Henry had cast us out. Not only from the hospital, but from our home. Henry said that we were wrong. We were an animal. And now that the sound of flies had subsided, we feared Henry was correct. Our memory of the age when we had been called Reprobus was a broken thing. And yet—yet we'd felt so strongly about our mission. We wondered if we might still be under the spell of some magician. Was it possible that we were two things at once? Two creatures in one body? We were Christopher X, who talked English and lived in a house and wore a fine suit. And we were also Reprobus, keeper of the boundary, guardian of the line.

We were without hope of understanding. Henry would no longer advise us. He would not let us live in the house or wear an English suit. He would not allow us to go on adventures or sit by the fire and reminisce about the day's events. Mrs. Hastur could not help us either. For she was gone. That too was our fault. We had not protected her.

Then, in the distance, we heard a sound—the call of a horn. Our ears turned. We listened. The sound rose again. It was the horn of freighter, a ship that floated upon the great black river. We could smell the Thames, its foul water, the very mire from which we'd been born. And we understood that the sound of the ship might be a kind of calling. The river bade us to return.

Such a request was itself a kind of answer. For if we could not live in the house with Henry and Violet and Mrs. Hastur, then what was truly left for us in London? We would not make our existence in alleyways as we once had done. We would not eat the flesh of men when we grew hungry. We heard the low ship's horn again. The river called. The river understood what we needed. We would return to it. And there, in that swift water, we would be unborn.

* * *

We crossed narrow empty streets, grim passages that had grown up at water's edge. The few rough men who lingered in these lanes did not look at our face. Instead, they watched their own boots as they walked. Before we saw the Thames itself, we smelled the quays, the black docks cut from the riverbank. We knew these waters well. We'd hunted here, searched for meat. We recognized the overwhelming scent of excrement. The river was a sewer. Beneath that smell was the scent of sulfur and pitch. Ship resin and brandy. When finally we emerged near an embankment, London Bridge rose in the distance, a regal, girded guard. And then we saw the river, the Thames. We saw scores of yellow-masted ships and metal cranes above sunken piles where birds cried out, hungry for fish.

We walked to the river's edge. So many colors its water: black of coal and blue of indigo, the purple dark of wine, the brown of a long-steeped tea.

Finally, a few men noticed us. They pointed and called out. We did not listen to their words. The thoughts of men no longer mattered. We would be a story for these harbor workers to tell their wives. "Such a monster!" they'd say. "It wandered out of an alley and dove into the river. Then it did not rise again. Thank God it did not rise. I hope I should never see a thing like that again. It made me feel as though Hell had come to London."

We wished we could assure these men that they never would see such a thing as us again.

Hell had not come to London.

London was a Hell.

We lifted a foot off the jetty, long enough for us to see the faces of Henry and Violet and Mrs. Hastur there in the water. And then we acted. We flung ourselves into the black and churning foam. We let the river claim us.

* * *

Down and down and down we went to be unborn. We drew water into our lungs. The water made us heavy and held us beneath the river. We allowed the currents to drag our body. And black water made us blind. Only when an object was directly before our face could we see—floating crates and bits of netting, the ghostly remains of a ship's sail that threatened to ensnare us. We disentangled ourselves and floated free, carried by swift waters. We thought of the ocean. Henry had shown us pictures. We imagined the ocean would welcome us. It would hold us in its cold depths.

As we thought of the ocean, we nearly struck the limb of a white and fleshy form floating in the water. We realized soon enough it was a corpse. Henry had once told us that bodies of Englishmen were sometimes disposed of in the Thames. The river was a haunted thing. A current of ghosts. We saw the long tendrils of the dead man's hair moving gently in the eddies. The body's arms drifted at its sides.

We pushed away from the corpse. We wanted to think no more of death.

After a few minutes, we believed we'd escaped the corpse. But soon, it appeared alongside us once again. A gleaming hand rose in front of our face, fingers splayed, as if to stop us. And that was when we saw the ragged hole in the dead man's palm. As if the man had been crucified. We turned to look at the face of the corpse and realized this was no Englishman tossed into the river. This was Mercurius, the magician. This was the man we'd murdered so many ages ago. We'd killed him, just as we'd nearly killed Violet. His eyes glowed white like marbles. His jaw hung slack, revealing a bilious tongue.

We tried to flee, moving our arms, kicking our legs. But Mercurius remained always at our side. He did not swim, yet somehow he clung to us. He followed our trajectory. The river's currents raised his hands once more. We saw the holes in his palms. He wanted us see. To know what we had done.

We attempted to cry out. Water filled our mouth. We dove deeper, moving toward the riverbed. Mercurius was always just behind us. We passed by the remains of a wooden house. It had fallen into the water ages ago. The house was covered in a green and floating moss. We saw formations of honeycombed stone. Deposits of iron. We circled around the deck of a Roman sailing barge. Gods stared down at us from the ship's railing. We dove again. Moving ever further down. Finally, we arrived at the very bottom of the Thames, and there we clung to the broken stern of a sunken barge. We looked everywhere at once for Mercurius, the figure that would not let us forget.

But he was nowhere to be seen.

We wondered if we had imagined him. If we had been imagining him all along. And we felt alone there at the bottom of the Thames. The rush of water was in our ears. We heard the beating of a heart in our own deathless chest. We thought of Henry and of Violet. We were so very sorry for what we had done. Our friends too were now alone. They would go to Nethersea. Toward a great danger awaiting. We thought of Mrs. Hastur's words: *Violet and Henry are strong, but they are not as strong as you.*

We looked toward the surface of the water.

The shifting hazy light was like an aurora.

A sign in the heavens.

Henry had banished us. But, at times like this, we needed to obey our own nature. And our nature told us that neither Henry nor Violet was safe. They should not be alone at Nethersea.

We let go of the piece of flotsam and began to swim toward the surface of the river. We would follow our friends. We would rescue them if we could. For even if we were meant to play some cosmic role—if we were intended to be a scourge or murderer as the memory of Mercurius indicated—that was no longer what we intended to be. We would be

Christopher. We would be good. We would protect the ones we loved.

VIOLET ASQUITH

WE DEBARKED THE train at evening time in the market town of Morley. Henry rented a coach to take us over what was known locally as "Owl's Hill," into the darkening countryside. The sky had gone from rose to rust. And brambles that lurked near stands of old oak trees were etched with shadows the color of funeral crepe. I admit the little rutted tracks that ran between the fields of wheat and barley set me ill at ease. Such roads did not, for me, evoke a sense of homeliness or the Romance of rural life. Instead, they seemed to open like a throat.

Brother James told the coachman to stop some distance prior to the village at Nethersea. Outsiders did not garner welcome. James informed us that, since the coming of the New Lord, approaching carriages were waved off toward Leeds or Kilner Bank. The New Lord had posted a watchman on the road, James said, a man called Brother Stephen who waved a lamp and looked himself quite like a wandering corpse.

We arrived through the fields on foot just as night fell, and James led us to a disused stable near the edge of the village. Seeing the shambling stone cottages, even from a distance, made me feel as if I walked inside a reverie, as if the mirror's own awakening had drawn me into sleep.

Thankfully, no men or women of the village peered at us from their houses as we passed the old mill and the bakery and a white stone church, the cross of which had been cut down many ages ago.

James opened the weathered door of a stable that smelled of the ghosts of long dead animals.

"Why don't we simply go to your house?" Henry asked, supporting himself against a wooden tethering post and pressing his hand against his ribs. "Surely, we could gather our disguises there."

James did not respond. Instead, he ushered us into the straw-filled dark and closed the door behind.

"You *do* live in the village, don't you, James?" Henry said.

"With my *wife*," James replied stiffly. "We cannot go to the house because my wife is there."

It was then Henry's turn to be silent.

"You're married?" I asked, knowing I shouldn't have been surprised. Father had seen to it that all the young men and women of Nethersea married nearly as soon as procreation was possible. He wanted the village line maintained. That way, he would always have a full stable of servants and soldiers.

"I am," James said.

"Is there any other secret you'd like to unveil?" I asked.

"I wanted to tell you earlier."

"But there's never a good time, is there?" I replied. "Wives—they're so *inopportune*."

James looked at Henry. "I'm sorry," he said. "But there's no time to talk now."

"It's all right," Henry replied.

"It isn't, though," James said. "I'll be back soon. I promise. I'll have more to say."

James opened the stable door and stepped out into the night. Henry and I huddled together in the cold dark, waiting for him to return with our new clothes. At one point Henry took my hand, but said nothing.

"I'm sorry," I said finally.

"For what?" Henry asked.

"For the way the world is, I suppose."

He gave me a half smile, and I felt as though I had not seen that smile for far too long.

"I don't want any harm to come to you, Violet," he said.

I looked down at the worn wooden floor of the stable. "This day loomed for some time, Henry. I knew it would come. I knew it the moment I ran away from Nethersea Hall. This is what I was made for, you see."

"You're made for more than just this moment," Henry said. "You made me feel as if I wasn't alone in this life."

"Do you think Chris is all right?" I asked.

Henry shook his head. "We'll deal with that when we return to London. But first the mirror. And your sister."

Noises came from beyond the stable door.

"Is it James?" Henry asked.

I raised my hand and whispered, "Stand up."

"What for? It must be James."

If it was indeed Brother James, he hadn't returned alone. There were too many sounds outside.

And then, before either Henry or I could rise, the stable door burst open, and what looked like an army of black-hatted men rushed in, all carrying muskets.

I lifted my hands and said: "Please should the boards strike them?"

Nails began to pop from the floor and walls of the stable, and suddenly, a barrage of loose boards flew toward the men, falling on them from all sides at once and leaving a hole in the back of the stable.

"Run, Henry!" I called. "I'll hold them."

He looked at me as if he would not go, and so I screamed his name, demanding that he leave. He did run then, ducking under the flying boards and beneath a blast of musket fire. I flung boards at the village men until their confusion seemed heightened and then I too ran for the back of the barn, crawling through the hole there. The villagers with their muskets followed, but I was already well into the woods. I fell to my knees amongst the shadows of black trees. Had James double-crossed us? I wasn't sure. I only hoped that Henry had gotten away. Surely I'd given him enough time. I considered whether I should try to look for him, but I knew it would be better if I didn't. I needed to go to Nethersea Hall alone, to finish the work of my infernal family.

ḣEⱤRY ꝘOXTOⱤ

MUSKET FIRE FROM the stable. Then a rending creak and the snap of boards. Violet was tearing the entire structure apart.

I ran, pain flaring in my lower ribs. I had to locate James. The two of us would help Violet infiltrate Nethersea Hall and find her sister.

I stayed close to the stony cottage walls, concealing myself in shadows. An alarm bell sounded. Villagers rushed toward the stable, and I realized that if I didn't find better cover, I'd quickly be apprehended.

I made for the only place in my vicinity that was not a cottage, the only structure that might reasonably provide concealment—the stone chapel with the steeple rising into the starry sky.

The oaken door stood open, and the chapel did, in fact, appear empty. But once I was inside, I realized the vacancy was not a boon. I was disturbed by what I saw. And frightened all the more because I was alone. The walls of the chapel, the pews, the altar, the windows, all of it had been painted a dull shade of black. At the center of the black room was a large stone basin raised on a pedestal. Perhaps it was used to baptize the villagers, to bring them into their lifetime of servitude. But it wasn't the basin that held my attention. It was, instead, what had been painted onto the black walls themselves. The images there caused my heart to stutter. For upon the walls were a series of great murals that appeared to tell a story. The very history of the villagers.

The first scene showed the time of plague. Men and women wasted in the village streets. Faces were skeletal, flesh pulled taut. Black and pustulent sores ravaged yellowed skin. Ragged dogs wandered, likely waiting for the dead to fall. Some of the villagers held their frail hands in aspects of prayer. Others reached helplessly toward the heavens. One woman knelt in the dirt with two dead children clutched in her arms. Another man held a scythe to his own throat. The sky above was crimson. Strange starlight leaked down from the firmament.

In the next scene, a new figure appeared in the midst of the dying: a tall, broad man in black armor. He stood in sharp contrast to the blood-red sky. The shield he carried bore a seal: a black unicorn in a withered ash forest. This was Violet's ancestor, the first lord at Nethersea. He held one gloved hand before him in some gesture of mystical significance. The villagers looked upon him with expressions of hope.

In the third panel, I saw the dark mirror itself, the shard of which had been described to me by Edgar Yarrow. The disk hung in the empty space of the red sky, looking like an open mouth. And from this mouth came pouring some substance, a gleaming *prima materia*. The men and women of the village appeared to bathe in the stuff, a look of ecstasy on their faces. Some of them were lifted into the air by fluid, cradled in its amniotic grace. And there, amongst their number, stood the dark lord in his suit of black armor, presiding over the great event with terrible pride.

The final panel was so dark that it was difficult even to perceive. From what I could make out, the village itself had disappeared, as had the raw, red sky above. The atmosphere was now composed entirely of the silvery-black miasma that flowed from the dark mirror. Strange forms hovered in the distance. Eerie bodies, like great misshapen dirigibles. This final image disturbed me the most, for this clearly did not present the end to suffering or an end to death that the lord at Nethersea promised.

"Well," an all too familiar voice said from behind me. "I never imagined I would see you here, my boy."

Phillip Langford emerged from the chapel's shadows. He was not dressed in one of his traditional woolen suits. Instead, he wore a dark mantel of some indeterminate age. His white hair shone like a flame.

"Phillip," I said, finding it difficult to even speak his name.

"I gather Brother James told you everything about this little affair?" he said, gesturing toward the murals.

"Where is he?" I asked.

"I'm afraid I'll be the one asking questions this evening, Henry."

"I know what you are," I replied. "But I didn't learn it from James. Violet told me."

He raised a white brow. "Well then," he said in an oddly pleasant tone. "At least that allows us to avoid dreary exposition, doesn't it?"

"Tell me where James is. I have to find him"

Phillip sighed. "Ever the detective. I suppose I taught you well."

"You taught me nothing. Eldora Tremmond—"

Phillip half smiled. "You finally figured it out, did you?"

"Why would you have laid so obvious a clue?"

"Because I knew you wouldn't be able to make sense of it," Phillip replied. "You were never very good at such things, Henry. Some of us are meant to rise. And others, well, others are like you."

"James told me you were afraid. That you felt threatened by me."

Phillip's mouth twitched. "James is a fool and a puppet. Do you really think he came up with the idea of *courting* you on his own? Of course not. I served the concept to him. Made him believe his feelings were real. I was well aware he wouldn't shoot you in the Tremmond house. And I knew you'd find him handsome—with his wiry strength and shock of red hair."

"But why?" I asked. "What possible reason could you have had to manipulate us both in such a way?"

Phillip considered this. "I suppose our James was correct about one thing. I do harbor certain feelings, Henry. But I am not threatened by you. And I'm certainly not afraid. I am, instead—how shall I say—*disgusted*."

"Disgusted?" I said, realizing I was allowing his word to affect me. I had to stop thinking of him as Phillip, my mentor.

"It was the hope in your eyes when I first met you outside the tavern long ago." Phillip said. "A jewel of hope still shone within you. I found this almost comical at first. But then, as you grew to be the leader of our ridiculous little firm, I felt increasingly troubled and finally repulsed. I myself was struggling with my role as the lord at Nethersea. It's more difficult than you might believe to steer the village. And I found that I wanted—I wanted nothing more than to crush the thing in you that made you think you could be something more."

"That's wretched," I said. "*You* are wretched."

"Yes...well...you asked about James. Would you like to see him now?"

Fear crawled in the pit of my stomach.

Phillip raised his hand, and from the ceiling of the black chapel, a form descended. Dangling upside-down at the end of the chain, bound and gagged with cloth, was James. The chain dropped until he hung just above the baptismal font. James stared at me, an expression of horror on his face.

"You are about to witness one of the most sacred traditions of the primitives here, Henry," Phillip said. "Death to remember death." From his mantle, he removed the ivory-handled dagger with the curved black blade that I'd seen on the table at this house in Mayfair. At the time, I'd thought the knife was just another antique.

"Let him go," I said.

"Oh, no, Henry. That would never do."

"I forced him to bring us here," I said. "He didn't want to do it. He shouldn't be punished."

James struggled, trying to speak through his gag. He'd been inverted for so long that his face had turned blood-red. I tried to let him know with my own eyes that I would rescue him. I wouldn't allow Phillip Langford to bring him harm.

"If it hadn't been for Sister Rose," Phillip mused, "all of this would have gone much more smoothly. We could have had a bit more fun before the end."

"I should have seen through you," I said.

"But you didn't. And the truth of the matter is, you still don't even see through me entirely, Henry. You think you've done something wrong. You think all of this is your fault."

I didn't respond.

"When you think about it, you aren't really any worse off, are you? When I met you, you had nothing. Life on a farm. Your ridiculous love affair with that gutter rat on board the *Daedalus*. What was the boy's name? The creature the sailors threw overboard?"

"Don't speak of him like that."

Phillip took several steps toward James, who still hung above the stone font. He raised his curved knife toward James' throat.

"Don't touch him," I said, rushing toward them.

"All right," Phillip replied. He pulled the dagger away from James and, in one smooth motion, he shoved it into my abdomen. Heat and pain exploded in my guts. Phillip twisted the knife, pulling it up toward my chest.

Blood spilled from the wound. I couldn't take a breath. I attempted to grasp the handle of the knife, to pull the thing out, but instead of touching the handle, I grabbed hold of the smooth coil of my own guts that protruded from my abdomen. I stumbled backward.

James thrashed on his chain.

"That felt even better than I thought it would," Phillip said.

I fell to the ground. Hands in hot blood. A red mirror, spreading.

And the dark chapel grew darker still.

CHRISTOPHER X

LONG AGO, WE had traveled differently. We had moved through the sky, born aloft on the wind. But enchantment had delivered us into confusion. Bound us to the earth.

As we emerged from the filthy waters of the Thames, we wished we could fly once more. We could go swiftly to Henry and Violet. We would protect them. But no matter how we tried to raise ourselves—extending our arms and rushing forward, leaping into the air with all our force—we were always returned firmly to the ground.

So, instead of flying, we ran.

Nethersea Hall was to the north. We understood that much from Violet's tales. When she drank red wine at dinner (a foolish custom of the Englishmen that led to all manner of divulgences) she sometimes spoke of the old village and of her father. She never revealed too much. Still, we believed we knew the direction. We moved north through London, tearing a piece of cloth from a fruit cart along the way and wrapping it as best we could around our face. We ran swiftly through the city streets, legs driving. There were those men and women who stopped to watch our progress. Perhaps they believed we were Spring-Heeled Jack, that storied devil, out to cause calamity. The beliefs of these men and women did not matter to us. We knew our aim. We understood our purpose. After we left the city—passing through the gray outer barrens—we paused twice, asking men who drove carts along darkening country roads if they had heard of a place called Nethersea.

The first, a young farmer in chaff-covered overalls, seemed startled by our enormous size. He mumbled a confused reply to our query and then drove his horses at a faster trot.

The second was a very old man with a long gray beard, the tip of which brushed his shirtfront. His hands, clutching the reigns of his horse, were leathered. He peered down at us from his high seat. "Nethersea? Did I hear you right?"

We nodded. We stood before his cart in the purple dusk. We had not lost our breath from running. We could likely run forever.

The old man grimaced. "My friend, if I may call you such, you would not want to go to a place like Nethersea. Not to the village or to the great stone hall on the bald hill. Both are cursed things."

"What sort of curse?" we asked.

"A spell of desolation and loneliness," the old farmer said. "The men and women of the village and the lord upon the hill, they are no longer part of the brotherhood of man. They've hid themselves, even from the eyes of God."

"You have been to Nethersea?"

"I'd never dared. I've seen it only from a distance—the black cottages and the terrible hall. You too must stay away."

Englishmen, even those who lived in the countryside, could be so difficult. "It is very important I find that place."

"That cloth you wear—" the old farmer said.

"I was burned," we replied, using Henry's lie, "in a fire."

"A *fire?*" the old man said.

"Rescuing orphans," we added. "The orphans were disfigured too. There was a great deal of disfigurement."

The old farmer made a low whistling. "A terrible tale."

"Indeed."

"A righteous man may have his troubles. But the Lord will one day deliver him. Those words are from the Good Book itself."

Henry had read to us from several books. One was *Thomas Shadow: The Ghost Finder*, a collection of stories of which Henry was very fond. The second was something by a Mr. Dickens. We did not remember the title. We did not know if either was the book spoken of by the farmer.

"I suppose I should not prevent a man such as yourself from doing what he must," he said finally.

"That is correct."

And so the old man raised one large hand and pointed. He spoke to us of a series of turns upon the road and how we must ascend a low hill.

And in this manner, we learned the way to Nethersea.

* * *

By the time we arrived at Nethersea Village, a yellow moon hung low. We emerged from a forest and hid ourselves in brambles. From that vantage, we peered at a dusty strip of road that served as the village's thoroughfare. Men in black hats and women in dark bonnets held lanterns and torches aloft. Alarms had been raised. From what we could gather, the villagers were searching for someone. Henry and Violet, we feared. We crept through the brambles, coming ever closer to the row of twisted hovels. A pale church stood in the distance. Beyond it, a creaking miller's wheel.

We thought we might grow bolder in our approach. We might capture one of the men and force him to tell us what was happening. Then, from behind the gnarled trunk of a dead tree, we saw movement. A girl-child, no more than eight or nine, rounded the trunk and stared up at us. She had long reddish-blonde hair that hung about her shoulders. Her eyes were sleep-ridden. She wore a nightdress. We studied the girl, wondering if she was going to scream. Wondering if she would bring the rest of the village.

"Do not be afraid," we said. We tried to make our voice sound less like a growl than usual.

The girl reached up and wiped sleep from her eyes. "Am I dreaming, sir?"

"You are awake," we replied.

"Then you must be—you must be the one Father told me about," she said. "The one who wears the mask."

"Father?"

"He's called Brother James," the girl said. "I am Sister Eloise."

"Brother James is your father?"

She nodded. "Have you met him?"

"I have. Where is your mother, child?"

"She's looking for Father. She's afraid. She told me to stay at home. To hide beneath the bed."

"Why did you not do as your mother said?"

"Because I wanted to see. Everything here has been so strange as of late."

"Well, now you have seen," we said. "You should return to your hiding place."

"But I know where Father is."

Our ears swiveled. Wherever Brother James was, Henry and Violet could not be far away. "Where?"

"I saw the New Lord take him to the chapel," she said, pointing to the painted white structure in the distance. "He did not seem pleased. I wanted to call out, but I knew better. Father told me never to speak to the New Lord unless the New Lord spoke to me first."

"That is wise," we said.

"Another man followed them into the chapel not long ago."

"What did he look like?"

"He wore outsider's clothes. A gray suit."

Henry. We pulled ourselves from the brambles and crouched beside the dead tree. "And the alarms. Why do the claxons ring?"

"Because the priestess has arrived. She who communes with the mirror. But something has gone wrong. It's believed she's gone to Nethersea Hall. Sister Rose is there too. The New Lord is not pleased with Sister Rose."

"And what is it that Sister Rose has done?" we asked.

Sister Eloise shook her head. "Mother didn't tell me. Perhaps she doesn't know. But it's something bad. Something that displeased the New Lord greatly, disturbed him in his work. No one should displease the New Lord."

"No," we said. "I suppose they should not."

"Will you help Father?"

"If I can, yes."

"Even if it means further disturbing the New Lord?"

"Yes, Sister Eloise. Even if it does mean that."

I turned then to walk toward the white chapel.

"May I ask you one more question?" the girl said.

"Yes. One more."

"Your head, sir," she said, attempting a semblance of politeness. "You wear the mask to cover it. But Father told me of your appearance. Is it truly a dog's head that you have beneath that cloth, sir?"

We cleared our throat, attempting to find a suitable answer. "No, Sister Eloise," we said finally. "It is my own head. It has never belonged to any dog."

* * *

We kept our nose raised high as we made our way through the thicket, attempting to catch Henry's scent. When we finally smelled him, we were troubled. For it wasn't only Henry that we smelled. It was his blood. Henry was *bleeding*. And if Henry was bleeding, then he must be hurt. And Henry could not be hurt. For we'd come here to protect him.

We crashed through another thicket and burst into the chapel, not caring if any man might try to stop us. We did not want to kill any more men, of course. We did not want to upset Henry. But we would do what we must to protect him.

And yet, when we saw him—our Henry—we knew we had not done our best. He lay on the floorboards in the church. Henry, in a pool of blood. Brother James was suspended upside-down above a stone basin at the center of the chapel. He struggled there, attempting to escape his bonds. Henry himself did not move.

We fell on our knees. Henry was still in the way that Mrs. Hastur had been still. We lifted his head and looked down at him. His eyes were half-closed. There was blood in his mustache. The hilt of a dagger protruded from his gut.

We smoothed his black hair.

"I have come to help," we said.

Henry did not respond. Yet he was not asleep. We knew what Henry looked like when he slept. We'd often come to sit on the edge of his bed and watch him dream. He frequently twitched and called out. Henry was a very good dreamer.

"We must go and rescue Violet," we said to him. "I have some understanding of how we will do it. It will be difficult, yes. But it will also be a great adventure. The greatest of them, perhaps."

Henry did not tell us whether this was a good idea or bad.

We placed our hand on his forehead. Henry was cool.

We hugged him tightly to us.

VIOLET ASQUITH

THE MANOR HOUSE, my childhood prison, sat darkly on the hill. Towers rose from low square walls. The eastern spire that had once belonged to Mother had crumbled, while my own western spire still stood strong. Father had once walked between the two like some roving spirit haunting us. Oak trees spilled from a shattered greenhouse, branches rising like the arms of dead giants. Windows shone, sick and yellow. How I remembered those thousand watchful panes, the eyes of a strange and dejected god.

Father once told me our house had not been built, it had *manifested*. As a child, I'd pictured some vast spirit descending from the heavens to sit upon the hill. The invisible creature had marked this place, or tainted it. Nethersea grew up from there. I pictured medieval quarrymen trudging out of a yellow fog, turning field-mud beneath their heavy boots. They dragged builder's stone under the watchful eye of an aged knight in black armor. That knight, the first magician in the Asquith line, knew the shape of the invisible beast and wanted to frame it in his eye. The bleached rocks of the old foundation protruded now like broken teeth from the house's lower realms.

Father had said there would always be a lord at Nethersea. And I had believed those words. For I'd seen the paintings in his gallery, black-eyed men in glittering mantles, holding swords and yellowed maps. The house was a site of power, and such power must remain. But who was the lord at Nethersea now, I wondered? Not Phillip Langford. For though he might call himself the New Lord, such a man could never truly assume Father's dreadful throne. Langford's blood was weak. The roots of his family tree could never be as damned as mine.

I quickened my pace, determined not to allow the house to rile me further. Yet the chalky smell of the ruin that wafted down the hill was nearly too much to bear. The dust of the Asquiths. The very end of my line. And yet I did not feel alone. I felt a watcher in the shadows. Something willing me onward. Something wanting me to come.

* * *

I entered Nethersea Hall through broken front doors, feeling as though I travelled through time. A massive fireplace spread against one wall, the last of its flames having burned out years ago. Figures of blackened stone decorated the mantelpiece. Perhaps the sculptor had meant them to resemble cherubs, but like so much else at Nethersea, they appeared diseased. These fat-bodied creatures were more like goblins, their faces not properly childlike, but instead somehow cruel and gloating. Above the mantle, carved in rock, the Asquith coat of arms: a black unicorn wandering through a withered copse of ash.

I held my breath and closed my eyes.

I would not become a hostage to the past.

"Rose!" I called, for I knew my sister was in the house.

Yet no answer came. Nethersea remained a grave.

I moved past the stair that led to the Western Tower. The Cedar Stair, as it had once been known, was still a breathtaking sight—a madly detailed piece of architecture, festooned in carvings meant to depict an ascent into the heavens. Here again were more of the monstrous cherubs. They crawled like insects over the railing, climbing toward some sickening vault, just as I had once climbed toward my long ago tower prison. And there at the top of the stair was the stone figure of Death himself, seated in an alcove, bones sheathed in funeral cloth.

But it was neither the Cedar Stair nor the figure of Death that held my interest. Not even the tower room called to me. My attentions, instead, were drawn to the arched door beneath the stair. For this was the door the led to the house's crypt, the place where all the Asquiths, even Father himself, were buried. I went to the door and touched the brass ring that acted as its handle. The cold of the metal made me feel as though an icy hand had suddenly grasped my own. And in that frigid thrall, I experienced the very moment I'd attempted to hold at bay.

The past, once more, came to claim me.

And I remembered.

* * *

Sunlight streamed through the tower window on that long ago day. Peacocks mewled in the garden. I was nearly sixteen, and Father was going to murder me. After all his experiments, all his terrible rituals, performed upon me late into the night, I had proven myself to be no priestess. I was nothing. I was less than nothing, in fact. He alluded to mistakes he'd made. There were failed experiments that he had not brought properly to a close. But *this* experiment, he would finish. He would seal it, as if inside a grave.

Father's heavy footfalls sounded on the stair.

I wept before the dark mirror. *Please should the mirror set me free? Please should I not die here all alone?*

Father's voice rang out then. He called my name.

Please, I said to the dark mirror. *He's coming. Please.*

I stared into the glass. Mirror Violet was sixteen too. The flesh around her eyes was swollen. She wept with me.

You must help, I said. *Father is wicked. He's going to do something terrible.*

I raised my hands. Mirror Violet raised her own hands.

Please, I said again.

Father appeared in the doorway. *What are you doing with the glass, Violet?* he asked. *Why are you speaking to it once again?* For he did not fully understand my relationship with the dark mirror, and this frightened him, I think. Perhaps that reason, more than anything, was why he had decided to take my life.

He came toward me. And it was when he raised his hand to strike me that the dark mirror shifted on the wall. Father and I looked toward the shining stone at the same moment.

Please, I whispered.

Then, with a tremendous and reckoning force, the mirror flung itself to the stone floor, shattering into three pieces.

Father's eyes turned black like stone. He knelt beside his shattered mirror.

I stepped toward the narrow slit of the tower window. I could not jump. The height was too great. I think I only wanted only to be nearer the sunlight. Nearer the world. Even if I could not make it out to safety.

"The mirror existed for eons," Father said. "And you destroyed it in a moment."

My heart filled with ice. I wondered what Father would do to me.

"I wanted to help the world," he said. "You've done nothing but destroy. You are death itself."

I looked again at the broken pieces of the mirror and thought: *Perhaps Father is right. Perhaps I am death.*

"Death in the shape of a girl," Father said.

I realized, in that moment, I no longer felt as though I should run. Father looked rather pitiful there amongst the pieces of his broken mirror. And I wasn't a child any longer.

"Maybe I am that," I whispered.

Father rose from his knees with a terrible swiftness. And he rushed at me, hands extended, wanting to grip my throat.

"Please should the lamp strike him," I said, pointing at the iron lantern that hung from the tower wall. I had not shown Father my power, my ability to move the world. I'd kept it as my own secret. Cultivated it in privacy. But now was the time to reveal everything. The time to demonstrate my strength.

The lamp flew at Father's head, striking him in the temple. He put his hand over the red welt, looking shocked, further filling with rage. I did not pause. "Please should the lamp strike Father again," I said. The lamp flew at Father once more, this time hitting his jaw, knocking him backward with the force of its blow

"Now the books," I whispered, raising my finger. "Please."

Father's sacred books, bound in animal hide and filled with magic verses, rose from the long table behind us. They flew across the room and struck him. He made a gasping sound like a man drowning. I wondered, for a moment, if all of this force was coming from inside the mirror. Or if, in fact, I now had a power inside of me. Whatever the case, I felt strong. "Please," I whispered to the room. "Please, please, please." And suddenly every object in the tower, every sheaf of paper, every bottle of ink, every ritual totem flew at Father. striking him. Pounding at his body. Father screamed, thrashing at the objects. I wondered when Mother would come. I wanted to see her face. She too should know what I was capable of. But the arched door of the tower remained empty. Father continued to scream. I could have left him there. I could have walked out at that moment. But part of me knew that if I did, he'd come after me. He'd find a way to finish me.

The objects that attacked Father dropped to the floor, one by one.

I pointed at one of the fragments of the dark mirror itself and said: "Please—should Father eat?"

Father, Lord Asquith, bleeding from his lip and forehead, turned to look at me with such horror when he realized what I'd said. I remember thinking, in that moment, that maybe I should stop. Maybe I should let him go. But I had already spoken. My will would be done.

The largest shard of mirror glass rose from the ground.

Father, whose mouth hung open—perhaps from exhaustion or from shock—had only a moment to act. Instead of crouching down or trying to hide his face, he merely closed his mouth. That, in the end, was the wrong defense.

What came next, I could barely watch.

The mirror shard, sharp and jagged, struck Father's mouth with such great force that both his lips split open. Then it struck him a second time and a third. His lips flayed. They hung like meat.

The stone struck him twice more, cracking his exposed front teeth. Breaking them off at the root.

When Father opened his mouth to scream, the mirror shard shot forward once again.

And suddenly it was in his mouth, wedging its way further and further inside. Pushing toward his throat.

Father's tongue attempted to push the stone out. He gagged, attempting to vomit the thing up. But the more he worked the more the stone pushed. And then, suddenly, I couldn't see the stone any longer. For Father had been forced to swallow it.

Father's eyes were pained at first, then somehow accepting.

It was then that I realized Mother stood in the doorway of the tower. Her white-blonde hair, her pale skin and dress, were like a shadow in reverse. A powerless white phantom that could only watch.

"My God," she said. "Violet."

* * *

Now, standing in the ruined foyer, I tried to push such memories from my mind. I pulled my hand back from the cold brass ring that hung from the door of the Asquith crypt. Fear did not move my hand. The knowledge of what I'd done to Father was always there in my memory, though I did my best to hold it at bay.

I pulled my hand back from the door because I'd heard a sound, the faint whisper of fabric against stone. And this sound, oddly, hadn't come from behind me. It had come from *above*. Slowly, I lifted my head and saw there—kneeling on all fours, hanging from the ceiling like a bat and grinning madly—was Sister Rose.

"So that's where it is," Rose said. "I knew you'd lead me to it."

I backed away from the door of the crypt. "Rose," I said. "Whatever you believe the mirror to be, whatever the New Lord told you it is, you're wrong."

"Am I?" she said.

"It's a living creature, Rose," I said. "It won't bend to your will. It only wants to be in this world. To feed upon it."

Rose laughed. "Such stories, Violet."

"If the mirror has indeed awakened, it will do us great harm. And that—that will only be the beginning."

"Look at us," Rose mused, still clinging to the ceiling. "Father's two flowers alone in his house. Which one grows stronger now? Which will get to the mirror first?"

She pointed at the door of the crypt and spoke words under her breath. The door fell off its hinges, exposing the stairwell that led to the crypt. Rose slipped from ceiling in one smooth motion. She seemed to be able to control the very atoms of the air. Perhaps her power had indeed surpassed my own.

I took the only action I could think of. I made to run at her.

A brick slipped loose from the wall behind Rose and flew at my head. I dodged the thing and continued on, but she'd already made her way halfway down the stairs to the crypt. I knew I had to stop her. I couldn't let her reach the third piece of the mirror. And so I leapt, throwing myself down the stairs and landing on top of my sister. The two of us tumbled to the stone floor below.

It was there, in the light from the open door, that I saw the state of the Asquith family crypt. One of the central sarcophagi, the box on which Father's own name had been engraved, was broken open. The lid lay in pieces on the floor. And there in the coffin was the body of my father, desiccated and gray. Strands of long black hair still clung to his skull. His broken teeth were bared. And from the place where his gut had once been grew what appeared to be an enormous shining tumor. The tumor, black in color, had spread liquid tendrils across the floor and up the walls of the crypt. The tendrils had leached into other coffins, pulling skeletal bodies of ancient family members from their graves. Bones were strewn about the room, all of them covered in the odd black substance. This was no tumor, of course. I'd forced Father to eat the mirror. That was where I had "hidden" the third piece of the glass.

As Rose began to disentangle herself from me, the corpses of our ancestors also started to shift.

"It's controlling them," I whispered. "The mirror controls them."

Skeletal remains stood erect, bones slick with liquid dark. They were incomplete figures, missing arms and legs, some of them even missing heads. Father's own body placed its frail hands upon the rim of the coffin and slowly began to rise.

Rose crawled toward Father, making her way to the great tumorous mirror that grew from him. She held out her hand. "He's come back to us, Violet," she said. "Look! Father has come back."

"Rose, stop," I called. "It isn't Father."

The creature turned to gaze at her, the sockets of its skull lined in mirror glass.

Rose was very close to the edge of the coffin. And the thing that looked like Father reached toward her upturned face with one shining hand. I thought of what Morgan Yarrow had told me in the other London. The mirror wanted to devour our world.

Before I could reach Rose, Father pressed his skeletal palm against my sister's face. The black material spread, oozing into Rose's eyes and mouth, moving up her nose and into her ears. Rose screamed in pain. Then she made an awful sighing sound. And then no sound at all.

ḣЄПRЧ ꞬOXꞱOП

THERE'S NO TIME, Mr. Coxton. A storm is on its way. There's no time, Mr. Coxton. A storm...

CHRISTOPHER X

WE PULLED THE one called Brother James down from where he hung, tearing the chain from the ceiling of the black chapel and letting him crash to the floor. Then, we went to sit beside Henry's unmoving form. We took his hand, as he had so often taken our own hand when we were troubled during the night. We thought of ghosts—the Nun of Barking, the Shade at Borely, the Fairy Man of Hinton Rectory. We had sometimes wondered if any of those creatures existed. We'd seen shadows, yes. Vague forms in cobwebbed halls. But when Henry showed the beam of his electric lamp over those so-called spirits, they had always disappeared. It was true that we ourselves had detected odors. And we'd gladly attributed them to the abnatural world, because such discoveries pleased Henry. But, in fact, we had no idea where those scents came from. Violet said ghost finding was nothing more than a boy's game, the sort of foolish thing that youths are wont to play at in abandoned barns or quiet forests on a warm summer's evening. And we knew, in our heart, that Violet was correct. Ghost finding was a game we played with Henry. A game that was good because it held back confusion, ours and Henry's own. It kept the world from falling into chaos.

But now, here was Henry in his own blood.

And there were no more games to hold back the dark.

* * *

Brother James came to stand beside us. He put his hand on our shoulder. He too looked down at Henry. We could feel his fingers trembling. "Christopher," he said.

"Do not speak to me," we replied.

"I must."

"If you speak, you may become a friend. And I no longer wish to have friends."

"I'm sorry," Brother James said.

"Enough. No more."

When we had lived as Reprobus, we had likely not made friends with men. We were a guardian then. The Dog of God. We came from the sky, we did battle, and then we moved on. It was the fault of Mercurius that we now remained upon the earth. The magician had taken our memory. And we no longer knew who or what we were, precisely. We had made friends with Henry Coxton because we needed him. We wondered if this was Mercurius' actual curse: that we should make friends with men.

"We have to go to Nethersea Hall," Brother James said. "We can't let the New Lord win."

We glanced up at Brother James. He had a handsome face. Henry had liked Brother James' face. We wished we could put all of Henry's blood back inside of him. "I met your daughter," we said to Brother James. "She is called Sister Eloise."

Brother James drew his hand back. "Where?"

"She is worried about you. Your wife is worried too."

"Christopher, I—"

We did not want to hear his human thoughts in that moment. "Henry believed you favored him. He died believing this. It was not kind of you to trick him."

"I didn't trick Henry. I *did* favor him."

We took a deep breath. "Henry was good."

"I know. And Henry would want us to move forward now."

"Where is Violet?"

"At Nethersea Hall," James said. "They'll all be at Nethersea by now. The mirror is awake."

We nodded. We placed Henry's hands upon his chest, crossing them in the same fashion as we had crossed Mrs. Hastur's hands. "Goodbye,

Henry," we said. With that, we stood and dusted off the remnants of our suit. "Take me to the house," we said. "I will finish this."

VIOLET ASQUITH

FATHER'S BONES LAY scattered. My ancestors too had fallen. Skulls and femurs, ribs and ulnae, the shattered dead of the Asquith clan. The creature had abandoned them. Forgotten its puppets. Its black liquid form had, to my horror, rushed with sudden greed and vigor into the living body of Sister Rose, a dark and shining river, flowing at great speed. She'd struggled at first, convulsing. Now, she lay curled in her gray dress at the foot of Father's coffin. Her hands covered her face. Her blonde hair hung in strands. The black material crawled beneath her skin, moving like some terrible new blood.

I heard her voice then, a strained echo: "Violet?"

"I'm here." I knelt beside her.

"I can't see you," she said, face buried in her hands. She sounded as if she spoke from deep inside a hole.

"You only have to lift your head," I replied.

"This—" She made some sound then that reminded me of the sighing I'd heard when I was trapped inside the mirror with Morgan Yarrow. A needful sound. Desirous. A hungry animal crying in a darkened wood. "This isn't what I thought."

"No," I said. "It isn't."

"The mirror wants—" Again the sighing sound. "It wants this world, Violet. I can feel its thoughts. No—that's not right. I can feel its *will*."

I wanted to put my hand on Rose to comfort her. And yet, I feared the thing that inhabited her now. I feared the swollen flesh and the black material that shifted beneath Rose's skin. "Is there anything you can tell about the creature's will?" I asked. "Something that might help me defeat it?"

"I know that it doesn't actually want me," she said. "It thinks—it thinks I am not strong enough. I cannot support its *appetite.*"

"Who then?" I said.

"It wants—the girl."

"What girl?"

"The girl with gray eyes and black hair. The girl who stared into it and spoke to it for so many years. She is strong. She is different. She's the one who'll finally bring it full into this world."

With that, Rose finally tilted her head to look up at me.

I stepped away, nearly falling.

For her left eye was entirely black, a dark mirror. And her right eye was still blue and clear. The right eye looked at me with such soulfulness, such sorrow. "You should run, Violet," Rose whispered. "My God, you should—"

"Rose?"

MY GOD, Rose repeated. Only it was no longer Rose's voice that spoke. The voice. if it could even be called a voice at all, was like metal scraped against glass. It was a mirror's voice reflecting back what it had heard. The liquid mirror shifted beneath the skin of Rose's face, pressing against the flesh. Her right eye slowly filled with darkness. I recognized, in those mirrored eyes, the god I'd been praying to for my entire life. I'd asked that god to move the world for me. It had obliged. But now it came to seek payment.

I stumbled toward the stair, nearly tripping over Father's skull.

YOU SHOULD RUN, VIOLET, the Rose-thing said in its scratching, scraping voice. It opened its mouth wide, and a narrow appendage protruded from my sister's throat—a second tongue, black and viscous. The tongue strained toward me, wanting to taste. I felt too frightened to move, and yet I knew I had to heed Rose's warning. And so I ran. Up the stone steps, two at a time. Fleeing the crypt and the beast. I glanced behind me only once to see the Rose-thing was in pursuit. The mirror did not fully understand human legs or arms. It caused Rose's body to crawl, just as Mirror Violet in Silent London had crawled. Rose ambled like some spider with a swollen human face, second tongue lolling from her mouth. Black material leaked from her eyes like tears.

YOU SHOULD RUN, the voice bellowed.

After I'd reached the main floor of the house, I rushed up the Cedar Stair toward the room in the Western Tower. Perhaps some reflex moved me there. The tower was my place at Nethersea, after all, the cell where I'd been forced to commune with a dark spirit. The awful cherubs appeared to laugh. I could hear the Rose-thing stumbling after me. At the top of the stair, I entered the tower room, slamming the door and bolting it. Then I pulled at Father's great oaken table, wanting to place it against the door before the thing arrived. "Please," I whispered. "Please should the table move?" Nothing happened. Of course it didn't. The awful god—the organism—would no longer answer my prayers. I heard it clambering ever closer, likely crawling on hands and knees. It spoke in the hideous voice again: YOU SHOULD, it rasped. YOU SHOULD YOU SHOULD MY GOD YOU SHOULD.

I sat with my back against the tower door, hoping the bolt would hold. Father had been so foolish. He and all the other magicians had believed they could control a thing that was not even imaginable. And in toying with its vast organs, they had unwittingly fed it. They'd given it strength over these many years. Then Phillip Langford and Sister Rose had found a way to cause the thing to stir. And I myself, in all my fear, had finally awakened it. Now the creature recognized in me something that it needed. All the rituals Father had performed—they'd worked. I was connected to the creature. Connected to such otherness.

YOU SHOULD YOU SHOULD. It was screaming now. The beast hurled Rose's body against the tower door, causing a fearsome crash. It shuffled back then before hurling itself once more. I heard what sounded like the breaking of a bone. It would destroy Rose to get to me. Shatter every one of her bones until it had me—the girl with the gray eyes, the girl it believed was strong.

"Stop!" I cried, pressing myself against the shaking door. "Please—please should it stop?"

PLEASE, the creature screamed. PLEASE PLEASE!

"I'm not what you think. I promise you. I *am not* what you want."

Miraculously, a silence fell beyond the door.

I waited. And then another voice came. Not the shrieking of the unimaginable organism, but Rose's voice again, quiet, plaintive. "Violet..."

"Rose." I pressed my ear to the door but did not move to open it. "Did it release you? Has the mirror left you?"

"I can still feel it..." she said, softly. "It hurts me, Violet... It hurts me so."

"I'm sorry," I said.

"It wants you to open the door. Please. If you don't, it's going to do something even more terrible. It will grow stronger until it can have you."

"I can't open the door, Rose."

"You would leave me out here all alone? Just as Father left me?"

"I'm sorry—"

I heard voices then from the entryway, male voices. One of them sounded very much like Phillip Langford. He gave orders, telling his men to search the house.

"Rose," I said. "Has the New Lord arrived?"

There was no response.

"Are you out there still?"

Nothing. Yet perhaps this was another ploy on the part of the creature.

I looked for some weapon. Hanging from the tower wall were a pair of ancient-looking swords. I remembered that Father had told me once that they'd belonged to the first lord at Nethersea, the great knight who wore the black armor.

I pulled one of the swords down and returned to the door, holding the blade close to my chest. I thought again about the beast, the organism. It made no more sense to me now than it ever had. There seemed no way to combat it. If I killed Rose—which I did not want to do—it could still use her body to follow me, as it had used Father's body in the crypt. Perhaps there was some way to exorcise the thing, to return it to its petrified form. I thought back to Father's story about the discovery of the mirror along the banks of the Nile. It had been more active then—it had stirred the soldiers' dreams. Driven them mad. They had called it the Eye of Osiris, the Lord of the Dead. And what had they done with the thing? How had they put it back to sleep?

Another voice called to me then. It was neither Sister Rose, nor Phillip Langford. Instead, it was the rough near-growl of a friend.

"Christopher!" I called. For it was Christopher, speaking to me from somewhere below the tower.

"Violet?" he said, voice echoing through the great house. "Tell me where you are."

"In the Western Tower," I said. "Follow the Cedar Stair. But you must be careful. The mirror—it looks like Rose now."

Two pairs of footfalls arrived outside the door. There was someone with Christopher. Henry, I thought. Finally, we would all be together again. And if we were together, we could figure out how to best the creature. We could do anything if we were together.

I moved to open the door, then paused. If the mirror could use Rose's body, what if it could somehow use Christopher's voice as well? What if the Rose-thing still stood outside, speaking now in the voice of my friend, attempting to lure me?

"Open the door, Violet," Christopher said.

"I want to make sure that you are you," I said.

"Who else would I be?"

His tone indeed sounded like Christopher's, but I had to be sure. "At Highcroft Abbey," I said, "tell me what Henry called the abnatural there." These words, the idea of our old expeditions, sounded so impossible to me at that moment, like some half-remembered dream.

"The Lonely Man," Christopher said. "He was said to carry his head in a lantern case. But we saw no heads. Nor even any lantern cases."

Tears burned my eyes as I fumbled with the bolt. As soon as I'd opened the door, I threw my arms around Christopher and hugged him. He put his great arms around me as well. And I thought nothing had ever felt so good as that.

"I'm sorry," I said to him. "I'm sorry for everything that happened—at the hospital and after."

I pulled my face back from Christopher's chest, hoping to see Henry behind his hulking form. Henry, gazing at me with care and attention. But it was not Henry. It was the tall redheaded figure of Brother James.

"Where's Henry?" I said to Christopher. "Didn't you find him in the village?"

Christopher peered at me with his gold eyes. His silence frightened me.

"Tell me," I said.

"Violet, you must remain calm," Christopher said.

"What? Tell me what's happened."

"Henry has—he has fallen," Christopher said, lowering his head.

My first thought was *where?* Where had Henry fallen and how could we get away from Nethersea to go pull him out of whatever hole he'd fallen into? But then, seeing the pain on Brother James' face, I realized what "fallen" meant.

"Langford," James said. "It was Langford who got him—some sort of ritual knife. Henry was trying to rescue me in the chapel."

"Henry was good," Christopher said.

It did not seem possible that the love I'd felt from Henry, the care he'd shown when he'd taken me into the fold at Coxton & Co., could be gone from the world.

I stepped away from Christopher and Brother James, back into the tower room. In my mind, I cursed my father. I cursed everything he had done. More than that, I cursed the awful mirror. The thing that had used all of us so it could eat.

"We have work to do," Christopher said.

"Henry's gone," I said. "The mirror's awake. We've lost."

"That's not the case," James said. "Christopher is here—he's here to bring an end to all of this. That's what he does, Violet. That's how he's written of in the Grimoire stolen from your father. Sister Rose told me."

I peered at poor Christopher, his bright golden eyes, the whiskers on his muzzle.

"I will try," he said.

"I'll lose you too," I said.

And then came the voice of the mirror again, a sound that seemed to shake the very foundations of Nethersea Hall. I thought the tower itself would crumble around us. The voice was so much bigger now than it had been, so much more powerful. It said: *IT HURT ME, VIOLET. MY*

GOD. IT HURT ME. YOU SHOULD RUN. Dust fell from the bricks around us

"What has happened to it?" Brother James asked.

"It sounds different now," I said.

"The two of you will remain here," Christopher told us. "I will fight."

I held firmly to the grip of Father's sword. "I'm coming with you, Christopher. We're stronger when we're together. We're Coxton & Co., remember?"

"Do you have another one of those swords for me?" Brother James asked.

I attempted a smile.

Henry had been right about James.

Henry—

ĦENRY COXTON

THERE'S NO TIME, Mr. Coxton. A storm is on its way.

Mrs. Hastur's voice in the darkness. A lilt, so like my mother's.

The sound flitted on dark wings, moving about a vast chamber. I imagined a bat in the black hall of an ancient pyramid, swooping, turning.

A storm. A storm.

How long had the voice been speaking?

I'd been absent. There was an ellipsis inside me. A caesura.

I hoped, for a moment, I might be lying in my own bed at Coxton & Co., velvet drapes pulled against the light. Perhaps I'd overslept. A client waited in the offices below. Lady Dorton had written several weeks ago. We'd yet to meet with her. She claimed to have seen an enormous Black Dog in her courtyard, rummaging in her azaleas. I'd spoken to Violet about whether or not we should tell Lady Dorton that Black Dogs were thought to be presages of death. Hellhounds, in fact. There were numerous examples: Padfoot in Lancashire, Hairy Jack in Helmswell.

A storm. Mrs. Hastur's voice again. The sound seemed to dive at me. *A storm. A storm.*

I opened my eyes, and I found myself in the dim hold of a ship. I recognized the symbol stamped upon stacked cargo crates: a compass and an oar. This was the *Daedalus*, the ship on which I'd set sail after leaving Warwickshire as a young man. A form lay next to me in the shadows. A body that I knew.

Paser.

He propped himself on one elbow to look down at me, eyes a thoughtful shade. A spider web of familiar scars spread across his shoulder. But how could this be? Paser was dead. Lost forever beneath the waves. Yet here he was—beloved friend, so full of life.

"A ghost?" Paser said, furrowing black eyebrows. "On deck? Really, Henry. Do you think I'm such a fool?"

The ship rolled beneath us. Paser and I were in the makeshift bed we'd often shared during our private rendezvous. It was little more than a pile of skins and burlap. But the bed was comfortable. And more than that, it felt like a kind of home. Paser said it reminded him of a tent he'd slept in for half a year near Cairo as a youth. Those had been oddly cheerful days, he'd once told me.

The ship rolled again. I could smell the sea and our precious cargo too: cinnamon and clove, ginger and saffron.

"You're here," I said, touching Paser's bare chest.

"Only for a moment," he replied. "We don't want the Old Man to catch us." The Old Man was what Paser called Captain Richards. "As I was saying," he continued, "we haven't any ghosts in Egypt. We have gods."

"Gods?" I said. I thought I half-remembered this conversation. "Have I been here all along, Paser? All the while with you?"

He peered at me, eyes half-lidded. "You were telling a story, Henry. One of your tall tales." He put his arm around me then. "You said you'd seen—how did you say it—a phantom walking back and forth on the deck of the *Daedalus.*" He kissed me lightly.

"Paser," I took his hand, clutching it too tightly. He was warm. This was not a dead man's hand. And yet, so much had happened since I'd last seen him. Since he'd drowned in the cold Atlantic.

A smile spread across his handsome face, as if he'd become aware of some secret. "You aren't going to frighten me, you know? I'm not that—" He paused, gazing out into the darkness of the ship's hold. "Henry, what is that?" He pointed toward the center of the low-ceilinged space. I saw nothing but crates and pale grain sacks. "What *is* it?" Paser asked again.

"I don't see anything," I said.

"It's coming closer now," Paser said, fear in his voice. "Henry. Oh God. It's moving toward us!"

"Paser—"

At this my friend began to laugh. He clutched me in our bed. "You are ridiculous sometimes."

Before I could respond, the ship gave a great lurch. I struck the crown of my head against the wall.

"On deck! On deck!" a voice called from above.

Paser scrambled to a standing position. "I was supposed to be on watch," he said, pulling on trousers and then his brine-covered jacket. "The Old Man—he'll murder me."

"Trim the sail!" another voice called. I recognized it as that of Captain Richards.

The ship lurched again.

"A storm," Paser said. "God save us. I'll see you on deck, Henry."

A storm is coming, Henry. There isn't time.

"Paser, wait," I said, because I knew what was about to happen. I remembered this moment. "It's the cyclone. This is when you—" But he was already scrambling up the narrow ladder. He was so afraid of what the Old Man might do. He feared the other sailors too. They loathed him, called him an aberrant, an unspeakable. I rushed toward the ladder myself, thinking I could protect my friend. I had to reach the deck, had to get him to safety before we encountered the towering black wall of the cyclone. A great gush of seawater fell through the hole above. I closed my eyes against the water, coughing, sputtering. In darkness then: *There isn't time, Mr. Coxton. There isn't time.*

* * *

I opened my eyes again. Rain fell in great sheets from a black sky. I was no longer on board the *Daedalus*. No longer at sea. Paser was dead. I felt that in my heart. I lay face-down on a crooked cobblestone street in London, and it wasn't seawater in my lungs. It was rainwater. I pulled my face from a puddle, coughing. Carriages clattered past. A flower girl chanted her wares. Gas lamps flickered over a painted sign: The Prince Alfred Tavern. Young men, handsome and dark, lounged on broken benches, smoking cigarettes. "Coxton!" one of them shouted. "Get out of the rain, you idiot."

"Can I help you stand?" said another voice.

Phillip Langford hovered over me in a woolen greatcoat, holding a wide black umbrella. The skin of the umbrella looked like a starless sky.

He extended a thin white hand toward me.

I coughed, lungs full of water. I couldn't call out. Could not ask for help from the young men at the tavern behind me. So I did the only thing I could think to do. I crawled away like some beaten animal. Phillip looked surprised. He called after me, but I couldn't hear his words over the sound of the falling rain. I found an alleyway and huddled in it. I closed my eyes again. *It's nearly too late, Mr. Coxton.* Mrs. Hastur said, her voice echoing from all around me. *You must leave these circles.*

* * *

A crack of thunder. I opened my eyes and found myself standing backstage at the theater known as The Dragon, watching Violet Asquith remove white greasepaint from her face.

"Are you some sort of physician?" Violet asked. "Or you've been sent from Scotland Yard?"

"Violet," I said.

She turned, face still half-covered in paint. "How do you know my name?"

"It's *me*," I said. "Henry."

"I don't know any Henrys. You're mad, aren't you? Another madman coming after me."

"Something's gone wrong, Violet. You're at—" I strained to remember. "You're at Nethersea Hall."

A look of horror spread across her face. "How do you know of that place? Are you one of *them*?"

"Just listen to me," I said.

"I'm calling for the manager." She threw the greasepaint-covered rag in my face.

I blinked.

* * *

I lay on the hardwood in the foyer of Coxton & Co., staring up at the flickering electric light that hung from the ceiling. Dull pain throbbed in my abdomen. I looked down to see the ivory handle of a dagger protruding from my shirtfront. The white paint on the foyer ceiling was grayed with soot from the office fireplace. I thought, absurdly, that I should have someone come to scrub it clean. We mustn't let clients see the office so filthy. Then I realized such things didn't matter. Nothing mattered. Phillip had once told me this place—every brick of it—was mine. But, in truth, Coxton & Co. had always belonged to him, to the New Lord. I thought of how many times I'd passed through this very foyer after returning from an investigation with Violet and Christopher. We hung our coats in the hall closet. Mrs. Hastur brought tea and biscuits. We sat together by the fire and talked late into the night.

A long shadow fell across my body then. I blinked. Mrs. Hastur leaned over me. She was dressed in her gray maid's uniform, rosy-cheeked and kind.

Upon her arrival, Coxton & Co. seemed momentarily transformed. Beneath the calm exterior of the foyer, I caught sight of the glimmer of something grand: marbled vaults lined with gold, high blue flames burning in tall pyres. As if the two of us were inside some kind of ancient temple.

"Have you finally come to your senses then, Mr. Coxton?" Mrs. Hastur asked.

Briefly, I saw something terrifying concealed within Mrs. Hastur's skin: a winged figure, vast in its proportions. It had an enormous face, an owl-like ivory mask. The figure stared down at me, its eyes and mouth made of blue fire. The light from a thousand thunderstorms. Stars gathered inside it. It seemed both a creature and the sky, all at once. "Good God," I said.

"What's the matter, Mr. Coxton?" The great winged creature said. Then it looked, once more, like humble Mrs. Hastur.

"Why—" I asked, unable to formulate any deeper question. "Why are you here?"

"This is where I belong, isn't it, sir?" Mrs. Hastur said. "I'm the housekeeper."

"You're not," I said. "You never have been. We played a game."

"Oh, this is no game," Mrs. Hastur replied. "Granted, I'm keeping house on a somewhat grander scale than you might have initially imagined."

I paused, wondering if this was all some death dream. A fantasy projected onto my fading sense of reason.

"Don't think about all this too much," Mrs. Hastur continued. "That's my burden, isn't it?"

Electric light buzzed faintly above us.

"There's a dagger," I said, pointing down at the knife in my gut.

Mrs. Hastur peered at the ivory handle. "So there is, sir. Does it hurt?"

"At times," I said.

"You must try not to think about that either, then."

"What should I think about?"

"I suppose you should wonder why the housekeeper of the universe came to you, to Mr. Henry Coxton, on that long-ago day during a thunderstorm."

I remembered the strange blue lights in the sky, the pounding rain, the manner in which the edges of the newspaper Mrs. Hastur carried had been singed.

"Why did you come?"

"There is a pattern at work, sir," Mrs. Hastur said. "A geometry of sorts. At times, I myself cannot see its logic, for it is not my creation. I only maintain its shape, you understand. And certainly, inside this rather pitiful body"—she held out her hands and indicated her maid-like form— "I am *simpler* than I would otherwise be. But I had to descend. To become flesh. For I was drawn, you see."

"But what could I have to do with any of this?" I asked.

"You are Henry Coxton."

"I know that."

"You don't," she said. "Not yet. I must admit, I made several errors."

"What errors?"

Mrs. Hastur shook her gray head. "I underestimated the Asquiths— Violet and Rose. I underestimated the curse that had been laid upon Christopher. And I underestimated you as well."

"I don't understand."

"It wouldn't help if I explained further, I'm afraid. The actions required here are, in fact, quite simple." With that, she reached down and pulled the dagger from my gut. Pain flashed. The marbled palace manifested around us once again. Mrs. Hastur's magnificent, astonishing wings spread. They were pale wings, full of stars. I put my hand against my shirtfront. I felt no wound. There was no blood on the black stone dagger either.

"Now," Mrs. Hastur said. "As I said before, the storm is coming, sir."

CHRISTOPHER X

WE DESCENDED THE Western Tower. Violet and Brother James followed, bearing broadswords. We believed we could best the creature that waited for us in the entry hall. Its form was sealed inside the body of Sister Rose. And she was a small woman. Certainly, we could overpower her. Yet we realized soon enough we had gravely misjudged the situation. For what we faced in the great stone room stood as an impossible sight. It was not Sister Rose who stood there, not as Violet had described her. Or perhaps we should say it was not *merely* Sister Rose.

The creature had grown, spilling forth in great tendrils from the body of Sister Rose, attaching itself to what appeared to be Phillip Langford and his entire army of black-hatted men. The dark substance, both liquid and solid at once, was wrapped around these men and *through* them. It had entered the mouths of the villagers, penetrating eyes and ears, forming a single massive and senseless figure. Its legs, if legs they could be called, were composed up of some three or four villagers each. Sister Rose hung from the center of the creature's torso, her skin split open everywhere at once. Some seven bodies were attached to her to form the giant's core. Phillip Langford, the New Lord, was part of the beast's single long arm, a tentacle of sorts. The creature had no head to speak of. Yet still, it observed us, staring with all its human faces. They looked from me to Brother James to Violet. And when the creature saw Violet, it made a great sighing sound using all of its many mouths. *MY GOD*, it said.

"Christ," Violet whispered.

The creature began advancing then toward the Cedar Stair. It appeared to crawl, using its single arm and two legs to drag itself across the floor.

"I will fight," we said to Violet and James. "If it bests me, you will run."

"Running is not a plan, Christopher," Violet replied.

"Brother James, you will carry Violet to safety," we said. "Do you understand?"

"I don't need anyone to rescue me," she said.

"You must remain separate from the creature, Violet," we said. "If you become part of it—"

The beast opened its many mouths and wailed: *YOU SHOULD RUN!*

"What about you, Chris?" Violet asked. "Who will get you to safety?"

"It is not my job to be safe," we said.

"But you don't know the first thing about this monster, do you? You don't actually remember much of anything."

"I am going to learn," we said.

And with that—we leapt at the great body, nearly flying once again.

VIOLET ASQUITH

CHRISTOPHER HOWLED AS he landed on the beast's massive shoulder, opening his mouth and clamping down on its impossible flesh. The two fell into battle then. The creature roared with many mouths, rearing back its great swollen arm that contained Phillip Langford, groping for Christopher with fingers made of human appendages. Christopher evaded the hand, crawling swiftly onto the creature's back.

"We have to help him," I said to James, raising my sword.

"You heard what he said, Violet," James replied. "We need to keep you separate from it."

"I won't lose another friend today."

The creature swayed back and forth, craning about, trying to grasp Christopher with its single, malignant arm. It appeared to be forming a second appendage too, this one made entirely of the black substance.

"Watch out, Chris!" I called. "Behind you!"

He turned, but it was too late. The material from the body of the beast wrapped itself around him, pushing him down into the great form. Christopher continued to bite at the black ooze, to struggle against it. But it proved too powerful. More tendrils rose, forcing him inside the body. Finally, he was buried, face-down in the muck.

James ran at the beast, sword held high. He swung, but he was no match for it. The creature flung its great arm at him, striking James with immense force. He flew through the air, and I heard his skull crack against the far stone wall. His body fell limply to the floor.

I was all that was left.

I held my sword at my side, staring up in to the many faces of the hideous body. So many mirrored eyes shining back at me.

VIOLET, the creature boomed from all its throats at once. *IT HURTS.*

"I'll make it stop," I said.

The thing attempted to grasp me with its great hand, and I lunged forward with the sword, cutting into one of the villager's legs that formed the creature's finger. The beast drew back, as if in pain. Then, after only a moment's pause, it redoubled its efforts, reaching for me again. This time, I could not move my sword fast enough. The creature suddenly had me in its grasp, lifting me off the floor. I looked into its churning mirrored surface and saw myself there, all alone. I saw myself as it wanted me. I was the vessel. The final body. The priestess. In this vision, my eyes were made of glass. I was infected. Filled up with black miasma. Yet I was not weak like Rose. I could withstand the beast's hunger. I saw myself hovering over London, great arms of the mirrored substance growing from me. The whole of my city had become a shining surface—every building, every cobbled street—all of it was transformed into an otherworldly plane. I saw myself alone in that city. For together, the beast and I were a thing that devoured. The Egyptians might have once called the beast Nun—the great chaos, the eternal sea from which creation arose—but it was not that. It could be given no name. For it was the opposite of names. The opposite of creation.

"You will not have this," I said. "You will not have me." I raised my sword and battered at the thing, slicing into its body. Trying in vain to free myself.

ĦENRY COXTON

THE WALLS OF Coxton & Co. parted like a grand curtain.

A theater.

Coxton & Co. had always been a theater.

Mrs. Hastur and I were once more inside the great temple, surrounded by marbled halls and burning pyres.

Yet even this was some façade.

The walls of the temple churned and billowed. They blew away like dark clouds.

Thunder rumbled.

Mrs. Hastur and I were no longer inside a room at all, but caught in the eye of a storm. "I used to drop Christopher from the heavens," Mrs. Hastur called over the sound of the wind. "It was me who did that. I organized the army of the dog-faced men. But we won't put you through that, sir. You've already been through so much." She stretched out her arms. The wind tore at her gray hair, pulling it from its bun. The vast owl-like figure appeared inside her again. I saw its fiery wings. Its ivory face.

"What I am I to do?" I said.

"The actions are simple," Mrs. Hastur replied. "They always are. Use the knife. The storm is coming."

"The knife?" I looked down at the ivory-handled dagger in my hand.

"You'll understand when you arrive. The pattern will be clear."

Thunder crashed.

"And don't return to the black chapel in the village, sir," Mrs. Hastur said.

"Why not?"

"Because you won't like what you find there."

"Am I still dead, Mrs. Hastur?" I asked. "Is my body there in that church?"

"It's more complicated than you imagine," she said. "Just bring the mirror to the storm. The waters of creation will fall."

CHRISTOPHER X

WE DARKEN. WE cannot move. Fastened to the vile body. The greater whole. We are with Sister Rose and Phillip Langford. The tangled mass of village men. Darkness binds our jaw. It binds our arms and legs. It wants to be inside us. To flood our cavity and become our body. And when it understands it cannot come inside because we are not the same as flesh, it wants nothing more than for us to die. It uses all its force, bending bones, stretching skin. And in this state of torment, we are granted a vision, the sort we must have once been privy to long ago when we were the Dog of God. We see the whole of the Earth. We see the cosmos where it sits. We see beyond that too. All of creation. So fragile and so small. Surrounding this fiber is the darkness from which the cosmos sprang. And the darkness would devour this tiny bead if it was not for us. For we are the keeper of the boundary. We are the soldier who fights. And we realize in that moment that we are not a monster. We have never been a monster. We are, in fact, the thing that loves. For we love creation. We love the life inside the bead. And that is why we protect it. We do not know ourselves as "I." For we are more than "I." We are like the world. And we are like time. We are like all of it.

VIOLET ASQUITH

I LASHED OUT with my sword, hacking into yet another black tendril rising from the body of the beast. Mouths moaned. Human bodies struggled toward me, propelled by viscous matter. Phillip Langford's own hand was suddenly at my throat. His gaunt, lifeless face stared at me, mirror-black eyes, mirror-black teeth. This was what his magic had wrought. This was his immortality. His end to death. I swung my sword, slicing off Langford's hand. Black liquid poured from the wound.

Bodies of the villagers clambered toward me in fury, hands grasping, mouths biting. There was no longer an above or a below. I knew only that I had to fight. And fight I did, slashing through men, releasing black material with my blows. All of us churned in an awful, oily ball. And then before me suddenly was Sister Rose herself, rising from the miasma like some diseased angel. Her eyes were dark. Her skin, torn. Tendrils wriggled in her flesh. I raised my sword, but hesitated. I could not plunge it into her. For in her face, I saw my own. Rose was like me. She *was* me. Rose, or more properly the mirror beast, saw me hesitate. And it grinned, opening its mouth. A black appendage extended toward me almost teasingly. Hands of the villagers fell upon me. The black appendage crept closer, pausing inches from my left eye. I struggled, but could not move. The appendage touched my eye, ever so gently, and I experienced fully for the first time what Rose had called the creature's will. A great chime rang inside me. I knew what was to come.

ᚼᕮᑎᖇᕼ ᑢOᕽᛏOᑎ

LIGHTNING. AND THE crash of thunder.

I found myself in a great stone hall, holding the black dagger that had previously been deep inside my own gut. I was alive. Quite irrationally and incredibly, I was *alive*. Before me, a scene of chaos. Violet was caught in the grip of what appeared to be a roiling black tower. Within the shape, corpses gyrated. "Violet!" I called. My friend tried to look, but the tower and its corpses held her in place. The tower pressed some appendage to her eye. I rushed forward and did the only thing I could think to do. I plunged the black dagger into the body of the tower. Twenty mouths bellowed all at once. I saw Sister Rose and Phillip Langford screaming. For they too were caught inside the grotesque architecture.

Thunder crashed.

Lighting streaked through the high arched windows of the hall.

The storm was coming.

I pulled out the knife and plunged it into the black material once more. I did this over and over again, tearing at the strange liquid form until finally it reached for me with one of its dark tentacles. I withdrew the knife and ran. The great churning beast, the black tower, followed, bellowing with its many mouths, using a single arm to propel itself.

I passed through the doors of the hall and into the open courtyard beyond. The creature broke through the doors after me, bursting into the yard. It seemed amazed to be in the wide-open expanse. It touched everything with its tendrils: the grass, the stones of the drive, the trunks of the blighted trees. It wanted the world. To taste all of it. And then it seemed to remember it had been pursuing me.

The corpses imbedded inside the creature looked at me with blackish eyes and screamed YOU SHOULD RUN. But, this time, I didn't run. I faced the awful thing.

And then with another great clap of lightning, the skies opened and rain began to fall. The storm had come. The waters of creation fell. Just as Mrs. Hastur said.

And as soon as the rain touched the creature, something in its physiology altered. Its body grew dense. Its form stiffened. The mirror was hardening once again. The waters of creation fell upon the waters of chaos. Violet dropped from the creature's grasp. I ran toward her, scooping her up and helping her away. Together, we watched as another body moved in the darkness of the black tower, struggling with all its might. It was a large form with a big bristling head. Suddenly, Christopher burst up through the dark surface of the mirror.

"Chris!" I yelled.

He looked down at me, eyes shining gold. He crawled from the back of the struggling creature, like something beautiful and new. "Henry!" he called. "You are alive!"

I nodded, pressing my hand against my belly where the knife had once been.

"I have a job to do, Henry!" Christopher called. "I remember now. I have to go."

I raised my hand to him.

He grinned a doggish grin. "I am so glad to see you," he called.

Then he grabbed the creature by its stiff and massive arm, heaving with all his might. Christopher walked, not off into the forest that surrounded Nethersea Hall but *upward* into the sky, as if some invisible staircase had appeared—or perhaps the hand of a great winged form, descended from the clouds. Violet and I held each other and watched him go. We watched until Christopher and the great mirror were mere specks of darkness in the storm.

EPILOGUE:
HENRY AGAIN

A GATHERING OF Christmas holly bound with a gold ribbon dangled from a nail above the crackling fireplace at Coxton & Co. Snow fell beyond the tall windows. The sound of carolers echoed in the street below. I sat in the leather chair behind my cluttered desk watching shapes move in the fire. Violet, in a gray silk housedress, lay on the velvet divan, a tasseled pillow beneath her head. In her lap, she held a pile of envelopes, all letters of solicitation. She used a brass opener to extract them and sometimes read aloud to me. "From a Mrs. Templeton in Cotgrave," Violet said. She read aloud: "'My husband, Morris, some days ago discovered a large femur bone in our garden. It didn't look as if it had come from an animal, but rather from a human skeleton. Morris brought the bone into the house, and much to my dismay, stored the ghastly thing in our bedroom cabinet. Now he claims to hear the bone speaking late at night. It told him once that his brother from Kent was going to call on him. And then his brother *did* call on him. Won't you help us, Mr. Coxton?'"

"Abnatural," I said, running my finger over the ivory handle of the black blade I now kept on my desk.

"To say the least," Violet replied.

"Write to Mrs. Templeton. Let's schedule a meeting."

"You realize we don't have time to take on every case, Henry."

"But we have time for most," I replied.

She sighed and inserted the tip of the letter opener into the edge of yet another envelope.

No one knew the truth about what had happened to our firm during the pursuit of the dark mirror. Yet our fortunes, in recent months, had changed. Apparently, we'd been recognized by a Mr. Tom Price, at both the fall of the Tremmond house and at Saint John's Hospital. Mr. Price was, of course, the caretaker at Number 15 Castle Crescent whom I'd spoken to about Edgar Yarrow. Price had taken more of an interest in both me and my ghost finding than I'd originally understood. He'd followed us. Reports of our connection to the collapse of the Tremmond house, as well as our involvement with the possible appearance of a "monster" at the hospital, were more than enough to garner publicity in the less reputable London newspapers. On top of that, we'd been interviewed by the *Times* about the mysterious disappearance of the occultist Phillip Langford. I'd told them I thought Langford might have gone off to India. He'd always spoken with some interest of that country.

"A doppelgänger in Shropshire," Violet said, continuing to move through the solicitations. "A vortex near Buckingham Palace. A sighting of the *Flying Dutchman* on the Thames. Sometimes I wonder if all of London is nothing more than one enormous grave."

"A haunted grave," I said. For when I dreamed, I often found myself roaming the narrow passages of the Tremmond house, only to discover soon enough that I'd arrived once more at the black chapel in Nethersea Village. On the floor, near the baptismal font, lay a body. At times, it was someone I knew: Violet or Christopher, Phillip Langford or Sister Rose. At other times, it was a stranger. I wondered if everyone in the whole world might eventually take his or her turn lying beneath the stone basin in the pool of blood.

A shuffling sound came from beyond the office door. James appeared, looking rather sunny despite the winter cold. His red hair was slicked into a neat part. He wore a checkered vest in current fashion and had a dishcloth draped over one shoulder. "I was just about to make some tea," he said. "Either of you care for a cup?"

Violet glanced up from the letter in her lap. "What's all this tea making, James? It's become something of an obsession."

He cleared his throat. "We weren't allowed tea in the village."

"Well, it's beginning to seem neurotic," Violet said.

"Tea would be wonderful," I said. "Neurotic or not."

James smiled at me. The look in his eyes told me he knew I didn't care about the tea in the slightest. I only cared about him. We'd talked about his wife and child many times, of course. I understood there were decisions to be made. But for now, James was here with us.

After he'd left the office, Violet sighed. "Let's not choose any more cases until we've drawn up a schedule for the week."

"A sensible plan," I said.

At that, there was a distant sound of thunder. We both looked toward the window. I stood and went to it, pulling back the drape. A few automobiles and carriages trundled through the snow on Bachelor Street. Everyone else had gone inside where it was warm. "Thunder in December?" I said.

"It happens," Violet said. "You mustn't believe it's anything too out of the ordinary."

I let the drape fall into place. She was right, of course. Violet was always right. "Do you think they'll come back?" I asked, not for the first time.

She turned the letter opener in her hand and looked at me. "No," she said. "I honestly don't."

I nodded.

Thunder rumbled again.

"I'm going to check on James," I said.

"Give him a kiss for me."

The front door chime rang then.

"I've got it," James called from the foyer. I heard the door open. James greeted no one. And soon enough, he entered the parlor, carrying a large plain-wrapped box that was damp with snow.

"Someone just left this on the stoop and ran away," James said. "I didn't see who it was."

"Maybe it's a Christmas gift," Violet said.

I stepped forward to stand next to James. The sender's address was written carefully in graphite on the top of the box. In reading it, I thought my heart would surely stop.

Mr. Winslow Crouch Harrington
No. 99 White Horse Yard
St. Dunstan and All Saints
London

"Winslow Crouch Harrington," Violet said. "Isn't that the name of the author of that dreadful book Phillip gave you? *Thomas Shadow* or whatever it was called.

"It is," I said.

"I thought he was dead."

"So did I," I replied.

James placed the box on my desk, and together we opened it. Inside, nestled in packing straw was a handwritten manuscript, some three hundred pages in length. The title, scrawled across the top of the front page, was SHADOW'S LAST CASE. Beneath the title, in the same hectic scribble, were the words: "I need your help, Mr. Coxton. Please. As soon as you can."

Thunder once more.

And then a crack of lightning.

"Should we read it?" Violet asked. "Is that what he wants?"

I shook my head. "I think we'd better get our coats."

ACKNOWLEDGMENTS

MY EXTREME GRATITUDE to Scarlett R. Algee and Christopher Payne at JournalStone for believing in this novel and bringing it into the world. Thank you also to my thoughtful and diligent agent, Eleanor Jackson, who has provided invaluable guidance over our years of working together. A big thanks as well to Matthew Revert for his incredible cover design. I'd also like to extend thanks to my colleagues and students at Vermont College of Fine Arts and the University of California Los Angeles Extension Program, all of whom consistently remind me of the wide and dynamic range of possibilities in fiction. Thank you to Brian Leung for reading many drafts of my work over the years and responding with intelligence, humor and compassion. For their help with my writing and for their friendship, I'd like to thank Chris Baugh, Christine Sneed, Scott Blindauer and Gabriel Blackwell. Thank you also to my supportive mother and father and my sisters, Sarah and Elizabeth. As always, my dear sister Sarah read countless drafts of this novel as I revised it, helping me every step of the way. And finally, thank you to my partner, the handsome, creative and funny Brad Beasley for his encouragement and love. He keeps Los Angeles bright and new.

ABOUT THE AUTHOR

ADAM MCOMBER is the author of two novels *Jesus and John* (Lethe) and *The White Forest* (Touchstone) as well as two collections of short fiction: *This New & Poisonous Air* and *My House Gathers Desires* (BOA Editions). His short fiction has appeared in *Conjunctions, Kenyon Review, Black Warrior Review, Diagram* and numerous other magazines and journals. He teaches in the MFA Writing Program at Vermont College of Fine Arts and in the Writing Program of the University of California Los Angeles Extension.

CPSIA information can be obtained
at www.ICGtesting.com
Printed in the USA
LVHW032124230621
690957LV00009B/1342